While You Were Mine

ANN HOWARD CREEL

LAKE UNION
PUBLISHING

Published by Lake Union Publishing, Seattle

www.apub.com

Amazon, the Amazon logo, and Lake Union Publishing are trademarks of Amazon.com, Inc., or its affiliates.

ISBN-13: 9781503953345 (hardcover)
ISBN-10: 1503953343 (hardcover)

ISBN-13: 9781503952232 (paperback)
ISBN-10: 1503952231 (paperback)

Cover design by Danielle Christopher and Jason Blackburn

Printed in the United States of America

First edition

For Laura Taylor

CHAPTER ONE

AUGUST 14, 1945

For days New York City drifted in a daze of nervous anticipation, awaiting the news of Japanese surrender. Already we'd been through the devastation of Roosevelt's death, the satisfaction of Hitler's, the celebration of Victory in Europe Day, and the stunning news that the United States had dropped massively destructive bombs on two cities in Japan, but one thing remained. The Japanese had yet to lay down their arms, and until they did, an electric restlessness filled the air, encapsulating us like a fog. I'd heard that crowds were already beginning to gather in Times Square. The end could come at any minute, and yet there was uncertainty, too, doubt about what the future would hold, a sense that maybe we were waiting for something we wouldn't be able to capture again.

My heart hammered inside my chest from time to time, and I would find myself clutching my blouse over my sternum. Call it instinct, but a feeling that something besides the announcement of victory was going to happen kept washing over me in waves. I hadn't a clue of the particulars, but as the world assembled and awaited the good news, that instinctual feeling was strengthening and spreading inside me, roots spreading like a ruptured seed.

On that Tuesday, I left my little daughter with the babysitter for a few extra hours after my shift ended so I could go shopping. I chose to do something pleasurable on that extraordinary day, perhaps in an attempt to calm the internal, gnawing sense of knowing something that held itself vague. It always gave me an extra spring in my step to shop for Mary. Since well before her first birthday in July, my little one had been outgrowing her baby clothes in weeks instead of months.

Still in my nurse's uniform, cap, white hose, and shoes, I went to Gimbels on 34th Street, took the clacking wooden escalator up to the children's floor, and looked through the summer sales racks. I picked up a couple of jumpers, some T-shirts, and a pair of pajamas, and then I took my bag of purchases into a diner for something to eat. I sat at the bar and ordered coffee and the special hot plate, and when I was about to head home, shouts came from the street. One suited man and then another came running into the diner, shouting, "It's over! It's over!"

My heart started hammering again, and I dared not breathe, dared not believe it. Tears came to my eyes, and I grabbed my handbag, flew out the door, and started running. People were already pouring into the streets. A crowd of cheering, smiling, crying, and laughing people swept me up. Fools, all of us, joyous fools. I fell in with the wave and let myself take the ride eight blocks to Times Square.

On the way, I asked a man who was striding beside me wearing a white dress shirt, pleated slacks, suspenders, and a hat, "Is it really true?" Beside him, two other men were carrying an American flag between them, and others were tossing torn newspapers high into the air. The man loosened his tie, looked over, and said, "Three minutes after seven. Truman made the announcement. Japanese surrender."

The men with the flag whooped, and I did my best to hold back a tear-laden cry of joy. Since the war had begun, my life had changed in so many ways. I'd left a dusty farm in southern Colorado, moved to Denver, worked in a factory, attended nurse's training, moved to New York—a city I'd always dreamed of living in—graduated as a nurse, and the most unexpected thing of all: Mary. The country had changed, too: blackouts and rationing and news of battles, deaths, and hardships every day. Life as it had been *before* had almost become a blur.

Dusk was beginning to come on, and the lavender-gold sky above seemed somehow bigger, wider, and more open. So soft and bright I felt as if I could reach up and touch it. The city was shimmering under the sunset and the glow of victory as herds of us hoofed it gleefully toward Times Square, all intent upon wildly reveling. The worst war in history was finally over. How uncomplicated and free our days would be in the future.

At the subway station near Times Square, people flowed from the underground as though a great subterranean river had swelled out of its banks. Already we were half a million strong. People of all ages were dancing, hugging, and drinking. American flags flew everywhere. As Times Square, with its electric waterfall and depictions of the Camel man and Budweiser horses, came into view, the fifteen thousand light bulbs of the Times Tower ticker spelled it out for us in just five words: "Official—Truman announces Japanese surrender."

The celebration was trance-like, urgent, joyful, and exultant; it drew me in, despite the fact that so many lives had been lost or ruined. Perfect strangers embraced, hats tumbled from heads, and beer sloshed. In the packed crowd, just as many people cried as laughed. Soldiers wearing fatigues and sailors wearing their blue denim shirts and dungarees, many of them just off ships returning from the war zone in Europe, ran down the streets, hollering and shouting, holding their bottles of beer high above their heads. There were other nurses in all-white uniforms, police officers, women leading children, store workers, chefs, waitresses, and businessmen among thousands of soldiers, everyone applauding and cheering. Men threw their hats in the air, and taxi drivers sat on their horns. Some kids beat a staccato rhythm on garbage-can lids, and a group of teenagers formed a conga line snaking through the masses. Couples jitterbugged to the music inside their heads. Sirens wailed and church bells clanged, joining the beautiful racket. Everyone moved and talked and laughed in crazy bursts, but later I would remember it in slow motion, like a lovely lingering dance.

Someone grabbed me from behind, and all I glimpsed was a flash of a face and a sailor's navy-blue uniform and white cap. He twisted me around, bent me backward, and laid a kiss on my lips. His kiss smelled of beer, but was not offensive. Nothing could be offensive during such a moment. Another man had a camera, and I blinked hard against the flash of light.

What happened next remains hazy. The celebration, the kiss, the exultation all around me, and the first taste of peace—all rushed together and held me still, as if time had ceased to flow forward. A bright white arrow of happiness struck me then, straight into my center, a point of glory that told me the world and everything in it had changed. And then the sailor and the photographer were gone. The celebration had obviously made some people act stupid. I touched my lips, kissed by a stranger, and then I laughed. I laughed in a way that pumped my chest and brought tears to my eyes.

A different sailor attempted another grab-by kissing, but I waved him away. More revelers surged past, and then the premonition I'd been having for days returned. It snapped up my spinal cord and tingled across the synapses in my brain, but I saw no images. Catching any details was like trying to catch fireflies, grasping at things that for a moment felt bright and close and then suddenly vanished. A fuzzy dizziness made me stumble, and with that—compounded by the crowd, the noise, the lights flashing—came an urgency to leave, to go home at once. I gathered myself together in an instant.

The subway stations would be packed, I knew; walking would be faster. But I had to go in the opposite direction of the crowd, so I hugged the buildings through an onslaught of smiles and cheers. Another strong feeling of knowing something, but not what it was, put me on the verge of fainting, as if I'd suddenly gone numb. A creeping sensation came over me, too, like a shadow crossing. A dark shadow that was growing thicker and rolling in faster by the minute. A waterfall of shadow.

A soldier said to me, "Hey, baby, you're heading the wrong way." Another said, "Come with me, doll."

I smiled at them all but kept working my way past the rushing crowd. For two years now, I'd made New York City my home. People might see me on the streets and think I'd always belonged here, but although I was a twenty-five-year-old living and working in modern Manhattan, it hadn't been all that long since the world around me was windblown and dust-enshrouded, the rivers and streams scorched dry, the fields yielding little or nothing beyond the bare essentials to sustain us. My father working late, backlit against the blank horizon, mending a fence, taking a tractor to field, tending to the ever-demanding needs of hungry livestock, or driving his battered truck to town for seed or feed. My mother counting coins on the kitchen table in between scouring endless piles of laundry and preparing three meals a day. My sister and I crying and clinging to each other when our livestock had to be slaughtered.

I'd abandoned that dreary farm life that was so dependent on weather and indiscriminate luck, and worked my way to New York. There were others here I recognized—transplants from the heartland with a hidden illness in their hearts they hoped the city would soothe or an inner dilemma they hoped it would solve. Once we arrived, we sought our places in the sprawling metropolis. For me it had always been the neighborhoods, each a small town with shopkeepers of all sorts who knew their customers, where people talked and smoked on the fire escapes, music and laughter drifted from open windows, and people sang and danced in the streets. Brilliant people—giants in their fields—lived beside the aspiring actor, artist, ballerina, playwright, and reporter. In the city, everyone, like me, was striving for something.

Did all of them harbor secrets, too?

I swam my way out of the eddy of humanity and picked up the pace. I'd always loved evening walks in the summer, but this was not a time to stroll. My feet seemed only to graze the sidewalks as I hastened along, driven by a hazy but insistent sense of urgency. The fog inside my head thickened. *Home.* Home, which meant my apartment. *Mary.* Something caught in my throat at the thought of her. Such a little person, such a sharp pang. I had to get there; I had to get there fast. I tried to tell myself that it was only the effects of adrenaline gone amok, that after so much sorrow during the war and then a sudden peace, I was suffering some strange reverse hysteria. But I couldn't shake the feeling of impending doom. I'd left my bag of clothes for Mary back in the diner, but I didn't stop to pick them up. I could go back for them tomorrow.

I was running by the time I turned the corner at 44th Street and Second Avenue. My street was quiet, all but deserted. It seemed everyone was out celebrating, and in the distance, multiple church bells were ringing at once, a fresh surge of horns were honking, and the loudest of revelers could be heard shouting above the crowds. It was now dark outside, and the windows of the few lit apartments cast yellow rectangular beams into the humid night air.

A man in uniform stood on the stoop of my building, his back to me. There was something familiar about him, but I didn't know him. I hadn't seen his face yet, and still I knew I'd never laid eyes on him before. I came to a stop. He turned to face me then, and it was all in the eyes. Eyes that suggested sapphire-blue seas.

Mary's eyes.

Realization bolted through me and fanned out over my world. A few moments earlier, the war had ended: the earth had started spinning on its right course again, and everyone was joyful. But now, for me, the planet stopped rotating around the sun. While in Chinatown dragons usually reserved for the Chinese New Year led the crowd in celebration through narrow streets, and in Brooklyn and the Bronx block parties broke out and music blared from radios and tables were laden with food and booze, my world split wide open. Every bone in my body felt fluid, and my joints melted.

My daughter, my Mary, wasn't really that, not in the natural sense. I had not carried her in my body and brought her forth into this world. But in every other way, she had become mine. This I knew just as sure as I'd known that someday I would be faced with this moment. Someday I would have to confront the truth. But not today! Breathing was the only thing that kept me upright. Because Mary was not really my daughter. And here standing before me was the one man who could take her away.

CHAPTER TWO

ONE YEAR EARLIER

A Sunday morning. I was wakened by a soft voice whispering my name. "Gwen, Gwen."

Slanting light coming through the venetian blinds told me the sun was already high in the sky. I'd slept in, as some other senior nurses and I had gone out the night before to celebrate the end of final exams. We had sampled the dry martinis at The Horse on Hudson Street, and I was just a tad hungover.

My roommate, Alice, stood fully dressed in the center of the room.

"Gwen, I'm leaving," she said.

I sat up in bed and glanced at the baby. Alice's six-week-old, Mary, slept soundly in her bassinet beside my bed.

I turned back to Alice, who was wearing an open overcoat over her best suit and a pair of nylons—our last pair, I guessed. The hat was perched squarely on her head.

"What did you say?" I asked her.

"I'm leaving."

She began to answer my questions before I could even ask them. "I don't know where I'll go, or when I'll return. I don't know when I'll call, or whether I will." She gazed toward the window, outlined in those bright bars of light. "Don't ask me."

"Alice," I said and pushed back the covers. "What are you saying?"

"I'm leaving."

I rubbed my eyes and took stock of the situation. In my hungover state, Alice appeared watery and unreal, like some ethereal creature not of this earth. The light slanting from the window trembled in her hair, and I could see that she was in a poor state. She hadn't been herself for some time now. Sometimes she arose from her chair in our living room and went to the door as though someone had rung the bell, but no one had. Then she would stand in the doorway and look down the hall, one way and then the other, and listen as though someone was speaking, but no one was. In my nurse's training, we had learned about the major psychiatric problems, but I had no name for what had come over my roommate.

"You're leaving?" I asked. "Do you mean you're going out for the day?"

"No, not for the day. For a long time. Maybe forever."

I pushed myself to the edge of the bed and stood. "What are you talking about? Sit down, Alice. Please. Let's talk."

She backed up. "There's nothing to talk about. I have to go, or I'll lose my mind."

Alice's cheek quivered, and then it was what I feared: she was worse off than I'd ever seen her before. I said, "Of course you won't. This is just a bad time for you. You're going through a tough spell."

"I'll have a nervous breakdown. I will."

I approached her and put my hand on her shoulder, gave it a soft squeeze. "You don't mean that. It'll get better. The war is coming to a close. Everyone believes that, and you must, too."

"Even that doesn't guarantee John will come back to me."

I said, "You must have faith. He's going to be all right; I know it."

Alice looked at me then, and her voice sounded a touch angry when she said, "I haven't heard from him."

I answered quickly, "He's in combat now."

Alice's husband was in the midst of the fighting somewhere in France or Germany. It would be difficult, if not impossible, for him to write. I had assured Alice of this on many occasions.

"He's dead," she said, gazing away. "He would've found a way to contact me; I know it."

I stood before her and tried to get her to look at me. "You don't know that."

"I do."

"It's just fear. And of course you're scared. I would be scared. Anyone would be."

Her anger vanished as quickly as it had come. Alice gazed down at Mary. "She'll be better off with you."

"Wait," I said and reached for my robe. "You don't mean to leave her."

Alice stared at her infant. "I can't care for her. You know it as well as I do."

My eyes darted over to Mary. Alice had grown increasingly exhausted ever since Mary's birth six weeks before. Even more concerning, Alice showed little interest in her baby and often seemed to have no inclination to pick her up, even when Mary cried. She showed no interest in buying baby things or in changing Mary's clothes. She washed bottles only when all of them were dirty, and when she fed the baby, she gazed blankly into the distance. Every act of mothering seemed a dreaded chore, and sometimes I wondered if Alice had even wanted this child. I had been trying to fill in the gaps as we struggled onward. I'd volunteered to feed the baby her bottle in the middle of the night so that Alice, who hated having to get up, could get some rest. Even so, she tossed and turned, fought the sheets, and stared at the clock, as if motherhood had played a dirty trick on her.

I'd never imagined myself a motherly person, and yet I had taken a liking to this little one. When I held Mary, something eternal and tender welled up in me. She fit snug and warm in the curve of my arm, her body surrendering to hunger and the need to be held, and her eyes locked onto mine as though there were nothing else to gaze at in the world.

Lately when Alice held her daughter, however, Alice's body grew limp, a faraway look began to swim in her eyes, and I was afraid she'd lose all control and drop the child. It was as if a strange transference were taking place, and the baby, who was growing and thriving, was somehow draining the life out of her mother.

I said, "You can't leave her. You're her mother."

"A poor mother."

I tried to give her a reassuring smile. "You're not a poor mother. You need some more rest, and help. I'll do more."

She took a step back, and I resisted the urge to grab her and hold her in place. She could not leave this baby with me! As fond as I was of Mary, I couldn't handle that responsibility! If only Alice had some family, someone I could call. But I'd never met anyone, not even her husband. Alice had answered an ad I'd placed for a roommate, and she'd come alone and taken my spare room on the spot. She told me her husband had deployed overseas and he wanted her to live with someone during his time away, because she had no living relatives, only a distant elderly aunt with whom she did not correspond.

From the beginning, Alice had struck me as fragile, perhaps not ample enough for this world. She was a delicate woman, the kind men wanted to rescue. She remembered every unkind word ever spoken to her and took every one of them to heart. Even her beauty, which was exquisite, was fragile. She had fine blonde hair, pale eyes and skin, and the smallest wrists I'd ever seen. If I was a sturdy young sapling, as my father had once described me, then Alice was a frail willow, bending in even the slightest breeze.

I said, "What am I to do with the baby? I have to work."

She finally looked at me. "Ask Lisen to help, or take her to one of the nurseries."

She started to back up again.

"Wait, Alice! Don't do this," I said.

"I'll send money if I can."

"Where will you go? Stop, please."

She shook her head. "I don't know where I'll go." She gazed off and continued backing away until she reached the door. "California, maybe, where it's warm."

"Alice, you can't do this! This is your child! Be reasonable!"

But by the look in her eyes, I knew that Alice was indeed leaving. She opened the creaky bedroom door, and whether it was the noise or this awful thing that was transpiring that awakened her, I'll never know, but Mary began to cry. She always woke up wet and hungry, gulping big breaths of air, and wailing in between them. She flailed her arms, kicked off her covers in distress, and clenched her hands as if demanding that someone come, and come now. She would not be quieted until she was picked up.

I stared at Alice, willing her to do the right thing. *Pick up your child.* Alice glanced in Mary's direction, but I saw no emotion there. Her helpless and hopeless expression chilled me. Then she met my gaze, and I could see that she understood what I was trying to convince her to do. The clock ticked loudly. The moment lengthened as though melting time itself, and the light brightened in the room. She had to do the right thing; she had to go to her crying child. I did not drop my gaze. I would not let her off easy.

Mary's cries reached a fever pitch, but I held my ground. One of us had to tend to the infant. Who would it be? Alice blinked once and didn't move in her daughter's direction. I thought I saw the hint of a shrug, then she stepped through the door, turned around, and closed the door behind her with a sound that made me think of a bone snapping in two.

I didn't move. Alice was her mother! How could she turn her back on her frantic baby and leave? Leave her with me? I had to take a few calming breaths. Mary was crying desperately now, but I stood frozen, in a state of shock. Then I ran to the window and looked down on the street, hoping I'd glimpse Alice, hoping she would turn around and change her mind. But she had already vanished. How had she disappeared so fast? It was as if she'd evaporated.

I went to Mary, as any decent person would, cradled her in my arms, and rubbed her back. Big baby tears streamed down her reddened face, but soon I had her soothed. I changed her diaper, warmed her morning bottle in a pan over the stove, and fed her in the rocking chair that Alice had brought with her. Mary sucked down the warm formula, her eyes fixed on mine. Though we must have appeared peaceful, my mind was swirling. What had happened here this morning was still plummeting into me, like a torpedo shot to the bottom of the sea. Alice had just abandoned her baby to a woman she had known for only eight months. I was about to graduate from nursing school and then take my skills into the theater of war overseas. But Alice obviously didn't care about any of that.

She had reached her limit, and it seemed she had been planning this, perhaps for a long while. I recalled her many staring spells, during which she seemed to be drowning in the past or suffering through the present. I had hoped those blank states meant only that she needed silence and solitary time, more rest or some such thing, but maybe she had been imagining a new and different life for herself, no longer bound by anything as burdensome as a child.

CHAPTER THREE

As I fed Mary, I tried to remain calm and focused on remembering all I knew about Alice. She had originally come to the city to become an actress. She had garnered a couple of small roles and then had gone to work sewing parachutes when the war broke out. She had rarely mentioned family. Although I'd never met her husband, I'd formed a mental picture through the stories Alice had told me. He had been a soldier at the army base on Governors Island, after coming to New York from my state, although from north of Denver, near Boulder. I had remarked to Alice that it was quite a coincidence. Her husband and roommate were both from Colorado.

Theirs had been a hasty wartime marriage, as was common in those days. Men in uniform swarmed the streets of New York City; many of them had popped the question and married near strangers in City Hall before they left to face uncertain futures. And many women were eager to accept these hasty proposals, swept away by the romance of the uniforms, the common cause of the war, and all that. Alice and John had married after only a month, and then he shipped out. These things happened.

The day I met Alice, I was struck by her beauty and poise. Alice paid for her room with a check drawn on a joint account with her husband, and when she told me she was pregnant, it gave me a moment of pause. I had wanted a nice apartment, but the rent was higher than I could manage on my own, and I needed a roommate to share expenses. I hadn't counted on a baby in the apartment. I was on the brink of turning her down, but then I saw something like loneliness in her eyes, and I relented. She had been the first to answer my ad, and she seemed quiet and sober. But now? I had never seen *this* coming.

Mary slept again after her morning feeding, and after I placed her back in the bassinet, my adrenal glands poured panic into my blood. I combed Alice's room, opened every drawer, and searched the recesses of her closet and under her bed looking for clues as to whom I might contact. I found her husband's letters and a Chesterfield coat he'd obviously left with her for safekeeping. Like so many other overcoats men wore in the city, it was long and black and sported a velvet collar and concealed buttons. Other than a comb I also found under the bed, she'd left only the letters, the coat, the rocking chair, and all of the baby's things.

I plopped down on the floor of Alice's room. What was I going to do now? I had dates to keep, new dance steps to learn, and places to see outside the good old USA. All this in addition to shifts at the hospital and the state board exams only a few weeks away. When was I going to study? How was I going to work? Now I had a baby to take care of, one that wasn't even related to me! Anger twisted in my chest, and my breaths came out in frustrated huffs. How could Alice have done this to me? And to her baby?

I tried to formulate a plan, but nothing came to me. Government people would probably intervene when a parent left a child, but what might happen to Mary? Would she be placed in an orphanage or given to people who didn't want her? I couldn't have that on my conscience.

I sucked in calming breaths. This situation would work itself out. This was only temporary—it had to be. All I had to do was stay calm and centered, take care of what I had to for now, and wait for Alice to come to her senses and return to Mary. Maybe she would be healed and ready to care for her child.

I would have to be patient; however, patience had never been one of my virtues.

When I was young and drought first hit the farm, my father predicted that I would not last long there. He was right. By the time the land kicked up clods of dirt and sprays of dust and refused to grow even the heartiest of grains, I had started making plans to leave.

My last Christmas there, in 1941, the country was in a new war, and there were job opportunities for women in the city. So just after the holiday, I took the money I'd saved since I was twelve, earned from babysitting and sewing, and I packed a bag and planned to ride the bus from Alamosa to Denver. As my parents drove me in the truck to the bus stop in Alamosa, I could not face them. I was ashamed I'd disappointed them. I could only look past the window at the pebbled patches of snow and straw-colored land that had failed us.

Despite being sad and worried about me, my parents hadn't tried to talk me out of leaving. I was the second oldest of their seven children and had finished high school in addition to doing my share of farm chores. Since graduation, I had worked on the farm and picked up small jobs, but nothing in the area paid well. I was almost twenty-one years old and had no future. My older brother, twenty-three, had long before decided to stay and try to save the farm, and my younger siblings were either not willing to leave or still in school. The hardest to leave behind, Betty, was three years younger than me and my only sister among my six siblings.

Betty was a beauty and a dreamer, who, as a child, climbed trees, fell often, and never cried. She often pretended to be the heroine of some fantasy story, and heroines didn't cry or show fear. She had long, thick hair she braided while wet so that it dried in long, raven waves, and in the spring she piled it on top of her head and tucked tiny flowers into the folds. We shared beds and clothes, chores and secrets, hopes and dreams.

I shook myself away from those memories, picked up Mary, and climbed the stairs to see my neighbor, Lisen, who had no children of her own and had been babysitting Mary when Alice needed time to herself. Lisen and I had met at the mailboxes on the first floor soon after I'd moved into the building.

Lisen answered the door, a quizzical look on her face as she looked at me and then Mary. "Vhat has happen to the mother?" she asked in her heavy German accent.

Lisen had prematurely gray-streaked hair that she wore in twirled braids on top of her head. She was only in her thirties but looked older; in addition to the hairstyle, she wore floral-print dresses with narrow belts at the waist and small collars at the necklines, clothes my mother would have worn. In between peeling carrots and potatoes and baking heavy cakes, she looked after other women's children. Sturdy she was, but there was a nervous way about her, probably because of anti-German sentiment in the country, aimed even at those who'd never been members of the Nazi party.

Lisen's husband, Geoff, had been in New York since he was a kid and barely remembered his homeland, but Lisen had come as an adult. Her accent had been a problem for years now, and on occasion she heard "Kraut" whispered as she walked on the streets. It didn't help that their last name was Dasch, the same as one of the German saboteurs who had landed in the Hamptons in 1942. She rarely ventured out and then only to places such as the Café Geiger, where they served Black Forest cake and Bavarian sauerbraten, or the Café Éclair, where German and Austrian refugees gathered.

At first, I didn't answer Lisen's question.

She ushered me into her apartment, which always smelled of soap and something baking in the oven. I was one of her only friends, and she was always eager to see me. But I had never shown up so early on a Sunday morning and with the baby in tow.

I sat down with Mary in my lap and finally answered, "Alice has left."

"Gone vhere?"

"I don't know."

Lisen looked at me with trepidation and then shook her head. "She leave the baby. I knew something vrong."

"In what way was something wrong?" I asked, curious to know what she had seen.

Lisen sighed heavily. "She start leaving the baby for longer and longer."

My back stiffened. "What do you mean . . . longer and longer?"

"Almost all the day. Each day. I never knew vhen she come back."

This was news to me. But I worked long hours at the hospital. I had no idea what Alice was doing during the day. Obviously she had been leaving her daughter and doing something. A shiver zinged up my spine and set the roots of my hair on end. I imagined I could look like a person who'd just touched a live wire.

"No, no," Lisen said, shaking her head. "I'm no surprised." She patted her hands lightly on her apron skirt and averted her gaze for a long moment. Lisen's voice was soft, her eyes concerned, but wise. "Something vrong there, something miss, lost. I was worry for her, but I do not know vhat to do."

I should've discussed this with Lisen before. I should've insisted that Alice talk to a doctor. I ought to have done more. I started to go down that path of self-recrimination, but then I had to dismiss all the should-haves and ought-to-haves. I realized that it was pointless. So with Lisen I figured out a schedule for Mary's care that would allow me to work my shift on Monday. Babysitting cost money I hadn't been expecting to pay, and the burn of resentment flared inside me again. How dare Alice leave her daughter and nothing to help provide for her? How dare she put me in such a spot?

"Vhat if Alice never come back? Vhat about the father?" Lisen asked.

Mary was starting to fuss, so I laid her in my lap, facing me with her head near my knees and her feet at my waist. I gently swayed her back and forth using my thighs. This movement always soothed and entertained her. It calmed me, too.

I shrugged. "I don't know. I don't know what to do about any of this."

"Maybe you call police?"

Of course that would be the right thing to do. If my parents had been here, that's exactly what they would *insist* I do. But my solid, God-fearing parents were not here, and they didn't know about the one thousand babies that were abandoned in this city every year. People left them at Foundling Hospital, and then the city did God-knew-what with them. We cared for the occasional orphan in the hospital, too, and their lonely gazes had always haunted me while I tried to work around them. I contemplated making the call.

"You vhant use the phone?" Lisen asked.

I should call the police; I should. But Alice had only left a couple of hours earlier; maybe it was too soon to get so rattled. Maybe she would rush back after she came to her senses. Maybe she would come back better prepared. Maybe I needed to give this more time. As I considered my options, I looked down at Mary.

She smiled. I hadn't seen her smile before, hadn't known she had passed that particular milestone. It wasn't gas, as some people claim, but a real, gummy, baby smile aimed at my eyes.

Oh, damn.

"I don't think it's a crime to take a vacation from motherhood. Alice told me she was leaving, and she gave me a general destination."

Lisen hesitantly nodded.

I said, "She isn't a missing person, therefore, is she? I mean, she hasn't been abducted or anything. She left of her own free will. No crime has been committed." I really didn't know if it was illegal to leave your child in the care of someone else without warning or not. "I wish she'd given me more information or some money to help with the costs, but I don't think that's a crime, either."

Lisen smiled sadly. "I suppose."

I continued to sway Mary until her eyelids began to fall. Once, twice, and then she took a long sigh and drifted off to dreamland.

Lisen was watching me. "So you care for the child."

I shrugged helplessly and fought hot tears that were forming. I didn't know if I was crying for poor Mary or for poor me. "I don't know what to do. Maybe I'll just keep her for a while and wait until Alice comes back." I also said that Mary was a sensitive baby, and I didn't know how she would fare if I turned her over to the authorities. She was still such a tiny thing, completely dependent on others in every way, and what if the authorities gave her to another person like Alice, or, even worse, someone mean?

"You should try, find the father."

"Alice is convinced he's dead, and he very well might be. That was one of the reasons Alice became so distraught. She hadn't heard from him. I went into Alice's room and found his letters, so I have his last military mailing address. But if he's dead, it won't do any good to write. And if he's still alive, imagine he's over there in the thick of it, and he's in such a bad place that he hasn't been able to write, and then he hears from me that his wife began to have mental problems and abandoned their daughter."

"Maybe the army let him come back."

I passed a hand in the air as if an annoying fly had flown near. "No way to know." I was remembering something. "You know, it just occurred to me. Her husband could've set Alice up in a place of her own, a place for her and the baby. But he didn't. He wanted her to have a roommate. Maybe he'd already seen something."

Lisen twisted her hands together. After a few moments she asked, "Vhat about you? You should be dating, find husband. You go around with baby, everybody think you are married woman."

"You can say that again."

Lisen held still, and I looked at her, hard, into her discerning eyes. "You don't think she's coming back, do you?"

Lisen looked away and then back at me. "Like I say, something vrong there. Something lost. In Alice."

Lisen was supposed to have comforted me, but a more powerful bolt of panic hit me now like a tank rolling into the middle of my stomach. I managed to say, "No kidding."

"Taking care of baby," Lisen whispered, her wise eyes registering the expression on my face, "is full time, day and night, and always. You are single girl. Supposed to have fun."

"No kidding," I said again.

Both in Denver and in New York, I had been a dating aficionado. My roommates had come and gone, most of them marrying and moving away to be with husbands or to stay with family while their husbands were away. But I was an anomaly; I enjoyed the dating and flirting, but deep down I was that commonsense farm girl. I was not interested in love based in fear and a rushed marriage. Poverty and worry had tested and strained the love my mother and father had for each other. True love did not come into being so swiftly and easily, I believed, and if it weren't true and tested, I didn't want it. I was holding out for the real deal, and I was willing to wait for it, even though there were times when I was filled with longing.

Lisen was still studying me. "Alice owe me money," she said after a long pause and some hesitation.

Of course she did.

Because Alice and I had shared housing expenses, I'd managed to put away some money, a small stash of personal savings that I'd never had before. Still, it wasn't a lot.

I said, "I'll take care of it."

CHAPTER FOUR

After paying Lisen what Alice owed her, I was cash poor. And the full rent for the apartment sat on my shoulders like a lead weight. I had to find a reliable roommate who would share expenses and accept that an infant lived in the place, too. I started by posting a notice on the bulletin board at the hospital. Soon after, a nurse who was interested contacted me and we met over lunch. Dot and I sat in the green-walled hospital cafeteria on slatted chairs and opened our sack lunches. A saucy brunette who wore cat-eye glasses and red lipstick along with her fashionably bobbed hair and tweezed, blackened eyebrows, Dot had been sharing an apartment with four other women and wanted more space to herself.

I took a deep breath before I said, "My roommate went away for a while and left her baby in my care. You can take her room, and I'll keep the baby with me. She'll be my responsibility completely, not yours." I felt each tick of my heart as I waited for her answer.

When I had first arrived in the city, I started to receive a small salary as a senior student, a so-called Senior Cadet. I opted to take $60 per month as a salary and find housing of my own instead of taking $40 and receiving free room and board.

In 1942, the need for nurses had been at an all-time high. When I first left home, I took an inexpensive room in Denver in a boarding-house near the gold-domed capitol building and found work at the Timpte Trailer Company, where we manufactured trailers for the army. I'd heard talk that our jobs at the factory would surely end when the war was over. I never wanted to be dependent again, so I entered nurse's training at St. Joseph's Hospital, which was run by the always rigid, but often kind, Sisters of Charity. Everyone said that nursing was a career with stability, since nurses were always needed. Then in 1943 Congress passed the Cadet Nurse Corps law to expedite and subsidize nurses' training in homeland hospitals, so that the more experienced nurses could join the armed services. I had already been in training and applied for the subsidy.

By early 1944, I had attained Senior Cadet status and could apply to spend the last part of my training just about anyplace in the country. I took all the money from under my dormitory mattress and bought a train ticket to New York City, where I'd always dreamed of living and where I had been accepted at Bellevue Hospital. Already weary of mandatory dormitory life during the first part of my nurse's training in Denver, I had missed privacy. Miraculously I found a furnished, two-bedroom apartment on the third floor of a five-story, red brick building not far from the hospital. It was a dour old edifice with no elevators, but it had central heating and a laundry room. A rug covered the living-room floor with faded but blooming flowers, and tall windows faced the street. It was a bit of an extravagance, but I could just make it work if I shared the rent with a roommate. My parents had taught me reason and restraint; they'd infused me with the lessons they'd learned from their hard lives. Those who'd mortgaged their farms for new equipment were the first to lose them when the Depression hit. Many who'd left for California had come back penniless. Steadfastness, solidity, and going forward slowly had been my parents' approach, but I had taken the risk and rented the apartment anyway. Now that Alice was gone, I was near desperate.

Dot frowned. "Why? I mean, why did the mother leave?"

I lowered my voice. "Alice hadn't been doing well. She hadn't been . . . well."

"Oh," Dot said and looked down. I'd known Dot only in passing at the hospital because she worked in Obstetrics, a department I hadn't been assigned to for a long time. "Sometimes that happens," she said barely above a whisper. "Some women get sad after the baby comes."

"Really? But the birth of a child . . ."

She finished for me, "Should be a cause for celebration. I know. But sometimes depression just creeps up on a new mother."

I didn't have any experience with patients with this condition, but Dot had been in nursing longer than I had, and she worked in OB. "Does the depression improve?"

"Most of the time, yes."

So there was something I could hang on to. A flicker of hope sparked inside me. Alice would improve and come back. It was just a matter of time.

Dot's expression changed. "You got dumped on."

I shook my head, thinking how complicated it was. "You could say that, I guess." I pictured Mary's face, and although I felt like complaining to Dot, I couldn't bring myself to when I compared my plight to Mary's. Poor little one, with two lost parents. "I'm hoping it's only temporary."

"So what happens when the wayward mommy returns? Will you give her back her room?"

"If she does, I don't know. I suppose we'll have to work it out."

Dot's face softened as she looked at me, and I could discern kindness in her eyes. She sighed. "I've always loved babies. Why do you think I work in OB?"

I inhaled, and it hit me then that my lungs had fully expanded for the first time since Alice had left. I asked for a little more rent money than Alice had been paying. It was still a good deal for Dot. Thank God she'd come along.

She was pleased also and said, "I'm lucky to have found you. They say that once the war is over, places will be even harder to come by. And mark my word, they might even try to force us girls out of the workplace. They're already saying that women who've kept the war factory alive will get their pink slips to make room for all the boys coming home."

I had done factory work, too, and knew the kind of woman Dot was talking about. Many women had lost their husbands or had come from tough circumstances. They needed their jobs as much as or more than the men did.

"It's only a matter of time," said Dot as she pushed her glasses up on the bridge of her nose. "In college I had a friend, a guy, no less, and he said that whenever a group of people is oppressed, eventually they rise up. Look at the colonists, look at the slaves." She paused. "We're next, my friend. But first we'll have to wait until the boys come home and let them think we're the same as before. Let them think they're still in charge, and we're still little floor rugs to be stepped on."

I smiled. "You mean we aren't? Someone needs to tell a lot of those girls on your ward."

After she moved in, Dot and I took our wartime duties seriously. We saved cooking fat and toothpaste tubes. We collected newspapers and participated in meatless Tuesdays. We joined scrap-metal drives, saved our sugar-buying cards for special occasions, and donated old nylons, which were made into powder bags for naval guns.

I found out that despite her freewheeling talk, Dot was also a vora-cious dater and went out without wearing her glasses so as not to appear too smart. She was already twenty-seven; her prime time was running out. She regularly met men at the USO, and occasionally I accompa-nied her, leaving Mary with Lisen for a few hours in the evening. Dot preferred officers, pilots, and navy men passing through. She made fast appraisals of each of her suitors and recounted those to me in great detail. One had what she suspected was a bad temperament, another had no plans for the future, and so on. We went out wearing high heels, leather gloves, and hats pinned to our heads. Men came to call bearing flowers and candy. An endless supply of soldiers passed through New York those days, and Dot made dating into a bright and happy hobby.

I envied her freedom, but it was uncomfortable to leave Mary with Lisen after she'd already cared for her all day while I was at work. Still I was tempted to follow Dot out on the town. I went out in this amazing city of mine only a fraction of how often I wanted to. Lisen had been ever so right: caring for an infant amounted to endless chores and work.

Lisen became my mentor and even loaned me a book about infant care. A huge responsibility had been heaved on me, and sometimes I paced the floors while Mary napped or after I put her down for the night. I hadn't felt trapped since leaving the farm, and I didn't like the feel of confinement on my skin. I hadn't been old enough to help with my little sister when she was an infant. So I had no experience to draw from, but I soon found out that the needs of a baby were, just as Lisen had warned me, time-consuming and relentless. Where once I had awakened just in time to throw on my uniform and head out the door, now I had to feed, burp, and clothe Mary. I also had to pack a diaper bag of her things before I dropped her off with Lisen. When I came home from a long day of caring for patients and comforting their families, I found another soul who had needs, too. There was no time for tweezing my eyebrows or soaking in a bubble bath. I'd once spent my days off combing through shops and discovering little cafés on my own or with another nurse, but those carefree and spontaneous jaunts had ended. Now every errand and outing required careful planning.

But Mary didn't ask for more than any other baby did. She didn't demand more than what her mother should have been doing. She was the innocent in this situation. It wasn't her fault, and through many hours of caring, Mary was becoming sweetly familiar to me. She had only in the last two weeks begun to show expressions of surprise, happiness, hunger, and gratitude—to name a few. So I did the best I could.

Just after Labor Day, I graduated and passed my state board exams to become a registered nurse. I was offered a position at Bellevue Hospital on the post-surgical unit, which had been my favorite. Still it was a far cry from what I'd once imagined when I left Colorado. I had dreamed of going overseas, seeing the world, helping the war effort on the front lines, but now I had to rein back those plans.

I accepted the job at Bellevue. At least I didn't have to lose my city. New York had opened up a new world for me; it had started to seep into my soul as soon as I arrived. The city was the smell of seafood and sewers, flower gardens, and Guerlain. It was painted toenails and feathered hats, tenements, docks, and haughty high-rises. The city could seem as desolate as a freezing night in the Bowery heated only by fires burning in oil drums, or it could feel as sweet as young boys fishing for minnows in the lake surrounded by dragonflies, daffodils, and birch trees. But it never felt dead. Always there were concerts and literary events, dancing and discussions, and a sense of something coming in the air, something about which we knew nothing except that it would take us places we'd never been before.

After work, I went home and did what I had to do for the time being. I still held out hope that Alice would return. But while Dot dressed up and prepared to go out on the town, I cared for Mary and envy tore through me. Everything had changed; I was no longer the center of my world. Middle-of-the-night feedings were the worst. Pulling myself out of a deep sleep, warming a bottle and patiently letting her drink it down, then changing her diaper was exhausting and had me yearning for a full night's sleep. When I awakened in the mornings to face a long shift at the hospital, I was as tired as when I'd gone to bed. Oh, what I had taken for granted in my past.

And yet there were some peaceful moments in the quiet of the night, too. Holding her blocked out some of the endless hullaballoo in my brain. I fit her in the crook of my arm, and like the most intimate of strangers, she studied me, and I studied her: the markings in her palms, the downy patches of almost sheer hair on her head—the same color as Alice's—and the soft, angel-shaped indention between her nose and upper lip. It was true she was a beautiful baby. She had a perfect, heart-shaped mouth, fine white-blond hair, and tiny wrists. Her eyes moved while she slept, and hair-like veins on her eyelids made a fascinating purplish web. She always took one final, elongated sigh before she fell into a deep sleep. These things I knew, though even her own mother didn't.

When Mary was three months old, I had a rougher-than-usual shift at work. At the hospital, we patched up many a soldier who'd had hasty or botched surgery along a front line somewhere, and that day we'd lost a sweet-faced, redheaded nineteen-year-old after infection finally took its toll. Here was a farm boy who'd stumbled into a world war not realizing how deep the fall could be. In his eyes, I could see the innocence lost and a soft, solemn question: Why? He was just a kid, a baby in my eyes, and he died fully aware, having never been in the oblivion of a coma.

I fell into a deep, dreamless sleep that night, so when my eyes flew open and the day was already dawning, I bolted upright. Terror zipped through me. I was off duty, and I'd slept in. Mary hadn't woken me; something was wrong. I flung aside the covers and flew to the bassinet, where Mary was only then opening her eyes.

She smiled. She smiled as if she knew she had just accomplished a major milestone. It was as if she were saying, *See what I just did? I'm trying to make it easier on you.*

My heart rate ramped down, and I whispered, "Good girl, you."

I picked up her rattle, gave it a shake, and then nudged it into her belly. She let loose a little cackling laugh—she was ticklish!—and I teared up. Her eyes held utter delight, and her silly, drooling, toothless grin touched me in my most sentimental spots. She was a huge inconvenience in my life, a vast responsibility I hadn't asked for, but at that moment, I allowed a little more than fondness to pump through the hollows of my heart.

In an instant I was back in the good days on the farm before the drought, standing in the grove of old cottonwoods down by the creek with Betty, and I remembered the way the wind moved through the overhead branches there, and the feel of fresh bark and damp soil underfoot. At night we would look up into the bowl of dark sky holding more sparkling stars than drops of water in a rainstorm and listen to migrating ducks call out as they flew overhead. The cry of a night-hunting hawk, insects humming in the air, and the clatter of deer hooves in the rocky hills surrounding us were the music of the land. For a time, life on the farm had been beautiful. And, for reasons I didn't understand, Mary was making me remember it.

I got her to laugh three more times that morning, and each cackle was more adorable than the one before it. I already knew she trusted me, but that morning I realized she loved me, too—unconditionally, the only way babies could love. And why wouldn't she love me? I'd taken the place of her mother.

CHAPTER FIVE

In late 1944 Allied forces were gaining ground in Europe and in the Pacific, and there was a spark in the air, a promise of impending victory. Despite the blackouts, rationed food, and gasoline shortages, New Yorkers partied the nights away at places such as the Stage Door Canteen, the Minetta Tavern, and the rooftop club of the Hotel Astor as they waited for good news.

On an evening in November, Dot urged me to go out on the town, since we were both off duty the next day. She had donned a crimson dress with black buttons down the back and was cocking a black felt hat smartly on her head.

"Take her back to Lisen's," Dot insisted. "Just for a couple of hours."

How nice it would've been. I would have loved to do that! I closed my eyes and swayed to some joyful, easy inner music. I missed male attention—having a man hold my hand beneath the bar, maybe whisper compliments in my ear over the sound of a band, clinking glasses, and laughter. Now I could hardly recall the days when I had dates, when I primped before the mirror and ironed my dresses before going out, when getting little sleep had been a choice.

Mary was four and a half months old by then and could sit propped up in her high chair. I'd just finished feeding her dinner, and her bib was covered in globs of baby cereal. Instead of staying home, cleaning her up, and washing diapers, I could let a man buy me a glass of champagne or a martini. My hair—shiny brown with a touch of copper, falling near my shoulders in coiffed waves—was still styled from that morning, and with just a swipe of lipstick and a change of clothes, I could escape all this.

I crouched down close to her and said in the soft, teasing tone of voice she brought out in me, "Should I go, little one? Should I go out for some fun tonight?"

She burped hugely, and it startled her, as if she couldn't believe that dreadful sound had emerged from her mouth. I laughed and she laughed back with a tiny bit of spit-up foaming on her bottom lip. I reached for the burping rag and touched it to her mouth.

She shook her head. Of course it was just a reaction to being cleaned up, but the way she looked at me, it was as if she truly wanted to send me a message, and it vibrated through me like the clanging of a bell.

In the San Luis Valley of my birth, there had once been a freshwater spring where the Utes went after winter hunts for rest and feasts. It was said that the waters rose from the earth and formed a quiet pool that reflected the sky above, and so they called the spring Saguache, meaning "water at the blue earth." I never saw this spring with my own eyes, because, like the Utes, who also left that once-abundant valley, pushed out by encroaching Spanish settlers, the waters of the spring gradually disappeared. But there was something in Mary's eyes that spoke to me of that place, something solemn and adult in her haunting blue gaze, a bottomless quality that held me still.

I let Dot go out on her own.

The evening seemed never to end. I played with Mary until her bedtime, and then the empty hours spread before me. The focus of my thoughts was beginning to fray in the air around my head, and there was a pang in my stomach I could not identify. It was hard to get Mary out of my mind, as if the biology of my body was changing. I went to check on her in the bassinet, where she lay curled up like a snail wearing pink pajamas, her rump high in the air. I gently placed my hand on her back and felt each of her silent, smooth, and regular breaths. I let out a long stream of my own warm breath as I registered a moment of quiet contentment. It reminded me of my early girlhood, of sleeping back-to-back with Betty when we were inseparable sisters. A sleeping baby is such a beautiful thing.

Good-night, Mary. Sweet dreams.

I owned few material possessions but had amassed a collection of small porcelain eggs—small, because of my wanderlust—so I could take them with me. While Mary slept, I touched the eggs one by one, then picked up my favorite and held its smooth coolness to my cheek. Maybe that collection of porcelain eggs had foretold a maternal streak I had not known was there.

Mary made a sound in her sleep, and I turned. Looking at her, I remembered my sister when she was little. One of Betty's first words had been "wah-ter," which she had said with a finger pointed toward the stream that ran across the southeast corner of the farm. The creek had been our favorite place on the farm, where we sought the cooler air and shade dusted with little spheres of light. I remembered us squatting at the edge of the creek, trailing our fingers through the running water, wishing we could go with it, though at that time, life was still good. Even so, Betty had wanted to leave the farm more than I had. As far back as I could remember, she had been drawn to that moving water, to something flowing away.

But when the Depression came and we witnessed neighbors losing their farms, businesses shutting down, and friends moving away in trucks piled high with meager belongings, she decided that money and greed were the roots of all evil, and she turned toward the solid land and embraced it as though there were nothing else, nothing else at all. When

I told her I was leaving, she begged me not to, and when I asked her to come with me, she declined. After I left, she rarely wrote.

Betty had made her choice, but I always felt as if I'd abandoned her and the farm. Perhaps this was why; perhaps this was destiny. Maybe my choices had led me to Mary, and this was a role I was meant to play, my small part in a war-ravaged world.

A few nights later, Dot and I had finished sharing an early dinner when someone rang the bell for the exterior door. We had been listening to the radio, and I turned down the volume. A male voice on the intercom said he was looking for Alice McKee.

Dot and I stared at each other. I pressed the button and asked, "Who is looking for her?"

"It's the United States Army, ma'am."

My heart fell into my gut, and Dot covered her mouth with her hand. They'd asked for Alice, but had they come for Mary? I had the horrible urge to flee with her down the back stairs. A flash of memory: Betty and I hiding premature baby piglets under our bed so our father would not drown them. He took them anyway, telling us they were destined to die.

Dot and I stood staring at each other for several interminable moments until I came to my senses. I blinked away the dizziness and breathed away the panic. I was a law-abiding citizen, and I could not hide Mary.

I said to Dot, "I'll go."

She replied, "I'll watch her."

I told the officer I'd be right down, and since it was cold outside, I threw on my heaviest coat. Two officers in full dress uniform, hats, and overcoats stood solemnly waiting, and I knew what it meant. My heart knocked against my ribcage as questions raced through my head.

If Mary's father had indeed perished, what would happen? The officers' faces were grave and still, revealing nothing, despite the cold wind pummeling them where they stood on the stoop.

I said, "You're looking for Alice?"

One of them answered, "Alice McKee, yes."

"She used to live here, but she left."

The same man asked, "Do you know where she went?"

"No," I said. "I don't."

"She left no forwarding address?"

I shook my head. I saw Mary in my mind. "No. I'm sorry."

The two men looked at each other and then said, "Thank you," at the same time and started to turn away.

"Wait," I said.

They turned back to face me, and I gulped. "What has happened? Has something happened to her husband?"

The one who'd spoken to me before said, "We can't say, miss. We have to find his family first."

"Has—"

"I'm sorry, miss." He tipped his hat. "We'll let you get back to whatever you were doing. Good evening."

Upstairs, I told Dot what had happened. She had put Mary down for the night while I'd been gone. She stared at me with sadness in her eyes. "He's either dead or missing in action. That's the only reason they would've come here looking for Alice."

"I know."

"Did you tell them about the baby?"

I swayed on my feet. "No."

She froze and then looked at me, hard. She was dressed to go out for a nightcap at the Monkey Bar with one of her recent suitors, and when she started moving again, she grabbed her gloves in a way that showed me she didn't approve of what I'd just done, or not done. "Why not, Gwen?"

I shook my head. There was no way to explain this feeling to someone who hadn't experienced it. I eked out, "I couldn't imagine what they'd do. Maybe they would've taken her to some horrible place."

"I doubt that."

"Well, maybe not tonight. But they might have sent someone to take her later. She would be so scared . . . terrified . . . You know how she is; she doesn't like strangers."

"The army probably doesn't even know he has a child. Alice was barely pregnant when he left, right?"

I nodded.

"You should have told them that his child is here, that he has a child here," Dot said in a low voice.

"But—"

"They came for information."

She was right, and in the silence that followed, the room shrank around me. Shame burned in my blood. I hadn't been as forthcoming as I should have been; I hadn't done the right thing.

I blinked quickly and said, "You're right."

I threw my coat back on and flew down the stairs and out into the cold night, the wind whipping my hair as I hesitated and looked in one direction down the street. I couldn't remember seeing a government car when I'd come down before, and so I had no way of knowing whether the men had come on foot or by car. Probably they had come by car. Traffic was almost nonexistent this hour; especially with rationing, few people owned or drove cars, and when I turned in the other direction, I saw the taillights of a sedan at the end of my block.

I ran in that direction. The cold wind stung my face, and as I ran, the inside of me began to tremble, as if an odd quivering clamp had come inside and grabbed a hold. I had not told the men as much as I should have. I had not divulged that Alice's husband was a father now, that he had a child here. I had turned my back on everything I'd been taught and believed to be good and true. I had acted selfishly, and as much as I hated to admit it, I had no rights to Mary. But how could the right thing feel so much like the wrong thing?

And still I ran as fast as I could.

As I neared the car, I called out, "Wait!" and waved my arms.

A truck rumbled past, momentarily blocking my view, but I was close enough to see the government license plates and thought I had stopped them. But then the traffic light changed, and the car rolled away. Farther, farther down the street. The men hadn't seen me, and I couldn't catch them. I stopped running and caught my breath, leaning over with my hands on my thighs, but I kept my eyes on those taillights until they had diminished from spots to dots and then blinked to nothing.

I stood up straight and then looked up into a black sky chipped with thousands of blinking stars, and I waited for those sharp star points to rain down on me, tossed angrily by the hand of God.

What had happened to me? Before I left home, I'd done all I could to be like my family, made of that land—the grasses, the soil, the sunlight, the rain, the stream, and the clouds. My family was the air that hovered above and the bedrock below, and even if they were to leave that land, its sediments would still flow in their veins, like rivers into more rivers. And yet I always knew I was different, that despite the moments of beauty, I was destined to leave. I wasn't different enough, however, to be criminal.

I went back upstairs, and Dot left shortly afterward without saying a word. I sat down on our small sofa and put my head in my hands. I ached for Alice, for her husband—dead or missing—for the whole miserable war and all the other dead and injured, too. Nothing horrible had happened to me, and yet I was selfish, effectively claiming someone else's child as my own. What had I done?

My back straightened as if I'd been struck through by an electrical current. My family believed in fate and the mysterious ways of a higher being. Again I thought that maybe what had happened here was in a strange way . . . right. It had been unsettling and entirely inconvenient, a single woman's disaster and a shocking turn of events, but again, maybe Mary had been left to me for a reason. The army officers would not have come here unless something awful had happened. *Her parents are both gone,* an inner voice whispered. Poor, sweet Mary. Life makes us no promises, no guarantees. Things move toward us whether we want them or not. Accidents occur, illnesses strike, and bombs fall. One street can be pulverized, the next one over not even scratched. Chance is so shifty and arbitrary. I closed my eyes against the memory of the redheaded soldier boy. I hadn't been able to save him, just as I hadn't been able to save our farm animals, and I'd seen countless other men, women, and children perish in the hospital due to unexpected illnesses and injuries. There was so much randomness in luck and life. There wasn't much, if anything, I could do about it; one person had so little impact . . . except when it came to a child.

The idea settled into my mind, and I remembered the feeling I'd had while standing on the bank of a pathetic creek on a Dust Bowl farm feeling sure that things would change. If I knew anything about myself, it was that I was resourceful. I'd made it from the farm to the greatest city in the world on my own.

And I could do this one small thing. I could save one life from an uncertain future. She didn't have to go through any painstaking placements in other homes. I knew nothing of her father's family; maybe they didn't want her, either. I recalled no contact they'd had with Alice. Mary could be sent away to strangers. Or worse yet, placed in an orphanage.

Maybe this was a part of my purpose here: I could save this one little lady.

After the visit from the army officers, my heart went through a mysterious transformation. In the morning, when I opened my eyes, Mary was my first thought. She had learned to calm herself and wait for me by sucking on her hands. When she saw me now, she smiled and cooed and gurgled. At work, my mind drifted to what she was doing at Lisen's, and I imagined her eating, playing, and napping. When I got off duty, I wanted to see her face. I missed the way she had begun to follow me with her eyes—that yearning gaze upon me—her laugh, and even her fussy spells. I knew how to get her past them. Lisen was good with her, but I was better.

Dot eventually forgave me for the army incident, and Lisen and Geoff said nothing to me about it, although they knew. They had little faith in government of any kind by that time and wanted to keep their distance.

For Mary's first Christmas, Dot and I put up a tiny tree and invited Lisen and Geoff over for a traditional dinner. Dot, Lisen, and I had made an elf outfit for Mary, and with her whitish hair and perfectly cherry-red cheeks, she could've been Santa's adorable great-granddaughter. While Dot, Lisen, and I made the food and took photos, Geoff joked about being around too much female company. In this large and boisterous city, I'd formed something of a new family. Dot's mother had died years earlier, and she did not get along with her father, a factory worker in Michigan. Lisen and Geoff were shunned by many simply because of a heritage they couldn't control, and I was keeping a child who wasn't mine. Separately we might have sunk, but together we moved beyond bloodlines and nationalities and backgrounds and formed a vessel that somehow stayed afloat.

And yet after Alice missed her baby's first Christmas, I had to do something. The day after the holiday, I finally went to the base on Governors Island to tell them that Lieutenant John McKee's wife had disappeared, but they turned me away at the gate, saying it was a local police problem. So I filed a missing person's report at the police station, but after I described the circumstances, the officer only shook his head and promised no action whatsoever.

On New Year's Eve, my newfound family went to Times Square; it had been decided the city was safe enough that the lights could be turned back on there. By then Italy had surrendered, but traffic lights in the city were mostly still masked in metal with only slits to show drivers whether they were red or green, interior trolley lights remained dipped in black paint, and every other streetlight was blacked out. That night in Times Square, however, it was full-scale dazzle and sparkle, and we were awash in golden hope. Maybe this was the last New Year's Eve at war. We stayed out too late despite the cold. But Mary loved the lights, and it was good to get out in the world again.

Mary crawled at seven months. I recorded all of these milestones in her baby book and took photographs with my Kodak. Her favorite toy was a mirror. Vain little thing—she was going to be a girly girl.

After work and on weekends, I took her along with me to the bookstores in the Village and the San Remo Café on Macdougal Street. I strolled with her on window-shopping adventures down Fifth Avenue, and afterward we would take rests on the steps of the New York Public Library, overlooked by its lions. We took our first boat ride together on the Staten Island Ferry. From the Brooklyn Bridge, we saw our first sailing vessel riding out on the ebb tide on the East River.

Once a week I volunteered at the USO, and I accepted dates when Dot convinced me I'd become a recluse. I spent an evening here and there soaking up the pleasure of male company. Some soldiers were lonely, and even desperate to marry. Many were boys who'd left towns and farms similar to my own and had enlisted for love of country and the adventure of a lifetime. Some seemed exhilarated; others seemed scared. But as I watched whirlwind romances and mad dashes to the altar, I had the feeling that some couples were, well . . . playacting at being in love, that the courtship existed mostly in their minds. Nurses I worked with married men after only a few dates and then later admitted they didn't know their husbands at all. Some couples who'd married at the beginning of the war were already filing for divorce.

Once I'd dreamed of a great romance followed by enduring love. I still wanted that grand love to come to me, but I had Mary now.

Besides, heaven help me, I met no one who stirred within me any sort of fire. And so I carried on without a ring on my finger.

There were times, however—once while riding the subway on a snowy day, once while drying dishes on a Sunday afternoon, and another time as a Gershwin tune drifted through the window and the breeze lifted the curtains like some beast softly breathing—when the loneliness came. So many decisions I'd made in my life had come from a sense of emptiness. The emptiness of the farm after the drought hit, the emptiness of my parents' bank accounts, and the empty opportunities where I came from. But now I had Mary. She had given substance to my life. Dreams I'd had of going overseas and experiencing an extraordinary life had begun to fade and feel flimsy. I missed those dreams from time to time, but I was surprised I was not sad. I would not have that exciting life filled with travel and adventure, but now I had this tiny, precious girl.

When she pulled herself up for the first time by clasping her chubby, beautiful hands onto the edge of the coffee table, she looked at me for approval with those saucer-huge eyes of hers, her white-blond hair about her head like a translucent halo, her mouth open like an *O*. Amazed that she had done it.

"Look what you just did," I whispered, leaning down to her and patting her back ever so gently.

She was growing up. *So quickly.*

She walked with the aid of furniture early, at ten months, and while she was learning, she often fell on her bottom. Startled, she would look up at me and then decide whether the fall warranted crying. If I laughed and clapped at her, she laughed back.

Once, when she had been struggling her way around the coffee table and had leaned in for her bunny just beyond her reach, she lost her balance, fell backward on her rump, and then waited. She fixed her searching eyes on mine and said, "Amma," in a soft, small, husky voice.

It took a moment for it to settle in: this was her way of saying, *Mama*, and, *Come help me up*. I hadn't realized until that moment that I had been calling myself Mama. I'd been saying to Mary, "Mama loves you," "Mama wants you to go to sleep now," and so on. The floor moved then, as if the earth had tilted on its axis. Of course I was her *Amma*. Her eyes and that one word said it all.

She looked to me for everything.

Love had crept up on me with the stealth of a cat and then pounced with an astonishing embrace. She had become my hold against the pushing and pulling tides that washed over the world. She had become my purpose in life. She had become mine.

As a toddler Mary was curious but reserved. She was much attached to me and to a lesser extent, Lisen. She was highly sensitive and also developed bonds to stuffed animals and blankets. But she also loved to be tossed in the air and flown around the room, a pale, tiny bird, silently soaring. Everyone said she was a beauty. Her hair was a color that no bottle of platinum hair dye could ever match, and it was so fine in texture that when I held her I could almost inhale those weightless strands. She had dimples in the oddest places—her elbows, feet, and hands. When I was at work, the thought of those dimples made me weepy.

Often I held her long after she'd fallen asleep at night. I kissed her velvet-soft forehead and whispered, "You're too much trouble," and then cocooned her longer. There was something so earthy about it. It kept me still; I was aware that she would not always be this tiny and dependent. Every day she changed. Every day we loved each other more. Every day I made a difference in her life.

I could've been more persistent: I could've demanded attention at the army base at Governors Island and perhaps made contact that would've eventually led me to John McKee's family. But I did not. At first I'd thought my guardianship of Mary was temporary, only an odd event in the midst of a war. But the feeling that I was her true mother only grew stronger with time. And with it the fear that, someday, someone would come to claim her.

CHAPTER SIX

Standing on the stoop of my apartment building on Victory over Japan Day, John McKee looked exactly as Alice had described—a tall, dark-haired man in uniform who wore the silver bars of a lieutenant. Everything went silent as I let it sink in. He had unusually sharp blue eyes, crystal-clear eyes, and although I could discern in the thinness of his face that something very bad indeed had happened to him overseas, he was nevertheless drop-dead handsome, with his sea-blue eyes and a shock of combed-back mahogany hair. And then there was that lovely, curious gaze. Mary's gaze.

How had my enemy arrived and managed to look like this?

"May I help you?" I asked.

The distant sounds of the city in full celebration returned. Sirens, music, horns, and shouts filled the air.

"I'm looking for Gwen Mullen," he said.

It took a moment for me to realize that my heart hadn't stopped altogether.

"That would be me."

"I'm John McKee." He said this straightforwardly, but I could see that he was nervous, a wreck, in fact—a red flush crept up his neck all the way to his chiseled chin.

I searched out my voice. It couldn't yet believe this was the father of my girl. Of course he had come for her. My life as a mother was being snatched away by a godlike, all-American soldier. I lifted my arms and then let them fall. "Welcome home." My chest was filled with a savage ache, but what else could I say? My mind filled with questions. What did he know? Did he even know that Alice was gone? Did he know anything?

"Thank you."

He seemed at a loss, and I'd been struck nearly mute.

"I arrived back yesterday. I had the address."

I nodded, stupidly.

"Could I bother you for a few minutes of your time?"

I pulled myself together and said, "Please come up. I'll make some coffee, or tea, if you'd like that better." I went through the motions, by rote.

"Coffee would be great."

Before I opened the door, I glanced behind me to remember the night, the taste of the air, and the feel of it on my skin. It would not be the same the next time I came out, or the time after that, or the one after that. I would never cross this threshold the same way again. Mary was to have stayed with me, to have kept me company and given me someone to comfort, teach, and watch grow. Now I would have to tackle the vast chasm of the future alone. Why had fate given me Mary only to take her away? Along the way the choice to hold tight had seemed so clear, but I had not asked myself enough of the tough questions. My throat tightened, but there was never any doubt what I would do. I had been found; I could no longer hide.

He followed me up to the apartment. Dot was out, and with Mary over at Lisen's, the place was empty. I turned on the lamp, and the light cut into the living room like the edge of a blade. I made the coffee and brought him a cup as he sat on the sofa, where I'd told him to make himself at home. I had cleaned up this morning, but Mary's bear sat on the end table, under the lamp. He seemed not to notice.

I took a chair opposite him. He didn't say anything, so it seemed I would need to start the conversation. "You were missing in action?"

He nodded once and never took a sip of his coffee. "German POW camp."

"It must have been terrible."

He shrugged and then looked me in the eyes with his shockingly blue ones. His pronounced cheekbones were covered with smooth, shaved skin, and his nose broke free of his brow in a nice planed line. I had to look away for a moment. He said, "I was one of the lucky ones. I got out."

He finally took a sip as though he were forcing himself. He set down the cup but kept his fingers wrapped around it, as if he needed to hold on to something. He worked himself up to what he needed to say, glanced at me, and then straightened his back. "I came here to find out as much as you know about Alice."

"Of course."

"I know she left here. They told me that at the base. But I don't know anything else. What happened?"

I chose my words carefully, not wanting to hurt this man any more than I was sure he had already been hurt. "She had been sad. Very sad. And she convinced herself that you were dead."

He took his hands away from the coffee cup finally and listened with glistening eyes, listened to each word as if his life depended on it.

"One day she told me she had to leave."

He cleared his throat. "Did she say where she was going?"

"She mentioned California; she said she wanted to go someplace warm."

A look of recognition came over his face. "She always wanted to live in San Francisco. The bay. The crooked street."

I gazed away, too, trying to recall Alice, who had faded so fast for me. "Yes, I think she once mentioned San Francisco."

He leaned forward again and clasped his hands before him. "I had promised her a real honeymoon there someday." He lifted a hand to his mouth and coughed self-consciously, and something pulsed at the corner of his right eye—a tic, it looked to me. Well, if that was the only physical damage the war had left, he had indeed been lucky.

The seconds went by, leaden and endless. I said, "I never heard from her after that day."

He clasped his hands together again and then let them go. "When was that?"

"August, late August."

He looked away and blinked a few times as if he were telling himself to wake up, that it couldn't be true, and yet knowing it was. "Almost a year . . ."

The tic worsened, and he blinked back the gathering tears. Men didn't cry, but the pain on his face was more heartrending than a hurricane of tears, a pain foreign and unknown to my heart. His expression wrecked me; I was a ship, capsized upon the jagged rocks. What I witnessed there—shattered hopes, shattered dreams, shattered love—was something I knew nothing about. What had Alice meant to him? What had she given him? I was completely unfamiliar with the bodily expression of yearning and loss that sat before me.

I eked out, "I'm so sorry . . ."

He shook his head. "I just can't imagine . . . I mean, what would make her leave like that?"

I was staring, and John was lost in disbelief.

I asked him, "You had no idea?"

He shook his head again and then met my gaze. "Her letters stopped coming even before I was taken prisoner. But I figured she was busy with the baby."

"She *was* busy." It didn't matter that . . . that wasn't exactly true.

"Did she read my letters?"

"I think so. I found them after she left, and I still have them. She had opened all of them."

He looked up at me with stunned, shimmering eyes. "She didn't take them with her?"

Tears were welling up within me now, for this man—or were they for me, too?—but I pushed them back down. "No. I'm sorry. Well, maybe she took some of them, but I do have a number of your letters, if you want to take a look."

"No," he said. "I suppose it doesn't matter." He looked down. If faces could tell stories, then John's was open to the page where all seemed lost. His wide shoulders had caved, and he couldn't face me. After several long, agonizing moments he said, "I have to find her. I can't imagine how she's taking care of herself and the baby."

I could've sworn the light in the room dimmed and then flashed back on. He didn't know. He thought Alice had taken the baby with her. But why wouldn't he have assumed a mother had taken her baby? It took me a moment to realize that this man in front of me had no idea that his daughter was sleeping safely one floor above.

I whispered, "I'll be back in a moment. Wait here."

I left the apartment and climbed the flight of stairs up to Lisen's place, a walk that felt endless. Could I place one foot in front of the other and finish what I was honor and duty bound to do? My eyes caught on the cracked paint in the stairwell and the triangular collections of dust and debris in the corners between the stairs and the wall. The air in the stairwell was cold, ever so cold, although it was warm outside. I reached for the walls to keep me upright. My enemy, the one whose arrival I'd been dreading for a year, was nothing but another lost and heartsick soldier. Another war-ravaged, broken man, who had but one thing left, who just happened to be Mary's father, and there was nothing I could do about it.

Upstairs, Lisen looked at me, and her face fell. She said, "Vhat is wrong with you? You are sick?"

I told her, "He's here. Mary's father is here."

She clutched my sleeve. "He is alive?"

"Yes," I gasped.

Her eyes teared over. "You give her back?"

I shook my head and laughed horribly. "What else can I do?"

Lisen wrung her hands, and then she started to sniffle. She magically produced a handkerchief from some hiding place in her dress bodice. "She sleep so gud tonight. You give her now?"

"I have to."

And so Lisen picked up Mary and held her close and kissed her sleeping eyelids. Then she turned away, her shoulders trembling. I bundled Mary in my arms and went down the stairs, opened the door to my apartment, and took her straight to her father. If I had stopped for even a moment, I might not have been able to make myself take another step. Or I would've barreled for the fire escape.

Mary hadn't budged; her sleep was that deep, and John still sat in the same place.

I placed her into his arms. "This is your daughter, Mary."

His face was so full of surprise that at first nothing else was apparent, but then, as he gazed down at Mary, I watched him go through a mixture of so many emotions: amazement, confusion, elation, devastation.

He didn't speak, but the tendons in his neck moved. He held his daughter in the awkward way that those who are not used to holding babies do. His elbows were wings at his sides, and his back was rigid, but his face quivered like a still pool of water barely touched.

Then he collapsed over her, his head grazing her blanket.

I whispered, "I'll leave you alone."

I stepped out into the hallway and pressed my back into the wall and waited while my life changed yet again. Mary had a father, a living father who would want her—no doubt—and that was that, even as it would tear my heart open. I brushed away tears and waited, giving Mary and her father time alone. No sounds came from the apartment; Mary continued to sleep. The innocence of the very young was such a gift.

When I returned he was still looking at Mary but appeared ready to ask questions. Questions I dreaded, such as, *Did you try to find me? Or my family?*

After I sat down again, he drew in a long silent breath. "She left the baby?" He shook his head. "What am I saying? It's obvious she left the baby."

It didn't appear he would indulge in a line of questioning about me. He seemed too crushed by what Alice had done, and my own sense of guilt waned. "I'm a nurse, and Alice and I . . . we were . . . friends. Friends to a degree." I paused. "I'm afraid I never knew her well, and she wasn't here long, but I had already been helping her with the baby. She didn't leave your daughter with a stranger. I think she was doing the best she could at the time."

He looked down at Mary again. "I guess I didn't know Alice well, either." There was not one ounce of bitterness in his voice, just bewilderment. "I can't believe she left the baby, but I'm . . . I'm overcome to have found her." He looked at me. His eyebrows were one shade darker than his hair, thick but well-shaped, like quarter moons lying on their tips. One eyelid flattened, sank lower, and trembled in some sort of odd squint, and he said to me without wavering, "Thank you. Thank you."

I had no words for the occasion. I couldn't tell him that I had loved her as my own, had become convinced she was my own, and that nothing else had ever been so sweet. I couldn't tell him I'd felt it would be forever.

Mary began to stir, and her eyes flew open. And then she reacted the same way she did to anyone she didn't know. She cried.

John McKee bounced Mary awkwardly and said, "There, there," but she only howled louder, and her face reddened.

He handed her over, and once she glimpsed my face and felt my arms, she stopped crying and wanted to play. She patted my face, and I pretended to bite her fingers. She cackled.

John McKee didn't speak, or maybe he couldn't. After all, he'd just met his daughter and heard her adorable laugh for the first time. Mary sucked on her fingers. I cradled her, and she fixed her eyes—which looked like strange and mysterious blue planets—on mine. She soon drifted back to sleep, safe and snug in my arms.

His voice just above a whisper. "You've taken fine care of her. She's been safe with you."

My eyes glued on Mary's precious face, I searched out my voice, and it sounded as if it weren't my own. "It's been almost a year." And then I could say no more. If I'd gone on, I might have bawled.

We sat in silence for a long time, I suppose to let our different but unexpected situations sink in. He had a daughter here, and I was going to have to give her up to him.

Finally he said, "I have to find a place to live. I'm not set up to take her now, and I have to try to find Alice."

I nodded.

"I have to go to San Francisco and at least give it a try. I feel sure she's there."

I had a hard time looking into his eyes. "I . . . I wish you the best of luck."

He clasped his hands again, looked down and then up. "In the meantime . . ."

I had to look away. "Don't worry. She can stay here."

"I'll leave money with you."

"It's not necessary. I've been managing."

"Of course it's necessary."

I simply blinked.

"I'll be back for her, and, Miss Mullen," he said and waited until I could look at him again. "Thank you. Thank you, again."

I managed to say, "My pleasure."

CHAPTER SEVEN

JOHN

At Grand Central Terminal, John bought a ticket for San Francisco. He had decided to travel by train, as he was sure Alice had, to better his chances of finding her. He boarded with only his duffel bag in hand and money in his pocket.

Aboard, he looked beyond the window and tried not to dwell on the reason he was making this trip. Instead he studied the different slant in the angle of sunlight that day, a sure sign that fall was coming, and he could smell the damp air and taste its coming cold in the back of his throat. In the city, the train swept past steel, glass, and brick buildings, on which hung patriotic banners. He saw "Welcome Home" signs on oil tanks and steamers, and flags draped outside windows. Beyond the city, the train picked up speed and clattered past forests and farmlands, towns washed in white clapboard and crowned with steeples, and across sandy rivers and networks of tracked roads.

A woman wearing thick glasses, bangs, and the shortest hairstyle he'd ever seen kept looking up at him, and John began to wonder if it showed, if the rest of the world could see what had befallen him.

He checked the front of his uniform and then his shave. Before leaving France, he and the other men had been given pamphlets offering "readjustment tips," ideas to aid them in their return to peace, but they said nothing about how to deal with a vanished wife and a country full of people who still had no clue about what the soldiers had experienced—who'd not seen bombed-out cities, dead children's stiff bodies on the streets, thirteen-year-old girls offering sex for a candy bar, and drowned and shot comrades by the thousands. *Hssst!* The sound of bullets passing through water. He jumped, a base-level muscular reaction. He shut his eyes—he could not, would not, think of D-day. The hills on the journey swelled in his stomach, and he had a hard time sleeping. He was still in the midst of battle, but who was the enemy now and for what was he fighting?

In the dream, he's running. Six feet away, down the ravine where he and his men have taken cover and are attempting to retreat, a grenade explodes. Only blood and bone and tissue remain of two of his soldiers, and then the rat-a-tat-tat of machine-gun fire pierces the air just overhead. He keeps his head low while more grenades boom nearby, shaking the earth and pulverizing twisted trees and showering the men with dirt and stones and thousands of smoking leaves. A smell of sulphur and burning flesh. He shouts for the medics and calls the order to keep withdrawing. Another volley of grenades and staccato machine-gun fire, and men screaming. They are surrounded. He staggers down the ravine grabbing men and yelling at them to move; cowering and praying isn't going to work. Another blast so close by he's momentarily deaf; a crater in the ground ruptures open before him, and he's thrown back into the dirt, and then everything goes dark. He tries to open his eyes, but they . . . wait . . . they are already open. He cannot see; he's blind. He has been told that you never see the one that ends it, but if it's the end, how would you know? Now he's helpless, and where are his men? He can hear more detonations, shots, and cries, the sounds of chaos. Have his men run the other way or been killed? Have they all been taken in ambush because of his orders? They have trusted him with their lives, have run through firefights, skulked through enemy territory side by side, and have been each other's eyes, ears, and instincts. Now he can do nothing but wait. Footsteps coming closer and then the warm, metallic butt of a gun against his cheek. "Say good-bye," a voice says. And then an earth-shattering boom.

John's eyes flew open, his heart racing, sweat flowing from every pore. He blinked; people on the train were staring. Had he cried out? He hoped not; a good soldier should never show weakness. A moment later, people politely turned their gazes away and returned to books and newspapers. He pulled out his handkerchief, wiped his brow, and then closed his eyes, summoning her face. When the dream first started, he was in combat, and he had soothed himself afterward by conjuring the face of his beautiful wife. Alice would appear like some otherworldly angel brushed by a breeze, her weightless hair flowing away from her face and a tiny smile of comfort forming on her lips. He closed his eyes and waited for that image to come and bring him back, give him a moment of peace, and he waited and waited . . . but for the first time ever, it was not there.

He'd been to San Francisco once before but had only spent a night and passed through, so he didn't know the city. On his first day, he looked for apartment buildings that had a view of the bay and asked the landlords about their tenants. Alice had once told him she dreamed of living with a bay view and singing in a nightclub on a slanted street. He also stuck his head inside clubs and asked if anyone knew Alice. So far he'd come up with nothing.

The next day he walked down streets lined with multistoried buildings, in and out of cool shadows, and then strode up hills on cobbled pavement, past machine shops, trash-filled alleys, produce markets, warehouses, tiny gardens, and homes with porticos, valances, and lead-glass windows. A gray sky made the bay look gray, too, only a duller, deeper shade of it, with gunmetal swells that rolled in unbroken except for occasional whitecaps. The wind brought with it the smell of fish and salt water and smoke from shoreline factories.

No rubble, no cratered-out buildings, no bloated bodies—everything working and in order. No pocked streets here, no apartments with blown-out walls revealing sagging sofas, kitchen dishes, and baby beds.

People rushed by, eyes down, collars up. Businessmen with stogies in their fingers, muscled Italian street fighters, and rugged cannery workers. There were other soldiers and sailors, Coast Guardsmen, bevies of laughing girls, and women with babies. Streetcars clanged up the hills with people hanging on to the sides. Spices and incense wafted out of doorways as people entered and left the small stores and restaurants. He thought he smelled sandalwood, then patchouli.

Finally he sank down onto a bench that overlooked the vast city. How would he ever find one person in such a huge, teeming metropolis? He had come without a plan. He had no automobile to broaden the search and no idea where Alice might have gone. He hadn't thought this through. Before he left New York, he'd combed through her letters again, thinking that perhaps Alice had left him a clue. But he found nothing.

He had assumed instinct would guide him. He thought he would know her scent or recognize where her feet had fallen before him. But now that he was here, he sensed no such thing. John pulled up his collar and turned his back to the wind that was spiking in off the bay, rattling windows and roofs. He could visit the police station, but he doubted they would have knowledge of a woman like Alice. He tried to remember if she'd ever mentioned anyone she knew in San Francisco, but she hadn't. In fact, she had barely talked about friends or family at all.

He picked himself up and walked some more. His legs ached when he stopped again and looked toward the clouds that swept across the moon like slim fingers. When he met Alice, she had charmed him with her musical talent and a reserve that hinted of something deep hidden inside. Her eyes spoke to him of special secrets he would soon share. She was lovely, smart, and mysterious. He fell hard. After they married, he learned of one mystery soon enough. Strangely, she turned to him most often during storms. Even the loud and violent ones had not frightened her but stirred her. During their brief marriage before he deployed, when rain soaked the streets and storms moved into the night, when their bedroom was lit by flashes of white lightning and claps of thunder boomed around them, she would let him love her under that angry sky in a way that had been better than beautiful. In those moments he hadn't thought about the combat zone into which he would soon be plunged. In those rare moments he was a lucky man, untouched by any of the world's ugliness.

But time waited for no one; it hadn't waited for them. The war tore them apart so soon. They could recapture what they'd had, couldn't they? He could help her overcome what she'd been through, and she could help him live with what he'd seen and done.

The next morning he bought a city street map. He could rule out the docks, the heavy industrial area between 3rd Street and the bay, Chinatown, the rail yards, and even the lighter industrial area west of 3rd. He could safely rule out Nob Hill mansions, too. But he would have to walk the rest of the city.

As the day wore on and after the sunset bled into a purple sky, the fog began to roll in, thicker than the mists of the day, and he felt touched by damp fingers. By nightfall, the wet coming off the sea was building in his head, raining behind his eyes. In the city alone, he saw how dangerous even this city, untouched by the ravages of war, could be—how it was filled with hazards, especially for a woman on her own.

He'd been spending his nights in a hotel, but he worried about how much he was spending. So he paid the bill and moved to a cheap boardinghouse near 19th and Mississippi in an area known as Potrero Hill, favored by Sicilians. The last hour before sunrise, John stole outside and watched the sun as it came up inside the clouds that were as dense and dark as a mantle, and he imagined those nights with Alice, his memories so fresh and real his skin tightened all over. He was soon roaming the streets again. He checked at boardinghouses, diners, and churches. Alice had worked many different odd jobs before they married, so he had no idea what she was doing here. He'd found no nightclubs that had employed her as a singer, seen her, or heard of her. She'd once sewn parachutes for the war, so he checked at clothing factories. He checked music halls, women's boutiques, and restaurants.

The next day, exhausted, he took a break at the western end of Golden Gate Park and sat on a bench to eat some bread and ham he'd bought at a small grocer's. As he took his first bite, he realized it was the first food he'd put in his mouth since the previous day. Still, hungry as he was, the food caught in his throat. He had to walk back to a diner and buy coffee to wash down the food, lest he choke.

Back on the bench, a nearby vendor was selling flowers, and the notes of a piano drifted down from a window. Perhaps in this pleasant spot, Alice would appear. Perhaps she would come and buy a bouquet for herself. But what money had Alice to take care of herself? Her allotment checks were sitting at the base. Gwen Mullen had returned them since Alice had disappeared. When he moved Alice into the apartment, she had brought only a little spending money and her personal belongings. She had received some allotment checks before she left, but how was she buying food or paying for a place to stay?

He closed his eyes and listened to the tune floating down from that invisible window. Alice had once played for him in the parlor of a hotel, and he remembered watching in quiet admiration as her hands, so small and delicate, had pounded out the loud chords. She had a pleasant singing voice, too, clear and high-toned. Odd, he thought now, that music had drawn him to Alice. He remembered that after they'd married, she not only had stopped playing piano, but also she had stopped singing around him. When he talked to her, she would touch her fingers to her cheeks and react as though he'd said something wise and important, but she seemed far away, distant. He tried to recall her hopes, her dreams, her fears, her secrets. But he'd known her only a little over a month when they became man and wife, and she had not divulged much about herself after they married, either. As he delved into that place of deep knowing and found it empty, he realized that Alice had been a woman barely seen, a woman made of mist.

The next day John found a police station and filed a missing person's report with a uniformed officer who looked as if chaos were his constant companion. The pen made scratching sounds against the paper, the most impersonal of sounds, and the officer obviously had much bigger problems to solve than this.

As the afternoon waned, John walked a new neighborhood. Men in golf coats, knickers, and two-toned shoes, and women in knee-length dress suits and coordinating hats, passed by him. Substantial homes of Victorian design stood near the tops of the hills; shops lined the streets he descended. Nearer to the wharves, there was a different class of establishments—breweries, pawnshops, stores filled with cheap trinkets, saloons—and alleys that smelled of cheap whiskey, smoke, and trash were populated by drunks, raggedly dressed teenagers, and vermin.

He finally ate something again, this time at a so-called Chinaman's restaurant, a table between vegetable stalls. He found that he could hardly eat the mixed, oily vegetables, which all tasted the same and came with a huge portion of rice. He caught a glimpse of the cook's reclaimed cooking-oil jar hanging from the griddle and lost his appetite altogether. As he walked away, hundreds of gulls cried out overhead, reminding him of the agony he'd heard in combat. He broke out in a cold sweat when he remembered the battles, the grenades, the artillery. Sloshing through water trying to dodge bullets, praying not to get hit. Bodies on a beach. Not D-day again. Would it follow him like this forever?

He looked out to sea and followed a wave sliding up the shelf to crash onshore. Then he walked uphill in brisk strides. He was out of breath long before he reached the top, but still he pushed onward.

At the top the view was enormous. Only a sash of cloud stretched out over the bay, and the sun was warm and lemon bright, just too bright a day to be dawning on such a dark awareness. He heard music from a courtyard, and between the slats of the outside gate, he could see flashes of color from girls' party dresses.

So others' lives would continue moving on course. He'd felt the same way overseas, too, when he first began to see the horrors of the war and knew that somewhere else, at the same moment, people were dancing a jitterbug or throwing a party. When they had to lay out soldiers' bodies in long lines for identification, somewhere else people were waiting in line to see a play or a movie. When he was eating scraps in a POW camp, people in other places were sitting down to five courses.

For another full day, he combed the streets. Alice had walked the same way; she must have. He wanted so badly to believe it that he convinced himself. Despite what she'd done, the thought of her physical closeness made him feel better. As he continued to walk, he imagined her eyes on the back of his neck. Sometimes he grew convinced she was near. Then he would stop, turn quietly so as not to startle her, and look. But the swarm of people only parted and maneuvered around him.

Other times he imagined her watching him from some tall and distant window, seeing him, experiencing a change of heart, and coming after him, her feet like ballet slippers padding the pavement. He stayed out late that night until he could see the flickering lights of Alcatraz out in the bay.

But as the next blue-sky afternoon came and went, he had to swallow the facts. The things Alice had done had a permanent ring. Alice's actions made it pretty clear that she didn't want to be found. He imagined her as she had risen early on the morning of her leaving. He could almost see her as she slipped away from the only place where he knew to find her, away from the weight of marriage and motherhood, weight that she would shed as soon as she rounded the corner.

He had survived the war and even a POW camp, only to return to a devastated life. His wife gone. A motherless child he didn't know. An uncertain future. Not even a home. Slowly it bled into him throughout the day, until he felt nothing but the pain and, finally, anger. How could Alice have done this to him? How could one person betray another like this?

In the POW camp, he'd imagined a sweet life in a tidy house, Alice playing the piano and singing to their children. He imagined getting out of the army, landing a good job that could support them all in comfort and even allow a vacation in the summers. He imagined going to dance recitals and baseball games, Alice sitting prettily at his side. These daydreams had given him hope. He'd had a reason to live.

Alice had given him a daughter. Then abandoned her, too. It would take years to sort through the complex multitude of feelings he had for his wife, but love was no longer one of them. In fact he'd not even known her well enough to truly love her; that was obvious. She was more strange than a stranger.

He clenched his hands down in the depths of his pockets. He'd fooled himself into believing he knew someone and loved her, he'd been foolish enough to marry her, and now he'd been fooled again. If Alice had come here, she had blended into this city like a thread woven into a vast bolt of cloth, and it was quite obvious: she had made it impossible to track her down. There was no point in continuing this search. He'd been blinding himself to Alice's obvious intentions. How ridiculous he'd been to think he could find her by wandering around this massive city, and even more pathetic was the naive belief that he could make everything better. He felt more cast off and alone than he had as a POW.

The next morning, he walked back to the train station and bought a ticket for a return trip to New York City. There was nothing else he could do here. Beyond the city, the train crossed the timber country and steamed up a riverbed, but John barely noticed their progress. Full of the cold and barren city he'd left, its chilly water still in his veins, John sat in silence all the way back.

CHAPTER EIGHT

Waiting to hear from John McKee was like waiting for a pot to boil. I had no idea what his next move was going to be, and often while Mary napped, I paced, scuffing out another faded path through the flower-garden rug.

A week had passed, and I hadn't heard from him. Every day Mary changed, and I knew that soon I would no longer be able to witness her daily advances. At night I was restless and awakened tangled in the sheets, longing only to hold her. I clung to her for hours before putting her down to sleep. When she was awake, she was a bundle of energy and curiosity, wanting to touch and taste and toss everything. Quiet moments were becoming rare.

Dot and I were off duty on Saturday, and she suggested we take Mary to the park. I think she sensed I needed to get my mind off the waiting, if that was possible. Dot wore one of her signature green dresses and high heels that showed off her legs. I wore slacks and flats, a match to my somber mood. In the morning, while the park was at its quiet-est, we walked with Mary in between us, both of us leaning down and letting her hold on by hooking her fingers around the tips of ours. Her balance was good, but she looked up at all the people we passed—that hindered her concentration—and I didn't want her to fall. Her delight in each new step gave me the urge to laugh and also to cry. How many more steps would I see her take?

It was a beautiful summer day with geese honking and flying in patterns overhead, lovers strolling, and the city still in full celebratory mood. Kites rose and dipped in the air, people played croquet on Sheep Meadow, and families rested by the boating pond. When Mary's nap time came, I put her down in the carriage, and Dot and I took a seat on a park bench to watch the parade of passersby.

Dot said, "Did you sleep last night? You look exhausted."

I crossed my legs and looked down at the grass. "Exhausted, huh?" I smiled at her. "That's a nice way of saying I look terrible. But to answer your question, I slept some."

She looked down at her hands. "Well, I know it's going to be hard on you. I've grown fond of the little monkey, too." She stopped to let out a sigh. "But look on the bright side. Now you can go into the army and travel the world like you once wanted."

I shrugged and felt the effort of it. "The war is over, and thank God for it. I don't know what the demand for nurses is going to be like now, certainly not like it was."

Dot turned toward me, leaned back into the bench, and asked, "So what will you do after she's gone?"

I shook my head. "Cry myself a river, I suppose."

Dot put her handbag aside and moved a little closer. "What was he like? Her father?"

The image came back to me then, the most powerful image I held of him—the moment I first put Mary into his arms. The forward tilt of his head, eyebrows straight across his furrowed forehead, and his eyes muddled, vulnerable, astonished puddles within the beauty of his face. For the rest of my life, that image would live in me.

I said, "He's a good man."

"What does he look like?"

"He looks like a man whose wife left him."

"You're practically related, you know. He's Mary's father and you're like her mother, more than her real mother was."

I sunk down lower and tried to get my neck to unwind. "Stop it. You'll truly make me cry."

"Can you imagine what he's been through?" Dot asked and then smiled at a group of passing soldiers.

I glanced at them, too, and then looked up and into a canopy of leaf and limb overhead. "He was in a POW camp, and he's trim," I said and looked at her. "I have no idea what he was like before, but he looks good despite the wear he's taken." I picked at a loose thread in the fabric of my slacks. "In fact, he's a looker, but Alice was beautiful, so that's to be expected. He wants to find her, but I know he'll take Mary away. He'll take her, no matter what."

"Can you imagine? Here he's been a prisoner of war in some god-awful cell somewhere, and then he finally gets out only to find his wife has left him. She couldn't have taken the time to write a 'Dear John'?"

I took a deep breath and held it for a moment, then said through exhaling, "I scarcely remember her. Isn't that awful?"

"Awful? What are you talking about? You did that woman the biggest favor in the world."

"Please don't sanctify me. I don't deserve it. When I first saw the man, I hoped it wasn't him. I didn't wish him dead, but I didn't want him on my doorstep, either. I thought only of myself."

"You took the place of a real mother, better than her real mother, so stop beating up on yourself. Of course you didn't want him to come, but now that he has, you're . . ." She looked down and glanced at me sideways. "You're free now."

We sat in silence then, and in the distance I could hear a siren and then a car's blasting horn. Two women, both pushing carriages, clacked past us wearing high-heeled shoes, just-below-the-knee-length skirts, and stylish hats. Teenagers wearing bobby sox and cuffed blue jeans skipped past.

I turned toward her. "Maybe we should join the navy, you and me, together."

Dot's eyes flashed toward me, surprised. Then she looked at me appraisingly for a long moment, and her eyes blurred. "Oh, Gwen, that's so nice of you to think of me in that way. You'll need to make a change, that's for certain, and thank you for asking me, but the army? The navy?" She shook her head. "Never interested me. All those rules and regulations. They would cramp my style."

"I've been cramping your style already."

"You don't say," she said and waved her hand about. "All these soldiers now set free to spend their money in the city, but they think we're married because of the little angel. Don't they bother to look at our left hands?"

I gazed off.

"It's not natural, anyway," she said in a softer tone.

I puzzled and turned back to her. "What do you mean?"

She looked down and then up. "Only that you should be married, you should fall in love with a man, you should have a honeymoon, too, before you become a *mother*. You'll never catch a husband this way."

I stared at her. "What has happened to my bold, independent Dot?"

"I'm getting older." She touched my arm. "Oh, Gwen. It will get better. And someday you'll get married and have a child, maybe several, of your own."

She glanced away. "There's something I've never told you before." She leaned back again. "A year before I was born, my mother gave birth to a daughter named Dolores Marie, to be nicknamed Dot. The baby died after only one day of life. When I was born, my parents gave me the same name and all of her little clothes and things." She paused only to draw breath and shake her head. "They honestly didn't see anything wrong with what they'd done. They just thought it would be simpler that way. But I've always felt my life was not my own to live . . ." She looked away. "First it belonged to my dead sister, then to my family, but now it's mine. Finally. Coming here and living this way is the only thing I've done by my own hand. I couldn't give up my freedom."

I couldn't take my eyes away from her face. I finally said, "I understand."

"Let's talk about something else. Let's ask Lisen to babysit so we can take in a picture show tonight."

"No date?"

She shook her head. "Only with you. The men can wait."

We sat a little longer, simply enjoying the silence and each other's company, and then she picked up a copy of *Life* magazine someone had left behind on the bench, and she began to thumb through it. On the cover was a photo of an underwater ballet swimmer.

Dot began to turn the pages. When she got to the section titled "Victory Celebrations" she scooted next to me so that we could look at the photographs together. A two-page spread had been devoted to kisses around the country, and the one that had been given a full-page display caught my eye.

I said to Dot, "That could be me," and pointed to the sailor kissing a woman wearing white in Times Square.

"Really?"

"A sailor kissed me just like that, in just that place."

"You don't say."

"Yes, just like that."

She looked at me. "Why, you're famous, Gwen."

I stared at the photo longer. Neither one of the faces in the photo was visible. And there had been many other people kissing that day. "Do you think that's me?"

Dot peered closer. "I think so. Maybe you should call *Life* magazine and tell them who you are. Get a little fame and notoriety from it."

For a moment I was back in that happy moment that had left me with a premonition that indeed came true. It was the moment I'd known my life was about to change. I scooted closer to Dot and perused the photo. I saw what looked like my hair, my nurse's uniform, and my shoes. I smiled. Here I was, just an ordinary person on the pages of *Life* magazine.

"Exciting!" Dot said and handed me the magazine. "You should keep this for posterity."

I held the magazine to my chest.

During the time I waited for John's return from California, I walked a sharp edge and noticed every detail surrounding me—the shadows cast by the Third Avenue El and the arching girders of the West Side Highway, the way the Chinese grocers stacked their vegetables in wooden racks like bookshelves, the slats of wooden produce crates, and the contrast of neon lights next to old filigree trim—as if it could soon be snatched away. The world was at peace, but within hours of Truman's victory declaration, telegrams had been sent out cancelling billions of dollars of war contracts. Tens of thousands of workers were being let go in the country's factories and shipyards. In Detroit alone, I read, over two hundred thousand had been fired. Already there had been an unemployment demonstration in the city, which harkened back to the days of the Depression.

On the other hand, people who owned cars could now fill up their tanks and head out for a drive to the shore. We could buy as many canned goods as we wanted, and we were told that new automobiles would be available next year. I surely wouldn't be in the market for one, but I loved to see the new models on the streets when they came out. The paper said we should have unlimited beef in just a few weeks' time, and my mouth watered at the prospect. We ought to have shelves full of nylons by Thanksgiving—no more bare legs with lines drawn down the backs when we ran out—new tires by January, radios in three months, and alarm clocks and ration-free shoes by October. I badly needed some new pumps, and I imagined the array of new shoes I would see in the stores. New telephones were predicted to be available in early 1946, but unlimited whiskey was to be had right away. I couldn't wait to linger in mindless thought while sipping a drink with Dot.

Each morning once the wailing sirens of the night had given way to the clunks and clatter of garbage trucks, I awakened with sunlight on my bedsheets and a temporary happiness brought on by the escape of sleep. But in the time it took me to turn my head toward the window and face that light, I remembered. *Mary.* During the day the thought lived as an ache in the arcs between my ribs. At night, sometimes I cried into my elbows, silently, so Dot and Mary wouldn't hear.

The next day John called and told me he had returned and that his sister had come to help him take Mary. I had known it was coming, of course, and yet the suddenness of it felt like a slap.

I finally formed my words and asked, "What about Alice?"

He breathed into the phone before he spoke. "I looked for her in San Francisco. I searched in apartment houses, boardinghouses, night-clubs, restaurants, you name it. There's no sign of her."

I didn't know what to say.

"Alice obviously doesn't want to be a wife and a mother." There was anger in his voice now, but who could blame him? "I think she's made that perfectly clear. I've spoken to a lawyer, who has advised me to get a divorce on grounds of abandonment and to seek sole custody of Mary."

"I understand."

"But enough of that. My sister has come all the way from Ohio to help me with the baby. As you saw, I have no experience with . . . kids, my own daughter most of all. But Catherine has raised three boys."

I clutched the receiver hard. "When will you be coming?"

"Tomorrow, if that's all right with you."

"I have to work the day shift at the hospital."

"When would be a good time then?"

"After dinner?"

"Certainly."

"I'll get all her things ready."

And so after Mary went down for the night, I folded her soft cotton shirts, flannel pajamas, corduroy jumpers, daytime rompers, and dresses. I gathered her blankets and stuffed animals, her bottles and baby dishes, and the tiny spoon I used for feeding her, and I packed everything in the diaper bag, a suitcase, and the bassinet that was already too small for her. I put her washcloths and diapers in the carriage and dried her bathtub toys and put them in there, too. I wiped down her high chair and scrubbed the tray and packed her remaining boxes of baby cereal and jars of baby food into grocery sacks. I washed the pacifier I'd managed to wean her off of and packed it, too, just in case.

Beneath all the grief, a sense of outrageous disbelief. Not only had I cared for Mary, I had loved her. I would love her still. And she would always be the better and stronger for it. My life, too, would always be richer for having loved her. And now . . . they were just going to take her away. Over and done. Outraged as I was, it did not take me all the way to regret. How could I have done it any other way?

I finished filling the bassinet and carriage, clicked the suitcase shut, and left the bedroom, where I'd put Mary down in the center of my bed.

All was done now; I went to the kitchen looking for something to drink. A good, stiff drink might be just what the doctor ordered. But I was overcome with nausea as I peered into the refrigerator and then the pantry. It was true that one can be sick with grief. My face crumpled, and I flew back into the bedroom, pulled out a T-shirt and a dress from the suitcase and held them against me. I would keep these things, just a few of them. Beyond the scent of the baby detergent maybe I'd always be able to breathe in the delicious baby smell of her.

CHAPTER NINE

The next evening they rang the downstairs bell, brutally announcing that the time had come. My stolen happiness had come to an end; my gig was up.

On the doorstep John introduced me to his sister, Catherine Daugherty, a thirtyish brunette beauty with a perfectly straight nose framed by high-boned, brightly rouged cheeks and penciled eyebrows. She wore a brown suit with wide, square, padded shoulders and held a clutch bag under her arm. She smiled hesitantly at me when I met her. I invited them inside, and then she had eyes only for the baby.

John was out of uniform and dressed casually in slacks and a blue button-down shirt that was open at the collar. The blue shirt enhanced the blue of his eyes—if that were possible—but he looked awful, agonized, as if he were the one saying good-bye to Mary.

Mary had been up since I'd taken her back from Lisen after work. Lisen had told me she'd had a tiresome afternoon, fussy and not wanting to eat. Maybe she was coming down with something, but she had no fever or signs of illness, and so perhaps it was her sensibilities, her child's intuition, telling her that something important was about to happen. She had been clinging to me ever since I'd come for her, and so I'd carried her around on my hip and talked to her in a soft voice and sang her favorite songs as I straightened up the apartment before John and his sister arrived. I put her down only to change out of my work clothes and into a pair of slacks and a blouse. Mary's daytime romper was soiled, and so I had dressed her in a white cotton dress with a strawberry print, ruffled diaper pants, and her white, high-topped walking shoes with lacy socks. She was the picture-perfect angel-toddler.

Dot had gone out for the evening, as she didn't want to interfere, but she had promised an early return in case I needed her.

Catherine sat perched on the edge of the chair opposite me and smoothed back her hair from her face as she looked around at my living room and then settled her gaze on Mary again. We had spoken little, but I sensed a rigidity about her that seemed in opposition to the kindness of her brother. John McKee seemed nervous, unsure of what to do or even where to put his hands.

"Where will you be going?" I asked him as we sat facing each other. Mary wiggled on my lap, wanting down. In the distance a siren whined, and I wanted to wail along with it. Composure, Gwen, keep it together.

Catherine answered, "We're taking her to my home in Ohio. Columbus to be exact. It's a fine place for families, and John is sure to find work there. We're members of the largest church in the area, and our schools are top-notch."

I nodded slowly. The light in the room darkened, as if outside a cloud had passed over the sun.

John looked at me and spoke softly: "I know enough to know I need help. The army has already released me, and I don't know if I'll find Ohio to my liking, but I need to be close to family. I know that." He looked down and away, as if unable to face me. He laced his hands together and then stared down at them.

Catherine said, "I've never adjusted to all these wartime changes, with women leaving their children behind and taking jobs and dressing like men. I'll take care of the baby as I've taken care of my own children, on my own, every day, in a stable household."

Her disapproval stained the air, and the mood became even touchier. I had become accustomed to women like her and their disdain for working women. Even those of us in nursing weren't exempt. I'd once been told by a woman not unlike Catherine Daugherty that working as a nurse was more acceptable because it was a helping profession, and I'd remarked that I was so happy to have her approval before walking away.

Catherine said, "Mary will have a solid, secure home. After what *that woman* did, leaving her . . . it's the least I can do."

She gave me a look that said she'd love to hear my feelings about Alice, but I had no interest in gossiping or berating someone, especially while my pain was so acute. I fought to make the conversation stay on a pleasant course. If I said how I really felt, all hell would break loose, and Mary was already feeling the effects of a long day. She rubbed her eyes with both fists and tilted her head against my chest and clutched at my blouse. Her eyelids were heavy.

I said, "Where will you be taking her now?"

John answered, "We have a hotel suite."

"And then tomorrow we plan to travel by train," Catherine replied.

"I hope you have a pleasant journey," I said and then looked aside at the bassinet packed with Mary's things so they wouldn't see the ache in my eyes. "Will you be able to take the bassinet and carriage?"

Catherine said, "There's no need. I have everything at home. I may have to bring down some things from the attic and dust them off, but it's all there. It worked for my children, so it will work for her, too." She smiled at me then, more of a real smile, and my tension eased, if only by a bit.

John said, "Maybe there's a needy family . . ."

"I'll make good use of the things," I told him, although I had no idea how I'd part with them.

"Hello, Mary," Catherine said in a soft, lilting voice as she leaned forward.

Mary turned away and buried her face into my chest and sniffled. Catherine stiffened and straightened.

"This is going to be hard on her," John said after a few long, tortuous moments.

"Well," Catherine said, "it has to be done." She sighed and looked at me and then at the back of Mary's head. "Let's get this over with, shall we?"

She stood then and took Mary from behind.

A shiver passed through me, even though the room was warm. I would never see her again. *Heaven help me*, I thought to myself as Mary howled and reached her dimpled arms in my direction, as huge tears streamed down her face, as she reddened and gulped in between desperate sobs, as Catherine sat and tried to comfort her to no avail. John tried next, and I moved beside him to stroke Mary's back in an effort to calm her.

But she twisted her body toward me and screamed, "Amma, Amma!" She flung around and writhed and kicked to get away from her father.

"Let me have her again," Catherine said, then took writhing and flailing Mary and began to pace the room. There was no patience in her voice or her stride.

The panicked howling continued, and then Catherine stopped and addressed me, "Perhaps this would go better if you weren't here."

"Of course," I said and stood, willing to do just about anything to ease Mary's panic. I headed toward my bedroom.

"No, wait," John said. The tic at the corner of his right eye had started hammering. "I don't believe that having the only person she knows leave the room is going to help. Maybe we sh—"

"No, John. I'm a mother, and I know what's best here. We must simply leave and get this over with. Prolonging things isn't going to help. It won't be any better tomorrow or the next day. It's going to be tough, and you, as her father, must be strong. Hold strong."

I could barely hear her over the sounds of Mary's cries. Mary was a tough girl when she wanted to have her way, and she nearly fought her way out of Catherine's grip and fell to the floor. Catherine hoisted her back up.

Then we all stood helpless as Mary continued to scream, her face red and wet, her hands grasping at the air in my direction.

"Take the clothing, John," Catherine said. "We could use that," and to me, "you have some diapers in there, I presume."

I nodded.

Mary screamed louder as Catherine moved toward the door. "I hope the taxi is still waiting."

John took the suitcase in his hand and said, "Is this it?"

I nodded.

At the door Mary's cries reached a frenzy, and I couldn't look at her, at any of them.

John said, "I can't take it." He dropped the suitcase, took Mary from his sister's arms, and put her into mine. She immediately fell into me and stopped crying, her fists grabbing my shirt.

"What are you doing?" Catherine said to him.

He shook his head, his face a portrait of torment. "I can't take it."

"It has to be done sooner or later." She let out a protracted sigh. "Listen, this is hardly the most difficult thing you'll have to do as a parent. You're her father. Let's get this done."

He looked at me. "May I call you later?"

I hadn't had a chance to answer when Catherine turned toward me with blazing eyes. "You, I blame you! You, you have made her into your child!"

Her accusation stung, but God help me, what she said was at least partially true. If she knew it all . . . but then again, how dare she blame me for loving an abandoned child?

John said, "Cath, don't."

Her eyes narrowed. "Why, what you've done is tantamount to kidnapping. Never reporting it to the authorities. Never trying to reach the army or John. Keeping her here and raising her as if she were yours."

My breath came out ragged and my pulse quickened. If she hadn't been Mary's aunt, how I would have given her a piece of my mind. How dare she criticize? Even if what she said *was* partially true, how dare she? I'd given Mary the best home I could. I'd thought that Alice might come back for her daughter, and I'd thought that Mary's father was most likely dead. All sorts of vile retorts came to my mind, but instead I focused on Mary. It would be horrid for this situation to deteriorate. She already had picked up on the recriminating tone that rang so clearly and forcefully in her aunt's voice. I swayed her on my hip and held her close.

Catherine said again, "You've made yourself her mother."

I couldn't contain it any longer. "I suppose I should've treated her like an orphan."

She harrumphed. "There are many things you *should* have done. First among them, sent a letter to John, then gone to the authorities, to—"

"I was a little on the busy side, working and taking care of a baby."

"What a pathetic excuse!"

John broke in with a soft but stern voice, "That's enough, Cath. I mean it." To me he turned silently and said, "I'll call you later. We're leaving you in peace for now."

"What?" Catherine glared at him.

He said to her, "I'll figure something out, something not as brutal as this."

"What else is there?"

"I don't know yet."

"There is no other way."

He held up his hand. "I'll figure something out."

"I have to return home tomorrow, John. I have my children and a husband and a house to take care of."

He said, "I know that."

And then John steered his sister toward the door.

"I'll call you later," he said again to me, before the door closed behind him.

True to his word, he called me later that night, after Mary had fallen into a restless sleep, clutching her blanket. I hadn't unpacked all her things, only enough items to get us through the night, because I had no idea what would happen next. I hadn't even been able to sit down and let myself relax. Tension and adrenaline streamed through me. Maybe they would be coming right back . . .

He said, "I'm sorry for what happened this evening."

I pressed the phone tightly into my cheek. "I'm sorry, too."

He exhaled into the phone. "You did nothing wrong. I'm sorry for what my sister said to you. It was uncalled for."

I swallowed. "Well, it's a difficult situation."

Had I made it more difficult by loving her so much? Had I made it harder for everyone? But when I looked back, my feelings had been inevitable. How could it be bad to love a child I thought was an orphan? How could love be anything but good for a baby, an innocent child?

John said, "I've sent Catherine on her way."

A tiny flicker of happiness. "She's gone?"

"Well, not yet, but she'll be taking the train tomorrow by herself."

"I'm sorry to cause such strife—"

"We've never been close, Catherine and I. She's much older than I am, and I never knew her well, not completely. She offered to help with Mary, and since my parents are frail now and I have no one else, it seemed the best idea at the time. But now . . ."

I waited for him to continue, and then he said, "I made a mistake thinking she could help me now. I'm sure you must be wondering, well, what I plan to do . . . and this is it: I think I should ease Mary into the idea that I'm her father, let her have a chance to get to know me and trust me."

He took another deep breath. "I was wondering if I could spend some time around her and you, as if I were a friend or an acquaintance. I'm hoping that, given time, she'll warm up to me, and then taking her won't be so difficult. What do you think?"

A ridiculous joy spread through me. I wouldn't be giving her up just yet.

"I think . . . that it's a wonderful idea, a very thoughtful idea."

Then he offered money for Mary's care, and I declined anything for me. But it was gentlemanly that he'd offered, and we did agree that he would pay Lisen to babysit.

"When might I see her again?" he asked.

I had been granted a glorious reprieve, and I filled my lungs with a cleansing breath. "Whenever you like," I answered.

The same evening that Catherine and John had come to take Mary, Dot had met a navy flyboy home from the Pacific. Once she'd been out with him, she didn't want to date anyone else.

"I tell you, dear friend," she said the next day as she powdered her face before the mirror. She was preparing herself for her second date with the pilot, and I was wearing a housedress and running Mary's bath. "He's Adonis in the flesh."

I tested the water for temperature. "When can I meet him?"

She shot me a reprimanding look. "Don't get any ideas."

I turned to her and laughed. "Come now! You know I'm all out of practice. I just want to get my eyes on the dreamboat who has sunk you."

She set down the powder puff and sighed. "Dennis Meade, that's his name. And he is handsome, I tell you. But it's more than that. He's exciting. I met him at the Onyx Club, and then he took me to Harlem. Harlem! We went to dinner and then to a jazz club called the Elks Rendezvous, and the music! It was the best music I've ever heard, and people were doing all the new dances. He taught me how to bebop. People came and went at all hours of the night. I know I promised to come home early for you, but I couldn't tear myself away."

I swayed my hands through the bathwater as Dot went on.

"And he's a pilot, you know. How romantic is that? You know I'm a sucker for pilots. When he gets out of the navy, he'll probably go to work for one of the airlines. Then we'll be able to fly anywhere we want for nothing."

As the tub slowly filled, I thought of all those harried marriages, some of which had already ended in divorce. Men shipping out, women settling in, with only a few memories to sustain them. "You're planning a life already."

She adjusted her shoulder pads and then her belt. "With him, I can imagine it. A life after all of this," she said and gestured around. I took her to mean single life and sharing a small apartment with another woman.

I said, "So you'll be joining the ranks of married ladies."

She sighed again. "Who knows? To pull this off, I'll have to put all my charms into play."

I was surprised that Dot, after having waited, seemed to be succumbing to such a rushed romance. I draped my hand through the warm bathwater and said, "I still want to meet him."

She shot me a look. "I don't want to scare him off."

"Dot!"

"Well, it'll be obvious I'm seeking your approval." She shrugged and then studied herself in the mirror. "Even after all he's done—he has some kind of medal for bravery—he seems shy or nervous or something. He's confident, he's manly, he's lots of fun, you know, but there's something ill at ease there, too. Probably because he doesn't have a job yet. And I don't want him to think I'm already parading him around as my own."

"So I'll wait until you're officially engaged."

"If I have my way," she said with determination as she fluffed her bob, "that won't take very long."

CHAPTER TEN

John had arranged to pick us up just after lunchtime on my next day off. All morning long, in nervous anticipation of the day ahead, I'd been getting Mary and myself ready and cleaning the apartment. I knew almost nothing about John. How would he react to spending a day with his daughter? Would he be saddened by his challenging situation and therefore withdraw, or frantic to form a quick bond and try too hard?

I donned a blue shirtdress and a pair of platform sandals, and I dressed Mary in a yellow romper and her white walking shoes. I put a red-checked bonnet on her head, which made her look country-baby adorable. Her father would be charmed.

Before she left for the day, Dot remarked that I seemed OK about the situation, and I told her I liked the idea of Mary warming up and getting to know her father. I liked the idea, even though it would still mean the end for me. But it would be a little less heartbreaking if I could see Mary go away more willingly when the time came.

Dot had just looked at me then and said no more.

John arrived wearing a white shirt that looked fresh from the cleaners and dark-gray pressed slacks. He was one of the few men I'd seen who looked as good in civilian clothes as in uniform, but obviously he knew little about playtime with a toddler. I imagined the white shirt soiled and perhaps even ruined by day's end.

In the yellow taxi, we all sat in the backseat. Mary clung to me and wouldn't so much as look at her father. John seemed all right with that.

On Central Park West, he paid the taxi driver, and we entered the park through one of the marvelous stone arches. As we walked toward the lake and the boathouse, I carried Mary on my left hip. It was a still and sunny day, the temperature a bit cooler than the heat we'd had in the middle of summer. The leaves drifted ever so slowly on their branches, and squirrels ran from one thick-trunked tree to the next across the green grass, making no sound at all. The air was like silk on my skin.

I put Mary down and held her close to me at the edge of the lake. She pointed her finger and said, "Wah-ter," the same way my little sister, as a child, had said it. I pulled out some bread scraps I'd collected from the kitchen so we'd have something to feed the ducks.

John crouched down next to us and watched as I showed Mary how to throw bread crumbs to the mallards that were already skimming across the lake in our direction, their webbed feet furiously paddling under the surface where we could not see. Mary loved to watch animals, and she had already spotted the ducks. I told John that when she was crawling, she had tried to chase after birds in the park.

He smiled. It was the first time I'd seen his smile, and it was transformative; his eyes creased just a little bit at their corners, seeming to erase some of the stress and worry that was normally present in his eyes. I hadn't seen that tic at the edge of his right eye today. I shifted my gaze and watched as he rolled up his shirtsleeves to his elbows. The brown hair on his arms and hands shone like gold leaf in the sunlight.

Mary stood transfixed by the ducks as they surged and plunged on the lake's surface in front of us, trying to beat each other for every morsel we tossed out. Sunlight danced across the water, and turned Mary's hair into translucent sheets.

"How is she?" John said as he followed her every movement. "I mean, would you say she's bright?"

I nodded. "I think so. Yes . . . very bright. She's met all her milestones so far, and she's been early in many. She's had only one delay—she's been a little slow to read and write."

He looked at me and then shook his head, confused for a moment. Obviously he didn't know what to make of me yet.

I said, "I'm kidding, of course."

Then I saw that smile of his again, and he went back to studying his daughter.

A few moments later I said, "Alice told me you were from Colorado, too."

He finally took his eyes off Mary and gazed at me. "You're from Colorado?"

"San Luis Valley, farming country."

He shook his head in a surprised way. "Not many of us came this way. Everyone I knew wanted to go to California."

I nodded.

He offered, "I grew up on a ranch between Denver and Fort Collins."

"When did you leave?"

"I went to college at CSU right after high school."

His parents had certainly been better off than mine. They'd had money to send their kids to college. The drought had affected southern Colorado and not the northern part of the state where John had grown up. "What did you study?"

"Business."

"What kind of business?" It sounded as if I was interrogating him, and I decided to stop prying.

He laughed wryly and looked down for a second before facing me again. "That's a good question. I didn't know what to do with it. I always wanted to open a business, but I couldn't come up with a plan.

I thought I should do something I knew about, so I was going to open a farm and ranch supply store in Fort Collins, but no one wanted to lend me the money for starting up."

Mary and I were almost out of scraps for the ducks by then. I whispered to her, "Just a few more now. See that duck out there," I said and pointed to a rather small female. "She hasn't had any treats, so let's throw some to her, OK?"

Mary said a big "O-K." It was one of her new words, and I told John that.

When she dropped a piece of bread, she said, "Uh-oh," very distinctly. That had been one of her earliest expressions, right after "wah-ter."

He said, "Uh-oh," back to her, and she stilled.

She had glanced at John a few times, and I could see that she remembered him. Her body felt it: *I've seen you before. You were one of the ones who tried to take me.*

He knew it, too, and was taking his time addressing her. When he watched her, his face showed but one emotion: wonder. And his gentle movements and sense of ease said, *I will wait for you.*

He said to me, "I also know about work boots."

A spurt of laughter escaped me.

He smiled, but he said, "A man will pay a lot of money for a good pair of boots. My dad will skimp on many things, but not his boots. Lots of working men do the same."

We walked out of the park, and back on the street the smell of axle grease and car exhaust and smoke from a man's cigar surrounded us. The sky was bright blue, and gold shimmered on some of the leaves, the earliest turnings of autumn. We stopped to buy an ice-cream cone from a street vendor, and I dug out a baby spoon from the diaper bag so we could feed some to Mary.

We sat on a bench, and I faced Mary toward her father as she sat on my lap. He licked some ice cream off the cone a couple of times and made some soft, satisfied sounds. He then held it out to me. I think he read my mind, because he knew what I had planned. I fed Mary a few spoonfuls of vanilla ice cream, and of course, she loved it. She started opening her mouth like a little bird long before I had the next spoonful ready.

And then I passed the spoon to John.

She didn't take the ice cream he offered, but she did look him in the eye for the first time. She wasn't scared. She simply studied him in the way that little ones do, curious and intent. *Who are you? Why are you here?*

He fed the spoonful to me, and she watched him place it in my mouth. Then he scooped up another bite of ice cream and offered it to her again. This time the pull of that sweet taste was too strong to resist.

He said softly to her, "That was good, huh?"

She nodded and opened her mouth for more. And so he fed her ice cream and told her about himself at the same time, as if he also wanted me to know his story. He told us that after college when he finally decided to join up, he chose the navy. But he showed up at the recruiting center in Denver only to find out that his draft notice had been sent in the mail. And sure enough the next day, it came. "Greetings," it said. So he ended up in the army instead. He went for basic training at Fort Riley, Kansas, and since he had graduated from college, he was then shipped to Officer Candidate School at Fort Sill in Oklahoma. After that, he was assigned to the First Army at Fort Jay on Governors Island.

He fed Mary until she could eat no more, and then he and I took turns finishing the ice cream, crunchy cone and all.

Now Mary couldn't take her eyes off John. She didn't want to go to him, but her curiosity had been piqued. Only the sight of pigeons finally drew her attention away. When we went back into the park, I let her walk. Her steps were a series of hard-fought triumphs. She was still not completely at ease while walking on her own, but how she charmed us with the blush in her pearly, cherub cheeks, her chubby hands reaching out for things long before she got close to them, her amazement at it all. She tried to get to a crow and then a butterfly.

"I imagined this," he said as his eyes followed her. "When I was in the POW camp, it was one of the things that kept me going. I thought of seeing Alice, of course, but I also tried to think what it would be like to be a father, to see my child in the flesh."

I'd never known a man who would or could openly discuss his thoughts and feelings. My father and brothers had never expressed such a sentiment in all the time I'd known them.

"The only thing that got me through it was thinking about the future," he said. He glanced up at the leaves above. "America has emerged from this war as the most powerful country on earth. When you've seen the state that other parts of the world are in, that feels even more true. We can do anything. I think about children all the time, too. I see them everywhere, and now that I know I have Mary, my perception of the world has changed. I see children as"—he paused and seemed deep in thought—"somehow more valuable, more precious. I hate to admit that I didn't feel that way before, but now . . ." He shook his head. "I think about the past, too, and what I've seen. I want history to be told truthfully. When I was in school I don't believe I was taught the whole story. The United States was always right. We never suffered great losses in war. We always won. We were invincible. Even at the beginning of this war, everyone said that once we joined in, the war would be over in six months."

"I remember that, too."

He rubbed his chin. "In the future, I want the children to know how the world really is, not just here, but everywhere. I want them to learn about the larger story. I'm just realizing this now, talking to you. This is what has been bothering me."

He gazed away. "I'm not sure where I'm going to fit in this postwar world. Owning a business, as I'd once dreamed, doesn't feel right any longer. I wanted to make some money and have an easy life, but now I know that nothing is easy. Nothing is simple. I don't know what I want to do, but I do know I want it to be meaningful."

I was never shy about giving unasked-for advice. "Maybe you should become a teacher."

He held still, and then his face went through what looked like a slow dawning, as if he was considering a new vision of himself. Every muscle in his face relaxed, but his pupils sharpened into obsidian points. He said, "Maybe I should."

He looked at me in a more direct way, as if he'd suddenly realized something. "You're so easy to talk to, Gwen. I had never considered teaching. My father would say it's women's work, but I love the idea of teaching history."

A few minutes later, Mary started rubbing her eyes with her fists and getting fussy. I knew she needed some sleep, so John hailed a taxi and we returned to the apartment, where I put her down for a nap.

When I came out of the bedroom, I found John sitting on the edge of the sofa. All day long he'd been serene and composed, but I could tell by the way he sat, leaning forward with his hands clasped together, tightly, like basket weave, that he was nervous. That tiny tic was pulsing, and his left knee was jumping.

I offered him coffee or tea, but he declined. Now *I* was nervous.

I sat down across from him. He looked away, searching out the window, as one often does when trying to arrive at a clear thought.

He turned back. "Did you enjoy the day?"

"Yes, very much. Thank you, and Mary thanks you, too."

"I think I made some progress with her."

"You definitely made some progress."

"She's a happy little girl."

I smiled, but I wished he'd get to whatever it was that was bothering him. "Most of the time."

He clasped his hands together even tighter. His hands were large and manly, yet there was something gentle about them, too, and he had clean, clipped nails. "I was thinking . . ." he said and faced me and then looked away again. Though his skin looked soft, there was tension beneath the surface. I could feel something stir in the air, too, a shift of sorts. Maybe he'd had a change of heart. Maybe he wanted to take Mary right now.

A moment of panic. I crossed my legs and waited for him to speak.

He held his hands in front of him, like an offering. "I was thinking . . ." he said again and then found my eyes, "that maybe we should make this a permanent arrangement."

I stopped breathing.

He looked away again. "My divorce should be granted soon, and then . . . I'll be free to do as I please." He looked back at me, and the question came into his eyes first. "Mary loves you like a mother. I don't know how I would take her away from you. But together . . ." He averted his gaze for a moment, then he looked at me again and drew in a breath. "Together we could give her a safe and loving home. Would you consider . . . marrying me?"

I sat frozen, disbelieving. I hadn't seen this coming, but why hadn't I? Through Mary we were more bound to each other than many war-time couples had been before they married.

Memories of the last three and a half years hammered through my mind. All the soldiers and patients in the hospital that I could've married, all the men who'd stopped me on the street or approached me in bars, and all the roommates I'd had that left to marry men they barely knew. And through all of it, I'd held out for something I didn't exactly know how to name. To say I'd held out for love was too simple. All the marriages I'd seen had happened because the couple was "in love." I wanted something that took my breath away, yes, but I wanted that feeling to settle inside me for a long, long stay. Let me truly, deeply know you and you know me in the same way. I had felt alone for many years, but I had not been afraid, and I had not settled or made an "arrangement." I couldn't marry for convenience, not even to keep Mary as my daughter.

I could've told him all that, but my lungs had become fists. I had to work past the small flare of anger his suggestion had ignited. I had been the substitute mother, and now he was suggesting I become the substitute wife? But of course his idea was more pitiable than insulting. How desperate he must be to make a home for Mary. It had hit him now, hadn't it?—the magnitude of being a parent. Now, he, too, knew what one might do to keep her safe and sound. But this man was not in love with me, and I was not in love with him.

There was so much I could've said; so many confused and contradictory emotions surged through me they left me shaken. His proposal was rash, but it could provide an easy solution. I could affix myself to this man, who was good and kind, and his daughter, whom I loved. I could have Mary forever. For a moment I was tempted to take an uncomplicated course. But for only a moment, because how could a marriage of convenience, without love, be the answer? I'd held out a long time for something better. I didn't know exactly what that was yet, but I was sure I'd know it when I found it.

I let all those thoughts dissolve unspoken. I drew in some calming breaths before I spoke, because his face was so hopeful. In fact, his hope was the saddest thing I'd seen in a long time. I stared at his hands, held together so expectantly. But I struggled to be brave and looked into his eyes and said an almost breathless, "I can't."

He held still, and then he nodded as if telling himself, *of course not, of course not,* but he said only, "I understand," with no discernible emotion whatsoever.

CHAPTER ELEVEN

JOHN

He left Gwen's apartment building and began walking. A layer of smoke and fog had rolled in from New Jersey and settled over Manhattan, and the brightness of the day was gone. He headed in no particular direction and fell into a regular rhythm, his steps the only regular thing about his life these days.

His wife had vanished, and he had a child he didn't know. He was seeking a divorce as soon as possible, but in New York, the only grounds for divorce was adultery. Many couples here had to stage a mock "caught in the act scene," aided by their attorneys and witnesses in order to get what they wanted. Even a "quickie" Reno divorce would not work for him without Alice being given some notice, and he had no way to find her. John had taken his problem to his commanding officers, who put one of the army's best legal minds to work for him, and that attorney had promised to push through a divorce on special circumstances, utilizing John's exemplary war record and an old friendship with a judge to his benefit. But John wasn't divorced yet. On top of that, the war dream flashed before him almost every night in his restless sleep, and he didn't know if it would ever stop.

And now he had proposed marriage to a woman he barely knew.

The day had been a good one, a rare pleasant day, and his daughter had looked at him with curiosity he hoped would change to familiarity and finally love. He had fed her ice cream, and the way she opened her mouth to take the spoon from him was so innocent and trusting that it rended his heart. And then Gwen—this woman his daughter loved as a mother, who had taken care of his daughter and asked for nothing in return—well, he'd seen the worst of humanity during the war, but in her he'd seen the best of it. With her, he could imagine that he might forgive the world.

But he'd asked too much of her. He swallowed down a huge lump of regret and kept moving.

New York City. He didn't think there was any other place on earth where a person could be surrounded by throngs of others and still feel completely alone. A man could keep entirely to himself if he wanted to, or he could tell his story to every shoeshine, waitress, and hawker in the city. He could isolate himself in a hotel room or go out on the town, surrounded by thousands of people. There was something sad about it, all these people rushing around, but a man would never feel dead here. Just take a new street, or turn the next corner. Everything was so busy and in constant motion, and maybe that was part of the problem. He still couldn't believe that all the things he saw around him—the tall undamaged buildings, the decadent shops and bustling eateries, the lights, the traffic, the gleaming windows, the healthy people on the street—were still here, were, in fact, untouched. As if nothing in the world had happened.

Everything had happened.

This city felt more foreign to him than when he'd first arrived on distant shores in that place of war. A pang of yearning for that world of desolation ran through his body like a shiver. He missed it, and he knew he should not miss it. It had been brutal, tragic, and horrific. But he ached for the camaraderie, the mission, the purpose, and all those men who hadn't come back. The enemy had been obvious, and each mission had started with a clear goal. But here, he was still fighting a war, only for what and with whom? Nothing seemed obvious or clear. He had planned on leaving New York and going back to Colorado. Now he wasn't sure he could do that, because of Mary. He couldn't do it soon; that was certain. He had to stay here for a while, even though he didn't even have a proper place in which to live or a job. If he decided he wanted to pursue teaching, it would take time and money.

He ducked into an Italian place on Mulberry Street for some dinner and then left after he'd eaten what he could. He headed to Third Avenue under the El where he'd heard soldiers could drink on the cheap. He found a barstool at a racy joint called the High Hat where revelers were still in a war's-end, wise-cracking, hard-drinking mood. Surrounded by the scents of sweat, malt, and cigars, he ordered a beer and before he knew it was talking to the soldier sitting next to him. The guy was in civilian clothes, but John could pick out the other GIs in a place.

"You out already?" the soldier asked him.

"Yeah," John answered. "Special circumstances."

"They're getting rid of all of us. I'm out soon," the man said and introduced himself as Charlie Hobbs, yeoman second class in the Coast Guard, originally from Highlands, New Jersey, across Raritan Bay. His buddies were Coast Guard, too.

"What are you planning to do now?" John asked him.

"We aim to stay here and get jobs. We got us some radio experience, so we're going to try our luck with RCA."

"Do you have a place to stay?"

Charlie nodded. "Man, Lady Luck was shining on us, I tell you. There's almost nothing out there. We hear his staffers can't even find a place for Mayor LaGuardia now that he's about to leave Gracie

Mansion. Like I said, Lady Luck. We just sublet an apartment on the Upper West Side. Size of a closet. But we're squeezing in."

"Any other apartments for rent in your building?"

"Not that I know of. My buddy Larry here, he heard about it, and we hustled over, but there were other people waiting before us. We played the patriotic card to get in. Plus it don't hurt to tell 'em you love their city and want to live here."

John took a long swig of his beer. He had been hoping to get a lead on an available apartment. What the hell was he going to do?

"You out on the street?" Charlie asked.

"No, I've got a hotel room at the Lafayette, but it's going to eat up all my back pay if I don't find another place. And I have to stay for a while. I have a daughter here."

Charlie leaned back and took a good hard look at him. "Where's your wife?"

The night rained her stars, and that tic in the corner of his right eye began to throb. John tried rubbing it away. "That's a good question," he said and drank again. "It's a long story."

The other man shrugged it off. "You don't have to say nothing."

A minute later Charlie followed with, "We got a couch in the place. It came furnished. I'll ask my buddies if you can have it, if we can help you out. Seems like your chips are down."

"Thanks, man," John said, overwhelmed with relief as he shook Charlie's hand. "I have no problem sleeping on a couch, and I've already put in an application at both Edison and Standard Oil. I'm hoping to hear from one of them soon. I have enough money to pay my share of the rent anyway."

John took down the address. He thanked Charlie and his friends and declined the advances of a strawberry-blonde, Wall Street–secretary type painting the town and looking for trouble. Up close she looked too bright and pretty to be parading around in a place such as this, and he was tempted. He was almost divorced and free, after all. But he'd not be fooled by a pretty face with mystery behind it again. John departed, telling his new buddies that he would come to the apartment the next day.

He began walking again, and as it got later, the face of the city changed before his eyes. New York City packed all manner of life—immigrants from every country, every race—into its convoluted streets and alleys and then blended food and music and the sounds of cars and swarms of insects. The sidewalks were flooded with people, the drunks slept out in the open, and the beggars asked him for a nickel for the subway. But he was OK, and it was safe. A popular war-bond poster of the day read,

> If my father hadn't come to America about 35 years ago, I'd
> be starving in Poland . . .
>
> I'd be sobbing in France . . .
>
> I'd be stealing in Greece . . .
>
> I'd be shivering in Belgrade . . .
>
> I'd be slaving in Frankfurt . . .
>
> I'd be hiding in Prague . . .
>
> I'd be buried in Russia.

But here he was, alive and walking on his own two feet. He had said good-bye to the First Army without a scratch on him. Only the dreams and the damn tic still haunted him.

He'd met Alice and had a whirlwind courtship and wedding while on leave from Fort Jay in the fall of 1943, then headed to the UK to prepare for his first combat operation overseas. In 1944, over a year ago, on D-day with General Omar Bradley commanding, he'd been among the first soldiers who had stormed Utah Beach in Normandy.

After Hodges took over command, the First Army had been the first American soldiers to enter Paris on their way across Northern France. They were the first to cross the Siegfried Line into Germany in September, but soon after they'd gotten over the line John and a small number of his men had been ambushed, captured, and taken to a German POW camp. The First Army, however, had reached the Rhine in March, and he was soon to be freed.

Before he saw combat, he'd imagined war as something different, nobler maybe, his side always in the right. He had pictured battle as something even spiritual in its purity; instead he had found himself leading raids, a bag loaded with hand grenades over his shoulder. John was a good marksman with a rifle. His father had taught him to shoot with a Springfield out on the ranch, but artillery bombardment was something else altogether. Invisible enemy weapons hurled high explosives to pulverize the exposed. He and his soldiers huddled together, well aware that they faced certain bloody, dismembering death if they suffered a hit. Often a shell or a grenade hit one man in a group and left him mutilated beyond recognition, while the others went untouched except for a spray of the fallen soldier's blood and bone and fragments of what was once a uniform.

The haphazardness of it was so incongruous with the merciful God John had been taught to believe in. As the whistling of shells rang out through the sky—no other sound like it—a soldier cowered and waited to find out whether that time, he would be the one hit. The smell of poison gas in ponds that used to float ducks and loons, the sea holding bloated bodies of fallen men, and the feeling that came after each raid and overhead attack—the elation of temporary survival followed by a dreadful, deep-seated regret and despair. In that place, John could clearly see how humanity had failed.

After capture he and his men had been marched off, many of them injured and suffering from dysentery and nightmares. By the end of the war, the German POW camps were running on empty, and he was taken to a ramshackle outpost that consisted of a few rows of wooden huts surrounded by barbed-wire fences, sentry boxes, and machine gunners.

The officers were stuffed into a room at the end of an unheated hut that sat off the ground. For the first few days there was no food at all, and until winter descended, the flies came in droves. Fuel supplies were running low, and Red Cross parcels ceased to arrive. The bathroom consisted of a separate shed over a pit pierced with holes that allowed the frigid wind to sweep through. Many soldiers became ill, and every morning the bodies of the dead were dragged away.

In the early days at the camp, the men talked and played bridge. But as the months dragged on, their nerves began to fray, and they irritated each other. They watched for signs that the Germans were moving out and the Russians were coming—surely the war had to end soon— but there was nothing. He remembered the cold at night, the meals of moldy bread, pea soup, and rotten potatoes, and most of all, the feeling of not being free. He had grown up with open land around him and beckoning mountains in the distance. He'd never had to endure confinement and was shocked by the way it affected his soul. He had to fight a rising tide of hopelessness at every turn. He had survived by dreaming of home, of his wife and child, and of a new life when the war was over. He had pictured his family reunited and forging new plans together. Maybe a business in Colorado, maybe a brick bungalow for a home. He would never forget Alice because of that. Even if what they'd had didn't, in the end, amount to much, she had sustained him during those long, bleak days and nights. And of course she had given him

Mary. If he'd known when he was there that she had fled, he wondered how he would've made it through.

He remembered his father's mantra to him, the advice he'd been given ever since he could remember: "Do right, and all else will follow." His father had said this to him on many occasions—on birthdays, at graduations, and when he went off to serve in the war. His father had always arisen every day before dawn, had never let up on his work or other duties, despite the weather or the seasons. Discipline had always been strict, but handed down with gentle eyes and big hands that held back their full strength. Those days belonged in a more innocent time.

Now, at midnight in New York, he heard the Queen Mary blow her horn and found in it the sound of departures and good-byes. He remembered the arrival of the Russians, more waiting, and then being shipped away in cattle trucks, sixty men crammed into each one. And then medical care, then taking the ship back home, watching fast clouds gallop across a full moon, the images and imaginings of home luring him onward, freedom fresh on his tongue. But he'd had no idea that Alice had left him. Something was wrong; he knew that from the lack of letters even before he was imprisoned, but he'd never imagined this.

On that ship over the vast black sea, there was nothing like the billions of stars wheeling above to make one feel utterly small, and also . . . conversely, entirely alive. Alive! How had he survived it when so many hadn't? All that black water flowing by held both complex and primitive life forms. Maybe humans, instead of being the highest form of life, were really the lowest. How weak men were, doing battle with each other endlessly. The long voyage home had given him too much time to think.

He walked on. If the apartment worked out tomorrow, he'd have to write Catherine and give her his new address. He and his sister hadn't parted on the best of terms, but he could still go to her for help once Mary was ready. For now he had a place to stay, but he still needed a job. All the jobs, however, had been taken by the first soldiers who'd come home from Europe months before he did, and now more men were coming back from the Pacific. He'd have to find something, anything, so he could take care of his daughter and himself while she got to know him.

And then what? Taking Mary from Gwen Mullen would be one of the hardest things he was ever going to have to do. No wonder he had proposed marriage. The woman was special and she put him at ease. Somehow he knew she had never spoken badly of Alice, even after she left. Others would have. That was the word he'd been searching for, the word that Gwen Mullen brought to mind: rare. Asking her to marry him had seemed so right at the time. Everything had seemed so clear.

But he hadn't played his cards right. He had gone way too fast. He would've been lucky to get her, but now he'd ruined his chances.

CHAPTER TWELVE

A few days later, Lisen and Geoff invited John and me to dinner at their apartment. John had been reimbursing me for Lisen's babysitting services while I worked. But the two had never met. Lisen was the reason I'd been able to keep Mary and also keep my job. I couldn't have done it without her, and John seemed to realize that. He told me he wanted to thank her in person.

He came to my apartment holding a bouquet of daisies and black-eyed Susans and a bottle of wine in his hands. He was dressed in a black suit, which made the pupils of his eyes pop like chips of onyx. All men look good in a dark suit, but John took my breath away. How'd he come to have the new suit? Had he bought it today so that he could better present himself to Lisen? He appeared to have spent a great deal of money in preparation for this evening.

He didn't want to come inside; I could sense that. This was the place where I'd refused his proposal. Gazing in for only a moment, he had a wounded look in his eyes that made me feel horrible. It was difficult to meet his eyes now. As nice as he was, John's presence made me feel a little awkward and uncomfortable. His history with Alice, his looks, his proposal—it all ran around in my head.

Before we went upstairs, I waited to see how Mary would respond to her father. I'd dressed her in a white shirt and a yellow-and-white-striped romper and her walking shoes. She looked as sweet as a daisy in the summer sky. She looked at John but registered no expression, although I was sure she recognized him. He spoke to her, and when he said hello, she toddled over to me and wrapped her arms around my legs.

I picked her up and said to John, "Lisen and her husband are immigrants from Germany from before the war, and it's been hard on them." I told him what I knew of Lisen's incredible journey—that she'd made it out in 1938 when she was twenty-six years old and working for a jeweler. A member of the Social Democratic Party, she opposed the Nazis, and sensing that the worst was yet to come, she sought help from Czech friends. She made it to Prague, where she was helped by what she called "art groups."

She still seemed fearful of revealing too much and exposing those who'd helped her escape. Before leaving Germany, she had arranged for other family members to follow her path to Prague, but none came and all their underground communications had been cut off. She heard later that those like her family who hadn't been able to flee or hide were arrested by the Nazis and sent to Dachau concentration camp, where they were executed for having once opposed Hitler's regime and for trying to leave Germany. I didn't know John well enough to divulge Lisen's family plight. Perhaps he would see them only as Germans. Now the full horrors of the Holocaust were coming to life as more and more death camps were found and emptied, many prisoners too far gone to survive despite their freedom and medical care. How would John react? It wasn't all that long ago that he had been imprisoned by Germans.

He smiled wanly and said, "Many of the German people, even over there, weren't Nazis. I know that."

I was relieved that he said this, but the pulsing at his eye was that tiny tic, that nervous indication of damage that seemed to express all the battles of his particular war.

I had no idea how the evening would unfold.

John, Mary, and I climbed the stairs, and Lisen opened the door to their place and immediately smiled upon seeing the flowers. She was wearing a pale-green dress and her wire-framed glasses. "Thank you," she said to John after I'd introduced him. "I put in vase."

John said, "My mother used to grow flowers like these in her garden."

Lisen said, "Very nice."

Geoff ushered us into the living room. Geoff had wild hair that reminded me of Albert Einstein's, and his eyes were green and streaked with amber. He was a big man with a voice to match. He shooed Lisen's cat, a Siamese that Lisen had named Gracie after Gracie Allen, away from the sofa.

"That cat. She is Lisen's baby. Gets better treatment than I do," Geoff grumbled.

John handed Geoff the bottle of wine. "I developed a taste for the stuff while in Paris. I didn't know if you indulged or not . . . but I found this bottle and thought you might enjoy . . ."

"Of course we do," Geoff said and laughed. "Only for special occasions, though." He looked at us. "Should I open it?"

We both nodded.

Lisen had returned with the flowers in a vase. "Very nice, very pretty," she said to John, and then, "I don't speak so gud English."

I looked for his reaction to her accent, but John smiled at her and said, "Your English is better than my German. And my French. I never picked up more than a word or two when I was in France."

"English," Lisen said, "is very hard for learn. Many, many words. Many long words."

"I agree," said John. "Here's one for you: sesquipedalian." He glanced at all of us and then settled his eyes on me.

"Don't look at me," I said as I put Mary down on the floor, and pulled out some of her toys from the diaper bag. "I've never heard of it."

John smiled. "Sesquipedalian. One who uses long words."

We all laughed.

Geoff uncorked the wine and poured four glasses. "You don't get any, pip-squeak," he said to Mary, who was entertaining herself well on the floor with her toys. She also knew where Lisen kept her stock of playthings and soon pushed herself up and toddled that way.

After a glass of wine, a pleasing warmth spread into my chest and all the way through to my spine. All was going so well. I looked up at John and found his eyes locked onto mine. His eyes were intensely blue and bright; I was bewitched again by the sharpness of his pupils, like two drops of India ink. For a long tick in time, we held each other's gaze. It was difficult to read his expression, but it spoke to me of something like enchantment. John had a way of flashing a revealing look oh so briefly and then quickly snatching it back. I wanted to reach out and grab it. *There, hold still.* But then, just like that, he stole it back.

I had to look down at my hands, cupped in my lap. They were clearly nurses' hands—a little rough and raw from so much washing. Dot once said we should be proud of our hands, because they showed we worked, and we made a difference. Alice had beautiful hands, I suddenly remembered. John's, too, were lovely—manly, but lovely. My breath escaped me like a sigh. The light in Lisen and Geoff's apartment was warm, as was the atmosphere, and it poured around us like heated cream.

When we moved to the table for dinner, Geoff pulled out a high chair he'd made for Mary and the other children Lisen took care of. I set her into it and placed her between John and me.

John touched the back of the chair. "Nice workmanship. Where did you get this?"

"He make," Lisen said.

Geoff said, "I make all kinds of chairs and tables. Coffee tables. Dining tables, barstools, end tables, bedside tables, rocking chairs. But I only use hardwoods. No pine. I do it all by hand."

John ran his palm over the back of the high chair. "Beautiful. Is it mahogany?"

Mahogany, like John's handsome head of hair.

Geoff nodded.

"He do all this, too." Lisen pointed toward the dining table and then gestured around the room.

"Very nice work. How's business?" John asked Geoff.

"Not bad. So many people are moving in, and they need furniture."

"I used to whittle a bit when I was younger," John said. "I remember, I got a switchblade for my tenth birthday, and I played around with it." He smiled as though recalling a nice memory. "I played too much, as I recall. I almost cut off the cat's tail."

Lisen said, "You to stay away from my Gracie!"

We all laughed again. I was pleased and relieved by the easy banter.

Lisen served traditional German fare, including sausages, kraut, cabbage, and potato pancakes. For dessert, she had made rice porridge, which John fed to Mary. Again she was reluctant to begin with but couldn't resist the sweet flavor. I helped her down it with some milk and then put her to sleep in the baby bed Lisen kept for her little ones.

I helped Lisen with the dishes, and then we joined the men in the living room. I sensed they had taken a liking to one another, but I was surprised to find them discussing the possibility of John coming to work at the furniture shop where Geoff worked.

"We need a man like you out front. A war hero can sell things I could never sell."

John said, "I have no experience in sales, but I'd like to give it a shot."

This was too good to be true.

Geoff asked, "How long do you plan to be in the city?"

My breath froze while I waited to hear how John would answer. If he said something along the lines of "a few weeks or so," I didn't know if I could hide my despair.

John thought for a moment. "A while yet. And I know plenty of other men who would take my place when I leave."

Whew.

"So you like the city?" Geoff asked him.

John winced. "I can understand the appeal, but it's not for me, not for the long run. I prefer a quieter life, and I think country living would be better for Mary, a better place to raise a little girl."

My gut wrenched. How casually he'd spoken those crushing words. All the earlier good feelings I'd had about John crashed down like a fine piece of crystal dropped to the floor. I'd almost forgotten that John held all the decision-making power over Mary, and I was at the mercy of whatever he chose to do. My role was merely temporary, and I didn't have any legal rights to determine Mary's future. What a fool I was to have been momentarily charmed by his looks and demeanor. I remembered the first thought that had rushed into my head when I saw him on my stoop on V-J Day. *Enemy.* He was my enemy again, pure and simple. He was the only one with a legal right to determine Mary's future—where she lived, where she went to school, and how she grew up. And probably sooner rather than later, he was going to steal her away.

Geoff and John went on chatting, oblivious to the creature that had resurrected itself inside me.

They made plans to meet at the shop the next day. John thanked Lisen for all she'd done to help me with Mary. And then I carried Mary down the stairs as she slept, and John said good-bye to me at the door.

I recalled his proposal, and another surge of anger rendered me almost mute. His audacity. His proposed marriage of convenience. Had he really thought that I would not only enter a loveless marriage, but also that I'd fall in line and follow him anywhere he wanted to go? That

I'd just walk away from the life I'd built here? I had made a home in this city he didn't care for, with a meaningful career and friends. I had my own goals and dreams. I suppose he'd thought I was so weak as to fall prey to his looks and charms and give everything up just to keep Mary. I couldn't do it; I hadn't done it, not even for the precious gift that she was.

He said, "Nice people."

I nodded.

"Hearts of gold, I'd say."

I murmured, "Yes."

"They have no children of their own?"

"No," I answered. "I never had the heart to ask why."

He said, "Well, 'night then."

When he left, it took all of my self-control not to slam the door behind him.

A few minutes later, Dot burst through the door, and on her heels was a handsome man who could only be her new flame. She said, "This is Captain Dennis Meade."

I smiled and shook his hand. He was tall, blond, and broad, looking every inch the Norseman. Chiseled jaw, thick neck, broad body, he had everything. Later I found out that before the navy, he had grown up on a farm, like so many of us had.

Dot beamed and thrust her hand in my face. "And get a load of this. My engagement ring."

I stared at the diamond, at all those facets reflecting the light. Then I hugged her and said, "Congratulations."

But even then, a strange sensation gripped me. Dot barely knew the man she had just agreed to marry. There was something rushed and frenetic about it that made me uneasy. What was the big hurry? Dot was so giddy that I feared she wasn't thinking straight. After they went out again—more dancing at Small's Paradise in Harlem, Dot said—I had to almost literally shake myself free of those bad feelings.

And yet they kept returning, creeping over any happiness I should have felt for them, like puffs of wind guttering out what should have been a glowing candle.

CHAPTER THIRTEEN

I needed a change. At the hospital I asked for and received a transfer from the post-surgical ward to the recovery room, where nurses monitored patients who had just come out of surgery. It wasn't what I'd once dreamed of doing overseas, but I sought something that would challenge me and take my mind off what was transpiring in my private life. In the recovery room, our patients ranged from civilians having appendectomies, gall bladder removals, and hernia repairs, to soldiers having surgical revisions to improve on or correct hasty operations that had been done in field hospitals under much worse conditions.

It was during my first days working in the recovery room that Dot married Dennis Meade in a civil ceremony at city hall with Mary and me as her attendants and a buddy of Dennis's as his. Dot had bought a cream-colored suit, something completely out of character, and she put her hair up in a French twist for the occasion. The day before the wedding, she had asked me if Dennis could move into our flat, and since she had her own room, there was no reason to refuse. So many people were living doubled-up in New York City, because like so many others, including our mayor, who was still living in Gracie Mansion, they had found no other place to stay.

The ceremony was brief and rote, but Dot didn't seem to mind. I took photos with my Kodak and promised to get the film developed as soon as possible. She wanted to send pictures back to her father and some cousins in Michigan. She and Dennis weren't taking a honeymoon because Dennis had an interview lined up with Pan American Airways on Monday of the next week.

So after we changed out of our nice clothes, we began to move in Dennis's things. He'd bought a double bed with a headboard to replace the single bed that was in Dot's room, and he had boxes of memorabilia from the war and a surprising amount of clothes.

John came over to help with the bed, and the men managed to maneuver it up the narrow stairwell while Dot and I nervously watched and cleared the way. When all had been done, John and I still had time to spend the rest of the day with Mary. John seemed unsure as to what to do. My nerves had settled somewhat, but John had a lost look about him. I suggested we take Mary to Coney Island as summertime weather had come back for a final tease, and this would surely be the last warm weekend of the year.

As we rode the subway I fell silent, alone with my thoughts. There was something about Dot's new husband that unsettled me. I couldn't put a finger on exactly what it was, but it had to do with the way his eyes shifted over things and rarely made direct hits. There was something yearning there, something unfulfilled. He talked fast and seemed nervous when he had to let another person speak, and he held his arms at odd angles to his body, the muscles tensed, as though he were a wild animal ready to strike. Something reckless lay just under his skin, ready to jump out and pounce. He was affectionate toward Dot, but it didn't look to me as if he were crazy in love, although Dot clearly was.

And maybe that was enough.

Also, I'd smelled alcohol on his breath that morning. Early in the morning. But what was done was done. Dot seemed elated, and I could only hope that my instincts about Dennis were wrong.

When I first came to the city, I was surprised to find out that Coney Island wasn't an island at all but instead a large sandbar between lower New York Bay and the Atlantic. A boardwalk had been built back in the twenties that made for an interesting promenade, and the first time I'd come here, I'd walked it alone.

Today I wore a white sundress with a flared skirt over my bathing suit, and I had dressed Mary in her first bathing suit and put a pink cotton bonnet on her head. Her feet were bare. The afternoon sky was as clear as the faraway ocean was glassy. John and I decided to look around before trying to find a spot on the sand, and so we strolled past bathhouses, sideshows, fortune-tellers, and snack bars. The air was rich with the smell of the sea and fried foods, and the sounds of screamers riding the roller coaster, and then there were the carousel organs, jazz bands, and dance halls. John looked captivated by the Cyclone and Thunderbolt roller coasters, and I told him to go ahead. Mary and I would watch. As he took his place in line, I breathed in the salty smell of the ocean as my eyes roamed over that wide, seemingly endless water. I'd grown up in a landlocked state; the ocean never failed to enthrall me.

After a single ride on the Thunderbolt, John said that was enough.

He was wearing a shirt with the sleeves rolled up to just below the elbows, exposing all the fine golden-gleaming hairs on his arms and wrists. He had an easy and graceful stride and had put on some weight. His cheeks were softer, the skin less taut—that and his obvious love for Mary made him even more perfectly soldier-boy handsome than when I'd first seen him. I hadn't seen that tic at the corner of his eye since just before he met Lisen and Geoff. An easy familiarity had settled over the three of them now.

The beach was packed, but we managed to find a spot where we could spread a quilt. We sat and took in the swells of the ocean, the small waves jeweled with sunlight. The tide was receding, sliding down the shore, revealing untouched damp sand.

John surprised me when he began pulling out things from his duffel bag. Mary was sitting on the quilt, almost overcome by the sheer number of people around us and the noise, but he got her attention when he said, "Abracadabra," and pulled out a yellow rubber duck.

She reached for it, but before he gave it to her, he squeezed the toy and made it squeak. Next he brought out a toy horn and blew lightly into it. She, of course, wanted that, too. Finally he pulled out what looked like a pair of old World War I goggles, and he put them on. He made a funny face, and she smiled at him. Her first smile directed toward him.

"Very clever," I said.

"I found them in a junk store."

He didn't appear to mind that the people around us must have thought him a lunatic.

"I found a set of marbles and almost bought them, too."

"Oh, no. She's too young yet. She'd put them in her mouth and choke."

"Yes," he said pensively then. "I figured that out."

Did he have any idea how much I'd had to figure out, mostly on my own, with no prior experience and only Lisen for help?

Mary watched him and cocked her head to one side, and he mimicked her. When she patted the quilt, he did the same.

We stripped down to our swimming suits, and he was totally unself-conscious about it. My suit was the sort women wore in those days, with little boy legs, pointed bosom, and straps that tied behind my neck.

We took Mary and a towel to the water's edge, where she could feel the sand and shallow water on her feet. She was studious about these new sensations, cautious, and skeptical. She said, "Wah-ter," just as Betty once had, and pointed out to sea.

"We can take turns going in," I said to John. "You go first."

He didn't hesitate. "You talked me into it."

He ran into the water and took a plunging dive under a low breaker. I couldn't see him for a moment, and then he surfaced out in the deeper water. He started treading, moving his arms like two fish tails, his hair slicked down like a cap of sealskin. He swam back to the beach, and when he stepped out of the water, he was smiling, and droplets clung to his eyelashes.

I handed him the towel. Our fingers brushed, and something pulsed through me, ardent and intense. I was sure he paused in return, and for a few seconds the air seemed to quicken around us. The distance between us shrank, and for another few moments I felt his gaze roaming over me, a sensation akin to sleeping in silk.

I blinked. I came to my senses as the moment flittered away. I told my foolish heart to stay in my solid center, where it belonged.

John took the towel, wiped his face, and said, "Do you think she'd let me hold her?"

"There's no other way to find out," I answered, and then I said to Mary, "Amma's going to go for a swim, too, so Daddy's going to hold you." I handed her over, and she whimpered and gave me a pleading look.

I said to her, "You can watch me swim. I'm going to swim like a ducky."

Then I didn't wait. The sun was hot on my skin. I stepped into the shallows and found it colder than I'd expected, or maybe the water felt cold because my skin *was* so hot. A shiver ran down me, and I crossed my arms and took a few steps down the gentle underwater plank of packed sand. The sand under my toes grew softer.

I took one last look back at Mary. She wasn't crying or fighting John, but her eyes hadn't left me, and she looked as though she thought I might disappear if she blinked.

Finally deep enough, I plunged in headfirst, and the gray-blue coolness of the ocean swallowed me. I had never understood women who wore bathing caps or never got their hair wet when they went for a swim. I loved the complete immersion of swimming this way. I pushed back up to the surface and then swam farther out. I treaded out in the clearer, darker water, its surface glimmering in the sunlight with the brilliance of phosphorescent fish.

Back on the beach, Mary and John were standing exactly as I had left them. I kept swimming and had to work against an undertow that was running strong. It felt as though it could sweep me to the churning cauldron of the far oceans, to the realms of fork-tailed mermen and their maidens. But I was not scared of the ocean. I was strong, and for those moments, the water made me feel suspended out of time and place.

When I came out, John passed me the towel, and Mary reached for me. I said, "You did just fine, little one. See? It wasn't so bad without your Amma for a few minutes."

After I did a quick version of towel-drying my hair, I let her come to me. I didn't want to push her too far in one day.

Back on the quilt, the sun now felt like warm oil in contrast to the air, which was cool and invigorating. I put Mary down in between us again and showed John how to play with her. I squeezed the squeaky toy up against her neck and tickled her with it. She laughed, finally, her adorable cackle.

It was kind of wonderful to be sitting with John in this cheery daylight beside the sunlit sea. A man as lovely as John should be surrounded by women in bars, restaurants, and in his bed. But here he was, both of us enmeshed together by this strange twist of fate. John was her father, and I was her mother in almost every way. Though we'd never been intimate, there was something there, like a string of connectedness that felt decidedly close, because we were both her parents.

"How's your new place?" I asked as I towel-dried my hair some more.

"Crowded," he said, "but I'm not complaining. At least I have a place. My roommates—most of them haven't found jobs yet, and so there's a lot of lounging around, boozing, and horseplay going on."

"And you're the stuffy old father." I said, even though there was nothing stuffy about him.

"Yes," he said with his quicksilver gaze, "it's no place for Mary. I won't be able to keep her overnight there."

Overnight. That seemed a faraway goal to me.

The moment stretched out, and I was lost in the warmth of sun, the rush of ocean waves, and the music drifting from the boardwalk down the beach. John seemed to be handling the day with the grace of a fish drifting in still water. But why wouldn't he? I was teaching him everything about his daughter, so he could do what he wanted with her as soon as he was ready. The weight of his former proposal hung between us like a touchable, living thing, and I certainly didn't want to speak of it.

So I was surprised when he said, "I scared you, didn't I?"

I eyed him carefully. I hadn't seen him in days; our work schedules had been at odds. He was a little more and a little less every time I saw him. A little more tangible and a little less damaged. And, still, he was a question mark. I knew almost nothing about him. I didn't really want to know more—the less attached I was to them both, the better. Soon, he'd be gone, and so would Mary. I had to do the right thing here, to help John, but I also had to protect myself. I fingered her rattle on the quilt and then looked up.

I said, "At first."

He nodded with his eyes, if such a thing was even possible. "But I imagine you were scared most of the time after Alice left."

Had he already seen through to my secret? Did he know I had intended to keep her and tell no one? I couldn't explain my reasons, even to myself, but I didn't want John to think poorly of me. I straightened my back and smoothed the quilt with my left hand. "Whatever do you mean?"

"It must have been difficult. You were trapped. No flitting about town while you had a baby in your care."

Full of relief, I laughed. "I'll have you know I do not *flit about*, with or without a baby in my care."

"Not even with that raven-haired, red-blooded roommate of yours? I mean, before she married, of course."

"Even without a baby in my care, I would not have been able to keep up with her."

He laughed and looked at his hands. Then, "I have a feeling you're more trouble than you're letting on."

There was an awkwardness to the silence, and a spark in the air. Was he being slightly flirtatious with me?

"Are you testing me?" Was I being slightly flirtatious with him? "If so, you can test me all you like. Just prepare yourself for what you might hear." I tilted my head, smiled at him, and realized a moment too late that I *was* flirting. Apparently the habits of being single could not be so easily erased. But this was dangerous ground. I should not be doing this, not with *this* man. Nothing but heartbreak could come of it.

"You can't fool me, Gwen. Deep down, you're still a country girl. Not like these city women, and . . . come to think of it, not like other women anywhere."

My breath caught. "Why do you say that?"

"No guile or gossip. You wouldn't waste your time with it. You wouldn't lower yourself to a level not befitting you. I saw that as soon as I met you. But you also don't shy away from taking a stand. You have purpose in your life."

Mary was beginning to scuttle away, and pure maternal instinct tore my eyes away from John to look after her. And still I sat paralyzed by the power of his praise, as if every cell inside me had been permeated by his words.

"Others must have told you to give up Mary. It must have been frightening, going against convention. But still, you did it."

I couldn't look at him. I hadn't expected this. *He* was the one without guile. He saw what I'd done as strength instead of weakness, and it dazed me into another moment of complete stillness. At that instant everything I'd done felt perfect, as if it had been directed by some benevolent hand.

Mary was struggling to stand, and it broke the spell. I let it fall through my hands like the seawater in front of me, because that's all it had been: a spell. The spell of being around a handsome, charming man who flattered me. I had to remember that soon I would lose what I cared about most in the world because of him.

Mary couldn't walk in the sand without help, and so we took her back to the water, each of us holding one of her hands. She loved to walk this way, on her own two feet but with the support of bigger people. We let go so she could stand in the wet sand on her own. Again she looked at the shallow waves that licked at her feet, but she seemed unsure of herself.

I looked over at John. "I think I'll take her in."

A wave slapped me on my shins just then, and in an instant Mary went down, her face under the water, her eyes wide open, seawater rushing over her face. I lurched for her, but in a split second John had her by the arm and lifted her up. His fatherly instincts had been even faster than my maternal ones. She had been underwater for only one second, but still it had terrified her, terrified me. She gulped and then started crying, desperately. He gave her over to me.

The day had taken a sudden, dark turn. "Oh my God, oh my God," I realized I was saying. "What was that?" I cuddled Mary against me.

"Is she all right?" he asked in a shaky voice. His face looked awful.

"Yes," I said and held her tightly against me. "She's just scared."

We headed back to the quilt, and I said, "I can't believe that just happened. What was that? I didn't even see it."

He said, "I don't know. Some kind of rogue wave of the beach variety. I didn't see it coming, either."

He shook his head and looked awful again.

I should've known better. He was only just learning how to take care of a child, but I should've known better. Life was so fragile. I had taken my eyes off her for one second, just one second.

Mary calmed down once we had her back on the quilt. I removed her dripping bonnet, and she put her cheek down on the soft fabric beneath her. I rubbed her back.

John looked down at her for a while, then straightened his back and squinted into the sun. We sat still for a long time, and my thoughts floated around the strangest things: first the polio ward with the eerie clacking and swooshing sounds of its iron lungs, and then Dot and her dead sister, and then on to Dennis.

I kept my eyes on Mary. "Did the war change you?"

He glanced my way and fixed his gaze on me. "Yes."

"I guess most of us back here don't know the half of it."

He shook his head. "You wouldn't want to know."

Was he discounting me? I said, "And why not? If we don't understand the horrors of war, then how will we do our utmost to avoid it? Besides, I know more than you might think. I've seen many of the soldiers who have come back. I see what has happened to them."

He looked at me. A moment later he asked, "How did it change you?"

I sighed and thought. "I left my old life, and then I grew up."

"Me too," he said. "War will do that to a person."

"Just leaving home starts it. Realizing that you have to make your own way. That it's up to you."

"I agree. So many choices and decisions to make, and there's no one else to blame if things go wrong."

We sat with that for a few minutes.

Then I stared out at the sea. "I wonder. What is it about the ocean," I asked him as I gazed out at the deeper water that moved like mercury, "that draws people?"

"I don't know for sure." He pondered for a moment, as if his answer to my question was important. "But maybe it's the size of it, the endlessness of it."

"Maybe," I said. "Or maybe it's something about opposing forces. The sea crashing into the land, or some such."

We studied it together, and then he turned to me, "Opposing forces? I've never thought of it that way. A battle between earth and sea."

"Powerful, and eternal."

He faced the water. "Wow, Gwen. You say interesting things. You make me think." He lifted his hand as if he were toasting me. "Beauty and brains."

It was a nice compliment, but it left me longing for more and wondering why his approval was becoming important to me. "That's rather a *line*, isn't it? Besides, I'm more brains than beauty." Why was I fishing?

"A *line*?" He seemed genuinely puzzled as he looked down at his hands. "I've never said it before."

A few moments later, as I touched Mary's hair, I said to John in a whisper, "I hope she won't remember this . . ."

"Or she'll be afraid to swim," he finished for me.

I didn't relax until I bathed at the end of the day. Sinking down in the water gave me a sense of escape. I let the tub fill almost to the brim, washed my hair, slicked it back, and then sat down low all the way up to my neck, my chin grazing the surface, letting the warmth soak all the way to my marrow. I slid the soap down my arms and legs and slowly made lather all over my body, imagining it as sleek and firm and lovely as John's was.

CHAPTER FOURTEEN

When I fed Mary her cereal in the mornings, I thought of John. When I dressed her, did her laundry, gave her liquid vitamins, took her temperature if she seemed not herself, powdered her bottom when I changed her diaper, I imagined John and all the things I had yet to show him about his daughter. If life was really a journey, then children had to be the center of the wheel that moved it. The thought of Mary going with her father, becoming the center of his wheel, was not a bad one. Try as I might to be angry at him, I couldn't stay that way. We'd both been put in an impossible situation. And yet a huge, heavy lump lived in my stomach, because I still couldn't imagine how *my* life would look without Mary at the center of it.

I started giving her finger foods—pieces of ripe banana, Cheerios, cooked potato I'd cut into cubes—and she loved being able to choose what she wanted next, pick it up, and shove it into her mouth. I was also introducing her baby cup and thinking of weaning her off the bottle. Such thoughts occupied a good deal of my spare time. Without Mary and now John, my days would be full of free time—and yet so empty.

Early fall was finally upon us. It was sweater season, and around street corners the city's small parks, adorned in tricolor beauty, gave me pause. In Colorado, fall came in shades of yellow and gold, but the oranges and reds and purples—yes, purples—of an East Coast autumn had come as a surprise to me.

John and I often met in the evenings, after we'd both eaten and Mary was winding down for the night. We took a walk, pushing Mary in her carriage as many businesses locked up, people arrived home and apartments lit up, clouds of steam billowed from manholes, and the stars blinked to life. Autumn was my favorite season, and fallen leaves littered the sidewalks and crunched beneath our feet. Even late in the evening, the streets bustled with people. There were flashes of khaki, polished boots, felt and feather hats, and the occasional fur. We crossed groomed parklets and passed grand storefronts; dark, mysterious, narrow passageways; small bakeries and cheese shops wafting rich aromas; and for the first time that season, our breaths made pale clouds we walked into. John always removed his hat when I came to the door, and he opened doors for me wherever we went. Sometimes as I drew near I could hear John jingling the change in his pocket, as if he was nervous.

I rarely could find a free moment, and yet my apartment, which had always been my refuge, was no longer mine. After Dennis moved in, I was intruding on a marriage that should have been private. For some reason, Dennis had not been hired by Pan American, and I'd accidentally overheard a heated conversation between Dot and him on the day he found out he hadn't gotten the job. Something about his navy record had interfered. And the atmosphere in the apartment became tense.

When I had to get out of the place, I called John to meet me somewhere in the city. We met for sandwiches at the automat and took Mary for a ride on the streetcar on 42nd. We showed her the El and taught her to say, "Choo-choo," since the word *train* was too difficult for her. Everywhere we went people remarked on what a pretty baby she was, and of course they assumed we were the proud parents, married and living a life together. Again, I experienced that intimate connection that people thought was there, only it wasn't. It made no sense.

Once, we were walking, and ahead of us, the wind blew the hat off an elderly woman's head and sent it alternately rolling and bouncing down the sidewalk. John ran after the hat and retrieved it for her. The woman had a face tracked with the evidence of years of smiling. She thanked John, patted his arm, and looked approvingly at me, and I felt a tiny burst of pride when she assumed we were together. John was the kind of man that any woman would want to have on her arm as a husband.

As if reading my mind, the woman said in a quavering voice, "You have a nice husband."

"Oh, he's not . . ." I began. "I mean, we aren't . . ."

"Married," John finished for me.

The woman said, "Oh dear."

And I said, "It's complicated."

Then she smiled. "It always is," she said and winked.

He steered me onward. We continued on in a sort of contemplative silence. Something tugged at me—those invisible threads that bound John and me together in this awkward and unnatural situation. I glanced at him. A little line ran down the center of his forehead when he was thinking, and I wondered what plans he was making to leave, and when. I could've asked him, but instead my strategy was not to push him, to stretch things out, to give this as much time as possible. No doubt the end result would be that I lost my girl, but I certainly didn't want John to think I wanted him to take her. So I let things play out and hoped he would take his sweet time making plans. I had to play nice.

As we strolled through Times Square, I told John what had happened to me there right before I met him on V-J Day. I stood right where the kiss had taken place. "A sailor boy grabbed me right about here," I said. "Then he twisted me around and leaned me back and planted a huge kiss right on my lips."

"Lots of clowning around on that day, I guess."

"Oh, I didn't mind. Everyone was so happy and celebrating the grand glory." Then I told him about the photo in *Life* magazine that I believed was me.

"I saw that issue," John said. "I remember that shot."

Of course I would remember it forever, that night, not only for the ridiculous kiss but because I'd come home to find John on my doorstep. Everything had changed for me on that day.

We went shopping for Mary's fall clothes, and he insisted that he pay. Even though his job with Geoff was going well, I was still pretty sure that I was better off than he was. But I let him have his way.

Mary became more comfortable with him. I could tell by the slightest ease of her muscles when she looked at him. And her eyes lingered a tad bit longer on his face. She didn't go to him on her own, but I could usually pass her to John without her making a fuss. After she sat in his lap for a while, she got used to the idea that he wasn't me. I could see that, given a few moments to adjust, she relaxed into the different feel of him, and I think she liked his size and comfortable strength. She seemed to sense that, like me, he was another person who would never let anything happen to her.

I cornered Dot in the hospital cafeteria the next day, and we shared a table. Her lipstick had faded, and she ate slowly, focusing on the corned-beef hash in front of her in a way that looked as though she was searching for something unseen.

I asked her, "What's wrong?"

She glanced up at me and forced a pitiful smile. "Nothing."

Her denial surprised me. It was obvious that something was wrong.

Instead of applying at other airlines, Dennis had begun to play solitaire for hours on the dining table. Often he was in the way when I needed to sit down and feed Mary. I would see cards set out on the table in squares, crosses, lines, and piles, and there were even a few games Dennis could play while holding all the cards in his hands. Once, he told me he had learned all the games while in the service. I never knew there were so many different ways to play solitaire, and I'd never pictured the soldiers, especially pilots, as having that much free time on their hands. Anyway, the card playing started to look like nothing other than a form of escape, but what was he trying to escape?

If he wasn't playing solitaire, he was smoking in silence, sipping a drink, which led to slugging it. Some spirit, some soulless grief, had overtaken my best friend's husband, and Dot wore sadness on her face that no pancake makeup or fake smile could ever cover. This was another thing I had not seen coming. How quickly a life can change. Something else had moved into our apartment besides just another person, something we had not let enter our place before.

I longed to hear Dot's laughter again.

Over dinner, sitting with the two of them, the silverware clinked loudly against the dishes, and sometimes I had the urge to grab Mary, run out of the door, and vanish into the streets. Mary had an instant distrust of Dennis. It didn't help that he never paid any attention to her or tried to get to know her. She turned her face away from him whenever he came near, and I could feel her body stiffen even when I held her. She clutched me with her small, chubby hands as if she was afraid I might hand her off to him.

When Dot and I worked the same shifts, we came home to the slipcover drooping off the sofa, brimming ashtrays, and dirty plates with sandwich crumbs attacked by flies Dennis had let in. Nothing had been cleaned or picked up.

Some nights Dennis yelled out in his sleep.

I just looked at Dot until she could stand it no longer. She took a bite and seemed to have difficulty swallowing. She set her fork down silently. Finally she looked up and said, "Nothing that can't get better."

"I'm worried."

Then she looked at me, really looked at me, and that moment of frankness broke her facade. "Oh, Gwen, something *is* wrong. Something happened to him during the war, and he's haunted by it. He hides it well at times; in fact he hid it all the time I knew him before we got married, but something terrible must have happened. The nightmares are just horrid. You must have heard."

"Yes."

"He can't sleep at night, so he's exhausted during the day. He says he has no energy to look for a job."

"He should see a doctor, maybe a specialist."

"I know," Dot said, "but he won't hear of it." She tried to eat again and then set aside her fork. Trepidation crossed a path over her face. "I imagined living happily ever after. Silly me."

"It isn't you."

She looked away, and then her face contorted when she gazed back at me. "Do you remember how once I told you my life didn't belong to me?"

I nodded.

"I feel that way again. I used to have a recurrent dream when I was a girl. I was lost in a big city. I was troubled that it might be a premonition, but I've never felt lost in this city . . . until now. I walk around and nothing feels familiar anymore. I don't feel familiar to myself anymore. And I don't know what to do. I'm so worried about him."

"I'm worried about him, but also about you."

She batted her eyes as though trying to shake something off. "Well, maybe we're overreacting, you and me both. He hasn't been back long, and sometimes I'm not a very patient person. He'll get over it; he has to. Any day now."

"I hope so." I had the urge to push the point, but I feared Dot wasn't ready to hear more. And we were at work; perhaps this conversation should have been taking place somewhere more private.

"Don't worry anymore," she said and forced a smile. "We'll be fine."

During one of my meetings with John, we sat outside at the Brevoort Hotel, where tables lined the sidewalk, and we ordered Cokes. Leaning back in his chair with his legs stretched out in front of him, he was maddeningly handsome that day, like a model in a cigarette ad. The evening was getting cool, but John had wanted to sit outside because he said it reminded him of Paris. I had dressed Mary in her new winter coat and warm tights. She wore a cap Lisen had knitted for her, out of which her hair sprung like silky curlicues.

After our drinks arrived, he straightened up and said, "I have something to show you." He pulled something small from his pants' pocket. It was a tiny porcelain hummingbird; he held it out between his thumb and forefinger and smiled the kind of smile that accompanies a precious memory. "My mother gave it to me to take overseas."

I shifted Mary to my other knee. He handed over the hummingbird, and I took a close look. "It's very pretty." The white porcelain was painted with black and green at the wings and red at the throat, like the ruby-throated hummingbird that lived in Colorado.

He picked up the Coke, threw back his head, and drained the bottle in only a few long swigs. *Oh, the things men do.*

"It means a lot to me," he said then, looking down at it in my hand. "Most people think of them as messengers and stoppers of time. But they're also called New World birds, because they're native only to North America."

"I didn't know that."

"They're the only birds that can fly backward. So to my mother, this was to serve as a constant reminder that I would come back home, back to America."

"What a beautiful idea."

"I carried it in my pocket the whole time I was away." He laughed softly as if remembering something funny. "I didn't show it to very many of the guys. They would have given me a hard time about carrying a little bird around in my pocket."

"I can imagine."

He went silent. I studied the hummingbird in my hand. "Did it help you to have it?"

"Yes." He took the bird back from me, and Mary reached for it. He pocketed it again. "Not yet, Mary. You're a little too young for this now. But I'll hold on to it for you."

He told me more of Paris, the place that obviously held the best memories of his time overseas. He described the cafés, bakeries, architectural treasures, and restaurants. He told me there really *was* something special about the light, even during the war. I closed my eyes. He filled my imagination like a flock of colorful birds blown in on an errant breeze. I imagined that the mist rolling in was the mist of Paris.

"People embrace love there, Gwen," he said. "They grab it by the throat. Lovers kiss with abandon out in public, as if no one else is there, as if nothing else matters."

He doled out his memories like precious gifts; he spoke more openly than any man I'd ever known, and there was a confident calm about him that night. In comparison, I was having a hard time catching my breath. Gusts of wind brushed over us, picking up my hair and whisking it about my face, and as I moved the strands away, he watched me with those piercingly clear blue eyes. My brain seemed to swim, and it was difficult to focus. I wanted him to touch me, and the shock of sudden desire ricocheted within my body.

"What's wrong?" he asked.

"What do you mean?"

"Your face is flushed."

"I'm cold," I said. "I mean, I'm hot." I shrugged out of my coat. "This thing is too heavy for this weather."

He just watched me, quietly, purposefully.

"It's your fault, you know," I murmured.

One eyebrow lifted.

"John, you have to know that you're a handsome man."

He sat back. And finally said, "I wish I could find a way to truly move you."

He had no idea what he was doing to me. I had to mentally free myself of this hold. Was I being drawn in by his good looks, his kind mannerisms, and his dedication to Mary? He was, after all, the most handsome man whose company I'd ever kept. I had to keep telling myself that he was way too good-looking, worldly, and charming. Despite my life in New York, in my soul I was still a girl turning corn, rolling hay, and hoeing vegetables in the drowning heat of summer, and in the winter sloshing to the barn wearing my father's gumboots. Growing up on a failing farm during the Depression had been tough, and maybe our pasts could not be excised cleanly as with a surgeon's knife, leaving nothing behind. Maybe every day, I still coughed up a little farm dust.

John had grown up better off than I had. He'd been to college. He'd seen another part of the world and had survived the war a hero. He was tested, well-educated, and intelligent, in addition to being strikingly handsome. Women followed him with their eyes and smiled at him from afar, even when he was with Mary and me. He had married an exquisite beauty who could sing and play the piano. I was practical; I'd gone to nursing school. He would find another wife more like Alice; I had to protect myself.

I gazed around and said, "I remember the first day I fell in love with this city. It happened on a June day full of bright sunlight. I bought a hot dog with mustard from a street cart, and then I sat down on a bench outside Central Park under a tree and ate my hot dog as the traffic on Fifth Avenue surged and flowed past, children ran by, and a ladybug landed on my arm."

He simply nodded. He didn't see the city the same way I did. Another reason to avoid more entanglements.

After Mary fell asleep in his lap, he settled her in the carriage and then pulled something else from his pocket: a deck of cards. "These came in handy over there, too, especially in the POW camp. I became a master at gin rummy. Do you play?"

"My brothers did."

"And you didn't join in?"

I shook my head. "My sister and I played dress-up, not cards. We pretended to be princesses, actresses, and madams in Wild West bars."

He laughed.

"Of course at the time, we didn't know what that meant."

He smiled and then explained the rules of the game, as he shuffled the cards on the small table that sat between us. I couldn't keep my eyes off his hands, which were like a sculptor's.

"So it's a game of chance," I said.

"Not entirely. For each play you must decide what to discard and what to keep. Any hand can be a winning hand; it's all in the way you make your decisions. Every choice means taking a chance. Now," he said and leaned back, "if I had to guess, I'd say that you're a risk taker. You'll go on gut instinct, or faith."

He beat me soundly three games in a row, but I finally took a win, or did he let me? His smile indicated that he was more pleased by my win than by his. A strong sense of foreshadowing entered me then. It said that John was sending me a message—something about taking chances and knowing what to discard and what to keep. Or was I simply imagining it?

The next day, Dot and I both had the day off. Mary awakened early, and as I was fixing her breakfast in the silent apartment, voices came from Dot and Dennis's room. Dot asked, "What is it?" in a weak voice. "What's wrong?"

I'd come to dread their confrontations. Dot kept picking and pleading, and I was afraid she didn't know what she was doing. I feared she would succeed in prying something out of him that she didn't really want to know about.

Dennis answered sarcastically, "What's *wrong*?"

I didn't want to hear this and shouldn't hear it. But the pain in Dot's voice held me paralyzed. She said, "I just want to help."

He said, "You can't come up with something better than that?"

"I'm sorry. I guess I don't know the right thing to say."

His tone was mean and dismissive. "Then don't say anything."

"OK," Dot said. "Then you talk to me."

"There's nothing to talk about."

"Of course there are things to talk about. I want to know all of it. I mean, I want to know everything you want to tell me."

"There's nothing to say."

I took Mary's food into our bedroom to feed her there. She could hear their voices, too, and I didn't want her to. Besides, I couldn't listen any longer. I hated what I'd heard, especially the way he spoke to her.

CHAPTER FIFTEEN

Uncertainty surrounding John continued and came upon me at unexpected moments. We spent time together, the purpose of which was to build his relationship with Mary, but sometimes our gatherings felt like dates. Sometimes they felt like lessons about baby care. I had no idea what he and I were doing.

He surprised me one morning when I was off by showing up on my doorstep and saying he'd made arrangements to take me horseback riding. My stomach gave a strange lurch, but I faked a smile. Seeing my reaction, he asked, "Do you like the idea?"

"Sure," I answered, though my throat suddenly constricted. "I've never really done much riding."

"You grew up on a farm, but you didn't ride?"

John's family had to have been better off than mine. "We had a couple of draft horses for pulling the plow. I remember my father setting me on top of one of them once, but he always maintained they weren't for riding. They were workhorses, he'd say, and deserved to rest when they weren't needed. They weren't playthings."

"I'll teach you then."

I shrugged. "If I'm teachable."

"Lisen is going to look after Mary," said John, "and I found a stable out on Long Island that will let us take a couple of their trail horses out on our own. A buddy of mine from the army works there. He cleans out the stables and takes care of the horses. Just temporarily until he can find something else."

"Sounds like fun," I said.

He was wearing a pair of jeans that looked new, dark denim and creased, with a red plaid, flannel shirt. He'd been getting some sun on his face. He looked like a gleaming star in a Hollywood Western. I said, "Nice outfit."

"All borrowed, but all meant to impress."

That was when I noticed the boots—cowboy boots with a pointed toe and a high heel.

"Nice boots, too," I said.

He picked up a foot and turned it in so I could get a better look. "Alligator. Real imitation."

I smiled. "Now if only I could do a real imitation of a horsewoman."

He took Mary upstairs while I got ready. I dug through my drawers and closet and finally donned a pair of blue jeans and a white T-shirt and then tied my hair back with a blue and white bandana. I looped a heavy sweater over my shoulders. It was the best I could come up with for the occasion, though what kind of occasion it was, I still wasn't sure.

I was even more taken aback when I saw the truck John had borrowed. He said he'd picked it up out on Long Island the day before and brought it back so we could ride out in style. The truck was about ten years old but freshly washed and waxed. Even the windshield was gleaming as sunlight streamed through, magnifying the heat of the Indian summer day. We put the windows down, and John drove us through Brooklyn and Queens and out onto the island with one hand dangling casually over the top of the steering wheel, the other elbow levered out the open window.

I didn't know what to think. In a way, I figured this was really a date—Mary wasn't even with us—but was it a *date* date? Or just a friendly gesture? Was John's kindness just the way he showed his appreciation for all I'd done for Mary? Or had he developed some real fondness for me? And if so, did I even want that? He was going to leave this place that had become my home.

We drove to the hamlet of Melville, a place known for its honeybees, and we turned right off the main road and drove past pumpkin fields to the stables that John had told me about. He said that Long Island was full of English riders, but here we could ride Western, the only way John knew to ride. His friend, Carlton, was there to make the introductions to the owner of the stables, a tall steel-gray-haired man wearing a Stetson and the tightest jeans I'd ever seen. His name was Stan, and he greeted us with a tip of his hat, a rather tight lip, and a bored affect. We must have looked like greenhorns to him, and I was certainly just that when it came to riding. Carlton was small in stature and had eagle eyebrows and a full smiling mouth.

Carlton told John that there had been rattlesnakes that morning along with some hints of cool clouds and lightning in the distance. He said some of the horses had been a bit skittish on a morning trail ride, and a bolt of fear shot through me. But I simply shrugged, put my hands in my pockets, and set a confident expression on my face.

"We picked out two easy riders for you," Carlton said with a smile. "Make a lot of noise, and watch out for snakes."

John turned to me. "Any last-minute doubts?"

"No," I lied. "Not at all." I was determined not to hurt John and ruin his day by showing fear. He had gone to so much trouble to make this a nice outing.

Stan had already saddled and readied the horses, two nearly identical chestnut brown mares with white stars on their foreheads. John packed a canteen full of water and brown lunch sacks into the saddle-bags. He handled the horses in a way that suggested he was comfortable around them, stole some glances in my direction, and made a show of stroking his horse. "You have to talk nice to a horse. Talk nice, but let her know you're the one in charge. Don't show fear. They can sense it."

"I won't," I said, and then, "I mean, I'm not. Scared."

He grabbed the pommel and swung up in one graceful move. Stan helped me mount my mare, and I let John take the lead. We rode toward the highest point on Long Island, Jayne's Hill, four hundred feet above sea level and supposedly a favorite spot of Walt Whitman's.

At first the sheer size of the animal made me nervous—that and the fact that I was so high above the ground. But soon I settled into the horse's gentle sway and saw that she knew her way, and there was very little, if anything, I needed to do. The only clouds were far on the horizon, and the sun spilled its light over the backs of our horses, John's hair, and my hands holding the reins. The earth was warm below us, and soon I relaxed and enjoyed the hush and hum of nature and the shape of John's back as my horse and I followed behind him.

We went from cleared, south-facing slopes into meadows dotted with oaks, birches, and maples. The hill loomed above, green and plush against a brimming blue sky. As we ventured higher, we rode through oak glens and stands of pine forest, and we crossed gulches dense with ferns. Creeks flowed past lichen-covered rocks. At the summit, the view was sprawling and encompassed fields and forests, patchworks and woods, all the way down the low slope to the Atlantic. We stopped to eat on top and sat on a smooth gray boulder under tree limbs and leaves.

John had brought peanut butter and jelly sandwiches. "It's the best sandwich ever made. What do you think?" he asked as he paused between bites.

For some reason, maybe because I'd eaten no breakfast, the mixture of flavors delighted my palate. I wolfed down the sandwich, and then John and I shared the third one.

As the sun crossed the sky, John's shadow crept from one side of his body to the other. Tilting back my head, I searched the sky for all of its invisible planets, suns, and moons, just to avoid staring into his hypnotizing eyes.

John talked of birds and flowers and his family back in Colorado.

I looked back at him. "Have you been in touch?" Then I stopped myself. "Of course you have."

He nodded. "They know I'm here. I told them the good and the bad, about Alice and Mary. My divorce will be finalized next week, and of course they're upset about that. They'd like me to come home."

His mention of divorce silenced me. I'd always found it sad when marriages ended, but John's situation had made it imperative. At least the army attorney had pushed it through quickly.

John said, "I could go back home, but my parents are getting on, and they deserve to have their peace and quiet." He grew still, and his eyes had a faraway expression. "Besides, I don't know if I can ever really go back home again. I don't know if that's possible. Things for me have changed so much."

I sighed, remembering my home before this one. Over the past year, I'd written to my parents about Mary and told them the facts, but I'd failed to mention that I believed she was mine. They would've thought I'd lost my mind. "I know exactly what you mean. Once, the farm was my home; in fact, it was the entire world. But I've found a completely different home now. Even if I went back, it wouldn't be the same." I paused. "But you know what? When someone asks me where my home is, I still say Colorado. Isn't that strange?"

"You remind me of home," John said pensively. He closed his eyes, giving me an opportunity to study his face; I admired his gorgeous bone structure; good, smooth skin; and lips with distinct borders shaped like a heart.

How easy it was to talk to John. I said, "Before the drought, I ran the rows in the corn fields, like a phantom weaving in and out of the waves of heat, wearing worn-out britches with a layer of dirt on my face. Then I was vanishing in the orchards behind walnut trunks, silent and stealthy." I sighed. "The world was rich and lush back then, and though we might have been poor, I didn't know it. The farm was full of adventure, and I could handle a hoe in the garden and milk the goat by the time I was four."

John's look said he understood. "It was a great place to grow up."

I didn't tell him that by the time I could hang my own laundry on the clothesline, my white cotton panties drying stiffly in the breeze, I wanted another life. Entertainment such as feeding the ducks or chasing a chicken or reading a book down under the cottonwoods could not compensate for running to the outhouse on a cold, slant-mist morning; slaughtering our animals; and watching crops die. But I didn't say anything about all that; I didn't want the conversation to turn dreary.

He grinned as if recalling something funny. "In 1935, my brother Bobby and I heard about the so-called Prosperity Club. A chain letter promised a return of more than fifteen hundred dollars if we sent a dime to the person on top of the list, put our names on the bottom, and mailed out five copies. I secretly believed it was probably too good to be true. Our parents forbid us the folly of sending off dimes in the mail for no good reason, but my brother had been convinced it would work, so we did it anyway. We found a way to save a dime and the cost of postage, which was hard to come by during the Depression. While we waited, Bobby chewed his nails down to the quick. When no money ever came, he dunked me in the pond, saying, 'You and your big ideas.'"

I laughed.

An hour passed in a few minutes. I looked up at the changed position of the sun in wonder. When I looked back at him, he was staring into my eyes, and everything around us froze as if fixed in time by a photograph. I considered all of these happenings between us and the ones still to come, and an ache bloomed in my gut. Something had formed between us, some invisible and, as of yet, unspoken bond, but I had no idea what to do about it.

We mounted our horses and began to make a slow descent. I didn't want the day to slip away, but here it was, doing just that. Although I loved listening to John talk about his life, I found that he went through long periods of silence, too, that he could simply enjoy being out in the sun, surrounded by birds and trees and sky, without having to say anything.

We came out of the woods onto a great, grassy meadow that backed up to a low, gold ridgeline. Overhead some sort of hawk was circling. The air smelled of grass, horsehide, berry brambles, and stream water. Surrounding us was the deafening hum of insects and birds.

John reined in and I drew up beside him, facing the meadow. "We could open it up here." He gestured out into open meadow. "You want to try running them for a little while?"

I shrugged. "Sure." I had gotten more comfortable on the horse, but running the mare was going to be scary. However, I played it cool.

He told me what to do, and then he extended a hand, palm up, toward the meadow. "Ladies first."

I sat tall in the saddle and faced that meadow. It was like the moment of silence before the orchestra begins to play. I picked up the reins, pulled in the slack, and dug my heels into the horse's sides. Even without spurs the horse lunged into first a trot, and then, as I stood up out of the stirrups and urged the mare on, a full gallop. I was holding on and hoping I could handle this. It was a pretty great feeling, with the wind in my face and the meadow spread out before me, lush and still. I glanced back once and saw John kicking up the dirt behind me, his face stretched into a grin, white teeth shining in the sunlight.

I faced forward again, and I could see myself as if the sky above were reflecting me, like the Saguache spring reflected the sky, as if I were on top of the sky looking down at this lovely scene, and yet I was there, too, pounding over earth like something wild let loose. The horse's hoofbeats matched the beats of my heart, and I gave myself over to this freedom. The mare was pushing herself in the heat, her breaths coming out in dusty spurts, and her coat rinsed in sheen. I was breathing deeply, too, and laughter came from a new and previously unknown place.

Then a jolt, and our forward momentum stopped, or at least my horse's did. I tried to clutch at the mare's mane as I went airborne, and then I was flailing and fighting at the air. I hit the ground with a sickening thud. The birds and insects went silent. I must have gone unconscious for a few seconds, because there was nothing.

When I opened my eyes, it was to a sky so big and blue that it was as if I'd never seen it before. The dome of the world was so huge and glorious, and the earth stood still beneath it, and everything around me was glittery, bathed in jewels. But I couldn't breathe. For a split second I thought the fall might have killed me and this place was heaven, and then John's face appeared over me. He was backlit by the sun and yet I could see his face so clearly. His eyes were blue, yes, and yet this close I could see that the irises were streaked with small gold strands and then speckled with tiny pepper dots, like a blue river suspending the substance of earth. His pupils were almost pinpointed in the sun, brilliant and dark, but somehow translucent, clear, letting everything inside of him show. The world changed in the time of that lost air, and it seemed the most pure and real thing to do, to kiss him. I tried to raise myself, to bring my lips to his, and yet I did not move. I could not move, and then I thought, *Please God, no, I've broken my back.*

John was down on his knees at my side, leaning over me, and I could hear him whispering, "Gwen, Gwen."

My chest moved, and I sucked in air. Then came the pain from the impact, and I could feel a grimace twist my face.

John was still saying my name, and then he was holding my hand and my wrist, checking for a pulse. *I'm alive, I'm OK*, I wanted to say, but I couldn't form the words. I could only lie there and witness John's torture. I could see it all in the expressions on his face. He clearly didn't know what to do. Should he ride for help, yell, stay with me until someone came by, what? He looked around desperately for a moment, as if a rescue squad might miraculously appear.

Maybe I was stunned more by his face and close proximity than by the fall and the pain that rushed in. I did want to be kissed again by a man, but only by John, only John. I wanted to feel his sweet lips on mine, his arms around my waist, pulling me close into his hips.

"Are you . . .?" he asked.

I didn't move, not even to blink. "I'm. OK," I finally managed to say.

"Don't move."

Then he looked straight down into my eyes, straight into me. "Dear God. What have I done?" he exhaled.

"I'm OK," I said again. "I just need. To catch. My breath."

He leaned in. He wore a look on his face that I couldn't describe. I could feel each warm breath he exhaled on my face, and I wanted it to last.

"I'm going for help," he said.

"No."

"I'll ride like hell. I'll be right back."

I wanted to tell him not to go, not to leave me, but air abandoned me again just as it had when I'd first fallen. I heard John whistle to his horse, mount again, and then begin to gallop away, as my breathing slowly righted itself. I hoped my horse was all right. For a long time I lay still, listening to the sounds of insects and birds come back and the horse tearing at clumps of grass with her teeth and then chewing. At least the mare seemed to be unharmed.

A few minutes later the life came back into my body, and I was able to ease myself up to a sitting position. I waited for a few moments, in wonder at the way the sounds of life had begun to hum and sing all around me so loudly. I looked around for what had spooked the horse, imagining that maybe a rattler was coiled nearby, ready to attack, but I saw nothing.

I slowly stood and tried walking. I winced with every move. My shoulders felt high and pinched, and I was walking as if my legs were strapped to rods. There was an odd leaning to the way I held myself. But each step was easier than the last, and whatever kinks and knots had been formed in defense of the fall began to ease and unravel. I walked over to the mare and stroked her forehead. I could swear, that horse was hanging her head in shame, and so I whispered, "Don't worry. I'm not mad at you." I'd been talking to animals on the farm since I'd been talking at all.

By the time I heard the thumping of galloping hooves coming closer, I could walk almost normally. John jumped down from his horse, a joyful look of relief spread over his face. "Thank God," he said.

"I'm fine, just fine."

Carlton and Stan had ridden over with him on their own horses, and both of them asked if I wanted to see a doctor or go to a hospital, but I saw no need. I said, "I wouldn't be walking if anything was broken."

"Maybe you should get an X-ray?" John asked.

Instead I mounted the horse, and the four of us rode back in silence. I could tell that John felt awful. Ahead of me, he rode with his shoulders hunched, and I could see him unconsciously shaking his head, facing straight ahead, and admonishing himself. It seemed so unfair to him; after all, the day had been so lovely to me.

On the way home, it seemed that remorse hit him hugely, and he didn't say much as we threaded our way back to the city. He clenched the steering wheel hard with both hands, but after the activity of the long day, he looked tousled and beautiful and incredibly vulnerable as he drove quietly, looking deep in thought, surrounded by the darkening sky. A breeze outside was picking up and tugging the truck to the side for brief moments at a time. His anguish lasted all the way home, for what felt like hours, until the daylight slanted away, and a huge burnt sunset ballooned in the western sky.

"I'll come up and get you settled, make sure you're OK," John said when we arrived at my apartment. He turned off the ignition.

"No—" I blurted out. I didn't want John to know about the atmosphere in my place now, the way it had changed, and just remembering what I faced inside closed a bitter fist about my heart. The apartment whispered and clicked with the tension between Dot and Dennis. If I told him, John would only worry about Mary being there and might even decide to take her sooner rather than later. "I mean, I'm trying my best not to invade Dot and Dennis's privacy."

When I had the nerve to look at him, his face seemed even more etched with anguish than before. I didn't know what to do with what I was feeling, the way he had touched me. And now, I'd hurt him once again.

"You know what . . . ?" I said. "Mary's probably asleep at Lisen's by now. We could go out." My bold suggestion made me gulp.

But John broke out into one of his gleaming, gorgeous smiles. He gestured at our clothes. "In this?"

"We could change and meet back here. I'll check on Mary, too."

John's eyes glistened. "You surprise me, Gwen. You always manage to surprise me."

I shrugged. "You took us to the country. Maybe it's time you saw what the city has to offer. Take advantage of someone who's been here longer than you have. What do you say we paint the town?"

He shook his head. "But you just took a nasty fall."

"I'm a little sore, but nothing more."

He placed his hand on the back of the seat, near my neck. "It gets worse by the hour, Gwen. You're going to be aching for a few days; trust me. I've come off a horse before, and I doubt jostling around in a crowded club tonight would be good for you."

"Come now. I'm tougher than you think." I gave him a flirty little smile. "Some not-so-fresh air could be just what the doctor ordered."

He shot me a look of amazement, waited, then shrugged. "If you're sure, it sounds great to me."

"You'll see."

He smiled. "Then A-OK."

We parted ways and I bolted up the stairs, already concocting what I'd wear in my head. I checked in with Lisen, who seemed as pleased as I was that I would be spending the evening out with John, and she had no problem keeping Mary overnight. Inside my apartment, I found that Dot and Dennis were out, too. If only Dot were here, I thought, to help me dress up. I wanted sexy, but not vixen. I donned one of my favorite dresses from my voracious dating days—cherry red with a swirl of a skirt landing just below the knee—a dancing dress with a fitted bodice and an off-the-shoulder neckline. I wore my imitation pearls and swathed on one of the new red, kiss-proof lipsticks Dot had bought for me. I blotted my lips and then sat and waited for John to return. As the minutes ticked by, a moment of doubt—a warning—nudged me. Did I know what I was doing? Did I just want to be seen on the arm of an extraordinary-looking man, or was I hoping for an opportunity to kiss John? I'd lost my chance in the meadow, but what would tonight bring?

John arrived, dazzling as usual, in his dark suit, and we grabbed a bite to eat at the automat and then hopped on the train. When we arrived at our stop, a light rain had begun to fall. John grabbed my hand, and we started running down the sidewalk. It was long after dark, and the lights were on in office towers, so their glowing reflections haloed around us. Speckled lights from windows and doors glistened on the sidewalk. Attempting to run in heels, I laughed, suddenly imbued with unexpected joy.

I had decided to take John to Swing Street, as West 52nd was known. There, the brownstone facades and basements had been converted to clubs; we wouldn't have to pay a cover charge and could linger over as little as one beer while listening to great improvisational jazz and bebop in any one of a dozen establishments. John had spent too much money on the day already, and I didn't want to burden him further. We stepped into Club Downbeat and brushed off the droplets of rain that clung to our clothes. John gallantly produced a handkerchief from inside his coat pocket, reached up, and gently touched the rain off my cheeks. Through the linen I could feel the warmth of his hands, and I had to close my eyes.

Inside, no lady wore slacks, and no man went without either a tie or a uniform. Women had adorned themselves with hats and nylons; the most dapper men wore their trousers suspended with clips instead of button loops. The music reverberated, waiters wove between tables lifting trays laden with drinks, cigarettes dangled from ladies' fingertips, and the atmosphere was one of cheery debauchery. The band was playing bop, and the place was swarming. We found seats at the bar, as all the tables were taken.

I started to order a beer, but John insisted on martinis.

"Mary's safe and sound. You're off duty for the night," he said over the sound of the music that trembled in the bar beneath my hands. Or was I trembling?

I tossed my hair and lowered my chin, just like I used to. "I suppose we don't have to be such *parents* all the time."

"I give you permission to let loose for one night. In fact, I insist."

John gazed at me with what seemed like a mixture of respect and desire, the exact way a woman wants to be looked at. I couldn't help but notice that women were staring at John. There were a lot of single gals out on the town tonight, and John captivated them as much as a faceted gem would. He didn't seem to notice, and that was one of the things I'd always appreciated about John. He wasn't vain.

When our drinks came, I took a significant sip of my martini.

John said, "There's my girl."

"I'm hardly a girl." The other women in the room struck me as just that—girls—probably no older than twenty-one or twenty-two.

John sipped his martini. "Wowza. They make a stiff one here, don't they?" He kept his elbows on the bar and tapped his fingertips on the polished wood, as if he wasn't sure what to do with his hands.

"You'll never find better food, drinks, or entertainment than in this city."

He shifted in his seat, just slightly. "You know what bothers me more than the noise . . . ? It's the lights on all these buildings, all night long. Messes up my sleep."

This was not a good topic of conversation. "I think the lights are beautiful. They make me believe man is capable of lovely, new, innovative things."

"Believe it or not, I slept better in a ditch in Germany. It was fantastically dark. Even with a moon in the sky, darker than this city."

"But you love Paris."

He lifted his martini glass to me. "No skyscrapers."

"Paris spoiled you, didn't it?"

He shrugged. "What do you think?"

"Is it really that much finer than here?"

His eyes twinkled, I swear. "Am I not convincing?"

"Do you always answer a question with a question?"

Laughter lit his eyes. "Do you?"

We grinned like kids.

"Here's another one for you, although I'll warn you . . . it's personal." He shifted his body closer to mine and lowered his voice. He was close enough that I could smell something lemony in his hair. "Why has no man snatched you up?"

I was becoming something of an oddity: twenty-five years old and still single. "Well, there have been many *potential* snatchers. But, you once told me you thought I was a risk taker, and yes I am, in certain areas. Leaving home, making my way here, and all that. But when it comes to men, I'm cautious." I waited while his gaze lingered on my face, and he sat perfectly still as if enraptured by my words. "Or maybe I've just been waiting for someone special."

We stared into each other's eyes for a moment, and it was as if each of us was waiting for the other to speak next. Then a man reached in between us to grab a couple of beers from the bartender, and the moment was lost. I turned away. The music boomed even louder, and we fell into a silence that was not uncomfortable at first, but then gradually became so. What were we doing? Did I want to be his girl? Was John just biding his time and having some fun, until he left and took Mary?

We were in a strange and impossible situation. We weren't going through a courtship; we were parents. Maybe I felt so close to him because he was Mary's father. Maybe he cared for me because of all I'd done for her. Even if those things weren't true, we wanted to live in different places, and so it was hopeless to think that we'd end up together. But despite all of my inner voices telling me it couldn't work, something was happening to me, and my breathing quickened. As deliberately as I tried to control it, I couldn't tamp it down.

He asked me to dance the jitterbug. The dance had become very popular while I'd spent most of my evenings at home with Mary, so I'd had little practice. And this was a fast-paced tune.

"I've hardly done it. I don't know if I can keep up."

He gave me a mischievous grin. "Of course you can. Just follow me."

He led me to the dance floor and started swinging me around. He whipped me into him and then out like a cowboy with a lady on a lasso. My feet started to fly in perfect synchronicity with the music. I smiled into John's face. He took my hands in his, and I knew he meant to slide me in between his legs. I'd seen the move a few times before. I was supposed to glide through and then pop up behind him. It required a slick step. Could I do it?

Oh, what the hell? If I made a fool of myself, what did it matter? John looked so adorable when I nodded, letting him know I would try it. I slid between his legs, smooth as oil, and only barely stumbled once on my way back up. Laughter flew out of me. John sure did know how to show a girl a good time.

People were watching us. I suddenly felt carefree, and I broke out in a cheerleader's smile when people looked at John and me as if we were a couple. A newfound joy and pride warmed me all over. When I didn't know if I could contain my lungs inside my chest any longer, we returned to the bar and then I excused myself to the ladies' room.

I had to wait in line for the facilities and afterward washed my hands, applied a dusting of face powder from the compact in my purse, and retouched my lipstick, all the while trying to slow my breathing and calm myself.

A girl in the bathroom said to another, "Did you see that knockout in the black suit out there on the dance floor?"

"Boy, did I. He looks like a movie star. *Fabulous* blue eyes. And wow could he move."

There were other good-looking men in the place, but I knew they were talking about John. However, they didn't realize I'd been the girl dancing with the "knockout." They had seen only him and not even remembered me. My exhilaration and pride slipped away like a balloon losing air. I was attractive; I knew that, but I was not in the same league as John, Alice, and Dot. I looked at myself in the mirror and reasoned myself down from what had come over me earlier. With John, I was in way over my head. Better now, I weaved through the throng of party-goers, waiters, dancers, and low clouds of smoke to find John surrounded by women—three of them dressed identically in lavender gowns, as if they'd come from a wedding in which they'd been the bridesmaids. I froze. John's adorers—a blonde, a brunette, and a redhead, how quaint!—lolled and giggled around him like circling butterflies. John was speaking to the redhead, seemingly intent on what she had to say.

Even though only moments before I'd tried to convince myself there was nothing between John and me, a pang of the most profound jealousy ran through my gut.

But what was John to do? He was too polite a man to rudely dismiss the girls. And yet, couldn't he simply say, "I'm here with someone"? With his looks, he had to have encountered situations similar to this before. He had to have learned how to extricate himself from entrapments.

Not sure what *I* was to do, I waited a few anxious moments that felt like eternity. If only he would see what was happening and take charge of the situation. *Look up, John. See me.*

I started to move toward him, but then he turned his back and addressed the bartender. Ordering drinks for the girls? My jealousy was so fierce I thought it would impale me. Irrational, of course, because John wasn't mine. I spun around in my shaking heels toward the dance floor through the throng.

I could play this game. In the past, I had played hard to get with the best of them, and I'd worked it so two men had to compete for me. I wasn't really proud of that behavior, but it had been exciting and good for my self-confidence.

I strode toward the dance floor and soon accepted a dance with a lonesome sailor in his dress blues. He was basketball-player tall with a firm grip and led me into a slower version of the jitterbug with practiced ease. As I went through the motions, I glanced toward the bar, wishing John would come after me. Once I caught a glimpse of him, still surrounded by the lavender ensemble.

So I kept dancing with the sailor, who told me his name was Chip. After a few spins on the dance floor, he asked if I wanted to sit for a while and get a drink. He had a table in one of the corners manned by his buddies. But I didn't want to sit with him. I didn't want to position myself so that John could not find me. But he didn't come to find me. So Chip and I danced on and on. As the place filled to overflowing, I lost sight of John altogether, and the evening dragged on, each song longer than the one before it.

My feet hurt, my neck pinched, and my body began to ache. I didn't know if it was soreness finally settling in after the fall earlier that day, or if I hurt all over because the night had not turned out the way I'd hoped.

A break in the crowd allowed me another glance toward the bar. The redheaded bridesmaid was urging John to the dance floor, grasping his sleeve, pouring herself into him, and dragging him off the barstool. He put his hand on the small of her back as they turned toward the dance floor. His eyes scanned the room, but it hurt my eyes to look that way. I could see him; why couldn't he see me? Part of me wanted him to seek me out, take me onto the dance floor, and pull me into his arms. Part of me wanted the night to spin out of control and spit us out in different directions. If only he hadn't touched her! I looked toward the band, as if the musicians could beat out an answer for me.

The party whipped into a frenzy, and the aching in my body became too much for me to bear. I suddenly wanted to be home. I disengaged from my dance partner and tried to find John to tell him I was leaving, but he seemed to have disappeared. Had he slipped away with a lavender lady?

Outside, the rain was pelting down now, cold and piercing. I hailed a cab. Just as I settled into the backseat and told the cabbie my address, a tapping came at my window. John stood crouched over in the rain, hands in his pockets, a baffled expression on his face. I guessed he had finally managed to untangle himself from the bridesmaids.

I rolled down my window.

"Where are you going? I've been looking for you," he asked with a hint of desperation in his voice. His suit was getting soaked, and he was batting his eyes against the rainfall.

"I'm hitting the sack. I feel the fall now."

He reached for the door handle. "I'll see you home."

I shook my head. The magic of the evening had vanished for me, and disappointment raged like a fever under my skin. "I'm a big girl. Go on and enjoy yourself."

I was being unreasonable, but I couldn't help it. The girls had cornered him, but why hadn't he removed himself? I kept seeing his hand on the lavender lady's back. Of course that was what men did; they guided a lady in that way. It was simply the way a gentleman would behave. It could've meant nothing, but the state I was in led me to realize how vulnerable I was. Mixed feelings bombarded me and made me dizzy, as if the earth were spinning too fast and I had to hold on.

I had to return to a more self-protective state. Even with the smallest slight, real or perceived, I knew then how badly John could hurt me.

CHAPTER SIXTEEN

After the dismal failure of my night on the town with John, I spent the next evening with Dot, Mary, and the miserable company of Dennis. Mary had the beginnings of a cold so John was not coming over, although he had called to inquire about how I was feeling. I was relieved to have an excuse not to see him for a few days. I was still reeling from that promising night that had not delivered anything but a short conversation, one exciting dance, and then jealousy and pain. My self-confidence had been socked in the stomach.

Dennis was drinking whiskey. At times he had slowed down or stopped drinking. The dry days seemed to follow nothing in particular, no unusual bad occurrences or good ones, and they seemed to have no relation to the nightmares I still heard at night. Out of the blue, he put the stuff away for a day, and I could see Dot's hopes soar that maybe he'd snapped out of it. For a while it looked as though he'd drunk the grief away.

But it always came back.

I could scarcely remember the days of their courtship. It had been such a romantic and exciting beginning. They had spent every possible moment together, and Dennis had splurged on everything in that short time. He took her out for fine dining, and then to the hippest clubs for dancing. He swept her off her feet with excitement, extravagance, and fun. It didn't hurt that he looked like a Viking king all spruced up in modern-day, stylish clothes. Dot had been sure she was standing at the open door of a charmed life.

I remembered the day when he came to take her for a ferry ride to Sandy Hook. Dennis was wearing his uniform with his jacket flung over his shoulder. He looked so lovely in those days—sometimes I could still see the handsome man Dot had dated beneath the bitterness—his strong Norseman's face, his satiny hair and deep-set eyes. I could see him smiling at her on their wedding day, his teeth a gleaming white band across his tanned face.

During the bad days, Dot did everything she could to reach out to him, and they no longer even tried to hide what was transpiring between them. Many times they argued with the bedroom door open, and then the arguments moved into the living room and the kitchen, too.

One particularly pitiful exchange started when Dot said to Dennis, "I want to help you." They were in the bedroom sitting on the edge of the bed next to each other. The door was open, and I was feeding Mary in the kitchen, only a few feet away.

He said, "You can't help."

Dot said nothing for a moment, and I could only imagine how she must have felt slapped by his words. Finally she asked, "What happened to you in the war?"

"I wonder."

"What happened to change you so much?"

He laughed. "We killed people."

It did seem unfathomable.

Dot said, "But you were supposed to kill people."

He hacked out another laugh.

Dot's voice, softer. "OK, I guess that would be difficult to live with."

His voice, more bitter. "You guess?"

"You can tell me about it."

"No, I can't. You don't understand."

"Then tell me so I will."

There was silence for a few long moments, and then he said, "I'm dead inside."

"Dead? Of course you aren't."

"There are many ways to die, Dot."

"Why do you say that?"

"I'm just as dead as all those soldiers in frozen graves."

"You're not. It only feels that way right now. It'll get better."

"No."

"I want to help you."

"You can't."

"I can, because I love you."

"You should never have fallen for me. You should never have married me."

This kind of conversation would go on until he walked away. That night Dennis ended the conversation by leaving the bedroom and coming into the living room to play cards again. He made himself a drink. Dot was back in their room, holding nothing but air in her hands.

I witnessed some moments of caring, enough to keep me hopeful of a turnaround. One day Dennis asked Dot to play gin rummy, and I could tell that he deliberately let her win. Over that game, I saw him smile. Sometimes we all sat on the building's front steps together, and he brushed off the stairs before she sat down. Another time as the three of us sat and looked out at the sunset and Mary toddled around, he reached down and dusted the powdery dirt from Dot's shoes.

The next day when I woke up, they were in the kitchen already. I heard Dot saying, "Dennis, you're still a good person."

"No."

"You're still a good person to me."

"How would you know if I was ever a good person?" he said. "We never knew each other, Dot."

I gulped. It was partially true. Two weeks did not make for much of a relationship. I was sure that Dot, too, knew that now. "OK, then we're truly starting from scratch. We can start over, begin again. Learn everything. We can go out on dates."

"Right. Let's go see a war movie."

Dot lowered her voice. "There are plenty of other things we can do." Finally Dot closed the door.

Once, they went to see a musical at a Saturday matinee, and I hoped that in the dark of the theater Dennis could forget about things for a while and maybe even hold Dot's hand. I never saw them touch anymore. That evening he seemed better. But the next day, inexplicably, he started drinking again.

And that night he woke up screaming, yet again. I saw a slit of light under my bedroom door, so I knew Dot had turned on the lights in the apartment. She had to make sure Dennis was fully awake before he tried to sleep again.

She said, "I love you."

No response.

In the silence of the night, every word rang clear. "You can't say it anymore, can you?" Dot said. I pulled the covers up to Mary's neck. She had kicked them off sometime earlier, but she was still sleeping.

"I can't say it, because I can't love anyone," Dennis said.

How those words must have cut and twisted inside Dot, but at least he was talking to her. "Why not?"

"I don't know."

"Let's talk to someone."

Dot had talked about Dennis to a doctor at the hospital, who had recommended a psychiatrist, but she was too afraid to say that word. Instead she said, "Let's go to a counselor or a minister or something."

He laughed.

The next day, Dot came with me when I took Mary for an evening stroll, down the straight lines of the streets, watched over by twisted filigree, hidden by shadows. She said, "I never fathomed having this problem. Growing up I always heard from other girls how much men would desire me, and as an adult I've felt that's always been true. I've been desired, wanted, sought after. I believed it would always be that way, at least until I was an old woman." She paused and swiped away tears. "It would be easier if he left me."

How quickly a life could change, how quickly hopes could die. I was watching it all fall apart for Dot in chunks the size of shattered dreams. Did she ever think of leaving her loveless union? Sometimes I would see her in my mind's eye gathering together all her money, buying a car, and driving away.

Ahead of us a stray cat prowled the moonlit grid on the sidewalk and then disappeared.

Dot said, "I envy the freedom of a stray cat."

Dot's marriage difficulties served to make me more determined than ever to practice restraint in my own life. I didn't particularly like this part of myself. Was I always going to be one of those people who could paint on a free-spirited facade, but secretly waited for the proverbial shoe to drop? Did my nature and history make me believe that a disastrous change was always just around the corner?

John had kept calling to check on how I was feeling and inquire about Mary, and as soon as her cold had resolved, he came by to spend time with her. When he arrived, I had a hard time looking at him. I couldn't describe the emotion—I was feeling angry but pitifully hurt, determined but defenseless. I sensed he was going through the same kind of confusion. Evident on his face were many inner thoughts, as if all his internal wheels were turning, the synapses firing.

It was rainy outside, but Dot and Dennis had gone out anyway. We took the opportunity to stay in, and I made a meatloaf with potatoes and green beans. We talked about the news and some mundane things over dinner. Nothing special had been said, but the atmosphere quickly changed for the better. There was an easy comfort about having John in the apartment. It felt sort of right. When we finished, I cleaned up the kitchen while he took charge of Mary. He cleaned her face and then put her in the living room to toddle about and play. He had bought her a new stuffed animal, and she was mesmerized by it.

He wandered into the kitchen, where I was filling the sink. He cleared his throat. "I've never taken care of a sick baby before. Has she ever been seriously ill?"

"Of course. She's had other colds and strep throat once. She gets cranky when she's starting to come down with something. And you can usually tell if she has a fever just by feeling her forehead."

"How did you know it was strep throat?"

"I always take her to the doctor if she has any fever. A doctor can diagnose strep throat, and it has to be treated with penicillin. She had to get a shot, and she howled."

He winced. "I don't think I could stand it."

"It's kind of terrible, but it has to be done."

He stood still as I washed the dishes.

"For colds, you just keep her home and give her lots of fluids, if she'll take them. She tends to lose her appetite when she isn't feeling well."

I told him she'd had all her required immunizations so far. I told him that my biggest fear was polio. He listened intently to it all, as if taking mental notes, and it struck me: he was preparing to take care of her, alone. Alone. Any contentment I'd been feeling quickly withered away, and all I could think of was losing Mary.

"About the other day . . ." John said in a softer voice.

"I'm planning to take riding lessons," I said.

"Really? I didn't know you had enjoyed it that much."

"Before I fell, it was wonderful. I want to feel that way again, that free, you know?"

I glanced over my shoulder, and he looked at me in that studious way of his. "Plus, I need to learn how to stay on a horse."

"You can say that again."

By now I'd washed the dishes and put them in the sink set to dry. I started wiping down the counter. John came up from behind me, put his hands on my upper arms, and turned me around.

"I was talking about what happened at the club."

I blinked. "You're a great dancer."

"We were having such a good time, and then those girls came and took over."

I kept my voice steady and low. "You let them take over."

He looked remorseful, and his shoulders slumped. "Look, I've never been good at getting rid of people."

I was filled with remorse, too, but the hurt hadn't left yet. I cared too much. There was a trembling in the air when I was this close to him. How would I make it go away? "You must have encountered a similar situation before."

"Yeah, and it's never easy. I can't stand to hurt people's feelings. It's a lousy quality. I eased away as quickly as I could."

"So . . . are you saying you didn't enjoy even a moment of all that attention?"

He looked taken aback. "Of course I enjoyed it, but I went there with you."

I wanted to scream at him, *Then why did you stay away so long? Dance? Touch the other girl?* But if I let my true feelings show, I would end up crying. I never wanted to come across as a jealous, slobbering fool. John was bringing out so many emotions in me—some of them good, some of them not so good—I didn't know what to do with myself. I sighed heavily. "I guess it was all just a misunderstanding."

He stared into my eyes until I had to look away. *He knows how I feel.* He said, "I apologize if I hurt your feelings in any way."

"I apologize, too. I shouldn't have left so abruptly. But why don't we let it go? Maybe we should focus on what's most important here: Mary."

He looked disappointed, but he plastered what looked like a fake smile on his face. "If that's what you want, Gwen . . ."

That night I showed John how Mary liked her bath—the temperature of the water, her favorite bathtub toys (ducks), and the way she liked to be wrapped in a towel when she got out. Mary rolled away from me and tried to get up when I was diapering and dressing her. John called her a "pistol." To my surprise, he squawked around the room like a duck to distract her while I got her ready for bed. I laughed so hard I almost stuck myself with a diaper pin. I showed him how to diaper her for the night and her favorite jammies and stuffed animals for bedtime.

After he left, I paced the floor. What was the matter with me? I could be going crazy. One minute I thought John was the finest, strongest man I'd ever met. Then the next, I worried about his need to never hurt anyone; he could be sucked in so easily. One minute I thought his looks weren't an issue, then the next minute I thought they'd always be an issue. One minute I wanted to fall into that sweet place within John's arms, and the next minute I wanted to pull back as far as I could. One minute I wanted to go everywhere with this wonderful, beautiful man who'd come into my life, and another minute I was convinced I could never leave here. I wanted him to go away and also to never go away.

The turmoil was exhausting.

CHAPTER SEVENTEEN

John worked every day at the furniture shop except for Sundays, and I worked every other Saturday and Sunday at the hospital, so it was a rare thing when we could take Mary out together for an entire day. On this particular Sunday, John had rented a car, a big four-door Edsel, so that we could take her for a drive in the country. It was the end of October, a time of autumn beauty. The fall colors were still evident in patches, and the air was tart and cool. I changed Mary into a long-sleeved T-shirt and overalls with heavy socks and her walking shoes. I put on wool slacks to make sure my legs stayed warm.

John and I never spoke again about what happened that night at Club Downbeat. Sometimes I could tell we were both thinking of it, but we avoided that sore subject.

We decided to explore the roads leading into Pennsylvania, where we could enjoy the colorful splash of leaves and visit the site of Washington's crossing on the Delaware. We drove out of the city beyond the Lincoln Tunnel and into dappled sunlight. Mary sat on my lap, and soon the motion of the car put her into something of a trance in my arms. Her eyelids started drooping, staying closed longer with each slow blink.

She needed this rest.

I looked over at John. I could smell that lemony fragrance from his hair, and his long legs were levered out in front of him as he drove. He'd tossed his jacket into the backseat and had rolled his shirtsleeves up to his elbows. The curve of his wrist was the same as Mary's. He drove with his shoulders squared but relaxed, his hands low and loose on the steering wheel. He looked ahead with a sense of anticipation, as if he knew that around the next bend, there would be something worthwhile to see.

After even the outskirts of the city gave way, the road wound past amber fields, orchards scattered with light, and woods aflame in reds, oranges, and golds. The air smelled fresh with moss and recent rain and river, and the sun was warm through the windshield. Houses and barns and outbuildings lay scattered on the land as though a child's set of blocks had rolled down from the hills and landed at random. Curls of smoke from chimneys and the occasional pickup truck and field hand were the only reminders that we were not traveling a deserted landscape. I hadn't been out to the countryside in a long time, and how it was working on me! The pace and packed-in feeling of the city slowly eased away, and a rare sensation that all was right in the world entered me.

As we crossed the wide Delaware into New Hope, Pennsylvania, John nodded down at the water and then glanced at me. Our eyes met, and I knew what he was thinking. The rivers of Colorado shot like chutes out of rocks and ravines, but East Coast rivers flowed across the land broadly on its surface, like thick veins track the skin of a muscular person. We didn't speak, neither of us wanting to wake Mary, and the river flowed beneath us.

At Washington's crossing, Mary awakened as soon as John cut the engine, and he got out and skirted the car to open the door and help me out. The air was as clear and clean as creek water scrambling over stones. Here you could smell winter on the way. The light was pale, and geese cried out as they flew in formation overhead.

Mary whimpered once when I passed her over to John, but he was already learning how to entertain her. She reached out her arms to me and gave me one of her "I need you" looks, but he said, "Look, look, Mary," and led her over to the closest tree, an old staggering pine, and he patted the bark with his hand.

He said, "Tree," and then repeated it, "tree."

He let Mary pat the bark and soon had her saying her version of *tree*, which came out as "tee," and then when she'd had her fill, he brushed away the tiny pieces of bark clinging to her palm. The breeze hummed through the trees, and the light shafted down like beams from some Almighty sending down grace on insects and squirrels.

Mary was mesmerized by the park and the breeze in her face. We stopped and read signs that told the history of this place. For many Americans, Washington's forging of the Delaware depicted freedom and courage. It was a place where one could still imagine stands of virgin forest climbing up from river to hill on undisturbed ground, where one could still conjure the faces of the Indians peering from between tree trunks and then disappearing, where every waterway our forefathers crossed ran clear and clean and unencumbered.

I said to John, "It's amazing to think that I'm walking on the same soil as George Washington did."

He nodded. "You get that feeling all over Europe. All that history, and everywhere you go, you know that famous figures have walked in the same places before you."

"Humbling, isn't it?" I said.

He shrugged. "Oh, I don't know. One thing I finally learned over there is that no one life is more valuable than another."

He lifted Mary to his shoulders, and she loved being up so high. She clutched John's collar, but her eyes were bright discs of wonder.

I said to her, "Look how big our Mary is. Look what a big girl you are."

She squealed. Then she pointed at the river and said, "Wah-ter."

We went back to New Hope for lunch and ate meatloaf sandwiches and corn on the cob at a place where picnic tables overlooked the old canal that ran straight as a rod along the western side of the Delaware. We drank warm cider and fed Mary a crustless sandwich I'd wrapped in waxed paper and packed for her in my lunch pail. I had also brought a thermos of chocolate milk I'd made with Hershey's syrup. I held her while John let her take sips from the thermos, and it was clear to see how John was falling in love with his daughter. I could feel her moving closer in his direction, too, and the taste of it was bittersweet on my tongue. I couldn't help being touched by the way John's eyes became misty as he looked at Mary, and also by Mary's slow adjustment into trust and love. It was obvious that they would be good together. John would be a caring and involved father, and she would be a daddy's girl.

But with every new step they took toward each other, it meant one step farther away from me. And that thought brought such a stabbing pain to my chest I almost couldn't breathe. Why had I been so ready to turn down John's proposal of marriage? I'd held on to my convictions, but now those convictions felt like nothing but words. Why had I been so sure it couldn't have worked between us? I had been so practical, perhaps my parents' daughter after all. And what wrongs had he really done to me? Our relationship had been moving in a promising direction, and then I had thrown it off course with jealousy and insecurity. At such a loss as to how to convey my feelings, I'd mucked it all up.

Today his hair flopped over to one side in the most enchanting way. A look at his hands made me teary. The skin on his face was always too close, tempting me to reach out and brush my fingers across the shadow of his beard. His smile brought on a choking sensation, and his lips looked sweet and soft, seductively pinkish.

I had no idea what to do with the thrilling ache that spread inside me along with a momentary dizziness. When had this man, this face, come to be the landscape by which I would measure all others?

I said in a gasping, halting way, "I've done the most foolish thing."

He shot a look my way, but he was absorbed in cleaning Mary's face after her lunch. My nerves were zinging with electricity and a battalion of tears threatened to charge from my eyes; I was that overwhelmed by what was happening to me.

I blurted out, "You're the most wonderful man."

John touched a napkin to Mary's lips ever so gently. "You don't need to say this. We've been through this before. I know where I stand."

I had to mentally clear my head. "What do you think I'm going to say?"

He smiled. "Any conversation that begins with, 'You're a wonderful man,' ends with 'but . . .'"

"No," I said and heard a crack in my voice. "Don't you know?"

He looked at me as if I were a riddle and then waited with that intense look on his face that I'd come to love.

"When I closed the door to us, I was too hasty."

He never blinked. But the sapphire sea in his eyes swam in a different way, as if new waters had rushed into them. He held still in what appeared to be complete serenity, and the look in his eyes said to me, *Don't be afraid, Gwen. Don't be afraid. I am the genuine article, and you can tell me.*

I went on, my voice only a whisper. "Don't you know by now? Don't you see that my feelings have changed?" I gulped pathetically. "Don't you see that I've grown to . . . care about you?"

"Because of Mary?"

"No," I almost whimpered. "Because of you, because of who you are."

A short chuff of a gasp escaped his lips. He set Mary down and without a moment's hesitation, stood up, and gently lifted me to my feet. He opened his broad arms and pulled me into him, where I fit like clay pressed into a palm. The breadth of his feelings were revealed, limb by limb, breath by breath, as if he were serving up all the parts of himself on a platter. All the old rusty gates inside me opened, and a new and previously unknown desire bloomed in my body. Everything around us fell away. Something between us was reborn, a second chance bathed in hope given and the shock of mutual understanding. He lifted my chin with his finger and unfurled his sweetest words so far. "You've just made me the happiest man."

He kissed me once briefly, sweetly, a bit hesitantly, waiting for my response. And then he kissed me again deeply, no holding back, and he pressed me against him from shoulder to toe with his hands traveling every curve of my back and his tongue exploring the inside of my mouth. I held his face in both of my hands and kissed him with all the abandon I'd been holding back. Embarrassed by my halting breaths and tripping pulse, I pulled away so I could gather myself. Then I found the most wonderful nook at the base of his neck and above his clavicle where I could rest my face and breathe in his scent. Mary was there, after all. Sexually inexperienced I was, but not naive, and I knew where this would take us. Where I wanted it to take us when the time was right. John pulled back, too. He held me and stroked my hair.

How could I be this happy? How could this gorgeous and kind gentleman love little ole me? Men had been attracted to me before, but this was the first time I'd allowed someone in. With John, the key fit into the lock that finally opened me up to love. He loved me. I loved him. It felt wonderful to drop the barriers and let everything I'd been secreting inside fly out on bright butterfly wings. Could joy be stolen out of the ruins of a horrible world war? Here it was; it had happened.

Mary was at our feet, pulling at blades of grass, frustrated when she couldn't pull one free and then cackling when she did. She was oblivious to what had just transpired, although it would change everything for all three of us. I felt each of John's breaths rise and fall in his chest as we watched her, together, and for a moment, everything truly was right in the world. But after the man I'd fallen for had kissed me for the first time, God help me, I thought about Alice. She could've had a fine man and a beautiful, healthy child. She could've had the family that so many other women dreamed of having. Did she guess what had gone on here? Did she have any idea that she was now divorced? Did she care?

But I forgot about all that when I looked back at John. He couldn't stop smiling, and he moved as if fresh silky air floated under his feet. He was as happy as I was. I could have stayed in that spot forever and ever, wishing the earth would hold still for us, even just a little longer, but the daylight was beginning to fade. A chill was flowing in from the river, and Mary would soon be cold.

On the way back to the city, Mary fell asleep. She'd had a long day, and John and I, too, fell silent as an almost full moon rose in the east at sunset. We didn't want to wake her, and the silence was somehow . . . perfect. Maybe we didn't know how to put such happiness into mere words. Ahead of us the moon shimmered liquidly in the mystical blue sky. John drew in a breath, and I had to marvel at the chain of seemingly unrelated events that had brought the three of us together on this beautiful evening. Looking back, it felt as if he had miraculously, simply . . . fallen into my arms. He took my hand in his and held it on his thigh. Out of the chaos of war and pain, John and I had found each other.

After being in the country, the city seemed smaller somehow, and yet it loomed as a shimmering black mass dotted with lights that brought to mind stars across a black sea. As John turned onto my street, a blackness fell over my heart, eclipsing all the happiness that had entered my life on that day. I hated the taut atmosphere of my home now because of Dennis. Each night I couldn't wait until it was time for bed, and I could take Mary into our room, watch her fall asleep with the tips of our fingers touching, and then indulge in thoughts and ruminations that hadn't had time to emerge during the day.

John pulled to a stop in front of the building.

"Thank you for a wonderful day," I said to him, and the flatness in my voice surprised me. It came from the thought of entering the apartment.

He said, "Thank *you*."

He started to get out but then stopped and peered my way. "What's wrong?" He could read my moods so well.

For a fleeting second, I considered telling him what was wrong— telling him about the change in Dennis, about the change in Dot, and the charged atmosphere inside the home where Mary still lived, but then I stopped myself. It would break a confidence. And it would worry him. My mind lay barren of explanations.

He took my hand and gave it the sweetest squeeze. "Gwen, I know you've turned into a city gal, and I'm a country boy. If you're worried about that, please don't. I know we can work it out."

It hadn't even occurred to me today that a problem still existed. I only knew that I loved him. "That's not it."

He waited.

"I'm tired; that's all."

I could already feel the tension coming from inside the apartment. How quickly it had extinguished the elation of the day, as if Dennis had reached out from the apartment and pinched dead the flame of a warm candle.

"You look more than tired," John said. Then quietly added, "You can tell me."

It was a strange mix of comfort and also disquiet to realize that another person could see inside me so well. This was one of John's particular gifts; he had the ability to look past any veneer into the depths of me. I couldn't hide from him, and for a moment I relished the feeling. He could see into who I really was and how I truly felt. It was the sort of closeness that my sister Betty and I had once shared, during those days when we had slept back-to-back through long winter nights and whispered our feelings under the pile of woolen blankets and quilts. With John, it was that sort of closeness and so much more.

But I still didn't tell him about Dennis.

The opportunity to confide in John slipped away as Mary awakened and we got out of the car. A stiff breeze tasting of salt water and smoke tore across our faces. John helped me wrap my thick sweater around Mary and then kissed her good-bye and pointed to himself, leaning over closer to her and to me. "Dada," he said. "Dada."

She just looked at him with tired eyes, not in the mood to learn a new word.

"Bye, Daddy," I said for her, and he walked us up the front steps and kissed me good-night until Mary reached up and patted our faces. Jealous little girl, used to my undivided attention. We both laughed.

John, always the gentleman, opened the door for us and said good-bye—a good-bye with a new tang of agony built inside it. The future ahead of us was so sweet now, parting was a new torment. John smiled, and tipped his hat as he backed away.

CHAPTER EIGHTEEN

Inside the apartment, I found Dennis wearing an undershirt and wrinkled slacks playing solitaire on the coffee table, a cigarette hanging from his bottom lip. His robust-looking, tanned skin had faded from so many days indoors, and now it had a yellowish cast that nearly blended into his pale hair. Next to his cards sat the usual tumbler of whiskey on the rocks. He hadn't bothered with a napkin or coaster, and the tumbler left behind a white ring on the wood when he picked it up to take a drink. It irked me; the furniture wasn't even ours. It had come with the apartment, and I'd always been extra careful with it.

He looked up lazily after I walked in carrying Mary, and his eyes were bloodshot. He was drunk. Surprise, surprise.

"Where's Dot?" I asked as I dropped my things in the empty chair across from him.

"Well, hello to you, too."

I bit my lip. "Sorry. We've had a long day." I looked down at Mary—easier to focus there—and I bounced her on my hip. "We had a big day, didn't we?" I said to her.

"Why do you need Dot? She's asleep. She turned in early."

I glanced at my watch. It was only 8:00.

"Oh, I was going to ask her to watch Mary while I take a bath."

He set down the cards he'd been holding. "I can do that."

I fell mute. I could think of nothing to say for a few long moments. Finally, I said, "Thanks, but she'll cry and make you miserable."

He laughed sarcastically. "I flew fighter planes overseas. I think I can handle a baby."

I tried laughing to lighten my response. "I'm sure you can. But she's a shy little rascal. She won't go to strangers."

"Strangers?" His face hardened, and his mouth became a narrow little nasty line. "What's the big deal? Jesus, I live here."

"I meant . . . you're still kind of a stranger to *her*. She's an odd little bird. Timid. It's taking weeks for her to warm up to her own father."

I turned when the door to Dot's bedroom opened behind me. She stepped out wearing a bathrobe. Her hair was up in pin curls that had obviously been slept on, and she looked drowsy and unsteady on her feet. Maybe she had been drinking, too. But I'd never known Dot to sit around and drink at home. We had a cocktail when out on the town, but otherwise we didn't often indulge.

She asked me about our day and then sat on the sofa next to Dennis.

He said, "Gwen wants you to look after the baby while she takes a bath."

"It's not necessary," I said quickly, perhaps too quickly. "I can see you're tired, and I can wait until she goes to sleep."

Dot looked at me as if not comprehending. Pockets of skin hung beneath her eyes as I'd never seen them before. She had lost weight. I wished we had been alone and she had been herself, so I could tell her about the beautiful thing that had happened that day. I wished I could shout for joy about John and me.

She said nothing, but Dennis's anger rode back over his face, and he stared at me.

There was a long, uncomfortable silence, as I gathered my things, preparing to retreat to my bedroom with Mary.

Dennis said, "Do you hear what I'm hearing?" he said to Dot while he kept his eyes on me. "I think Gwen here doesn't want either one of us to touch the baby. I think your friend here doesn't think we're good enough."

Dot managed to roll her eyes, and then she rubbed them and afterward looked more awake. Lately she walked around looking full of shame, her eyes always averted downward, her smile mostly forced and short-lived and rimmed with barely concealed pain. It was almost as if she'd done something wrong. I had tried to get her to talk about it, but most of the time she wouldn't even let me broach the subject of her husband. Instead she seemed determined to prove everything was fine.

I grabbed the lunch pail and thermos, dropped them in the kitchen, and then headed for my room, Mary still curled against me.

Dennis said, "Isn't that right, Gwen? Don't want to admit it? Well . . . you don't have to. It's pretty damn obvious."

I stopped, not wanting to be so rude as to walk out on them, but I had no idea what to do or say.

Dot said, "Good God, Dennis. Leave her alone. She didn't say anything."

"Didn't have to."

She reached for his pack of cigarettes and matches. "I hate it when you do this. You just want to fight. You'll do anything to start a fight."

Mary said, "Night, night," as if telling me to get her out of there. She was the most sensitive and intuitive child I'd ever known.

"I'm not starting anything. I'm telling you what's happening here. First I offered to look after her while you were in the bedroom, but it sounds like I'm not acceptable. Then you come out here, and now you're not acceptable, either."

Dot lit up, drew in on the cigarette, and glanced at me. "We've been drinking."

He said, "So? What are we going to do? Drop her?"

Dot blew out a line of smoke, set the cigarette in the ashtray, and then touched her temples with her index fingers. She looked at her husband again. "You know what, Dennis? If I had a child I wouldn't want you to look after her, either."

"Nice," Dennis said, and that was the last thing I heard before I took Mary into our room and shut the door behind me. I turned on the radio to drown out the rest of their conversation.

Mary's body had gone almost rigid, and I had a hard time getting her to bed. She fought sleep as though it were a form of surrender to a battle she wasn't ready to give up. Every time her eyelids fell and stayed down for a second, she roused herself, rolled over, and batted her eyes to stay awake. She held on to her stuffed bunny that we'd named Carrots and pulled on his eyes and nose.

"Carrots is so sleepy," I said. "Sooo sleepy. If you don't hold still, he can't get his rest. And bunnies need rest."

She looked at me and then sucked her fingers.

I gently pried them out of her mouth and tucked Carrots in beside her even closer. She wrapped both arms around him. I lay down beside her and turned off all but the nightlight. Once the radio was off, the house was silent. Mary finally slept, but I kept focusing on the ceiling, trying to find something that made sense in the bumps on the tiles and the shadows that clung there.

My apartment was now a miserable place. And my best friend was going downhill, dragged by her drunken husband. I was disappointed in my own character as I found that my compassion for Dennis was changing into disgust and downright dislike. He was probably suffering the aftereffects of the war, but I hated what was happening to Dot.

The night wind whistled against the windowpanes, tree branches rattled against each other, and a night crow cried out. The walls came to life with short pops and creaks. It had been the best day of my life, but I'd come back to this. I had moments of joy and fantasy about my life with John and Mary, but my happiness was tainted. Dot's marriage to a troubled man in our apartment haunted me like the most unholy of ghosts.

I'd had no premonition or foreboding about this. I wished I'd never agreed to let Dennis move in here, but then again, I wouldn't have wanted Dot to go through this alone. The future had played a devious little trick on her, and now Dennis's sadness was absorbing our lives like a sponge.

CHAPTER NINETEEN

Despite Dennis, it was a time of happiness. John and I were a couple, sweethearts, seeing each other at every available moment, sometimes alone and often with Mary. Dot proclaimed she'd always known it would happen, and I'd called her a know-it-all.

John and I glided about in a dazzling, dizzy exhilaration. In the evenings we went to the automat and tiny cafés. An unseasonably warm spell allowed us to spend a Sunday in the best spot of all, Central Park. I dressed Mary and donned my sweater, and we took her out in her carriage. The wind gently puffed from time to time, and John pulled me in close to him, effectively saying, *You're mine now*, and my heart swelled. In the wooded area of the park, we let Mary pat trees, their branches gnarled and twisted like old growth in forests over which fairies would choose to fly. Couples wearing Sunday church clothes strolled arm in arm, and children ran ahead of their parents. We settled down on a quilt in Sheep Meadow when Mary was ready for a nap.

We hadn't discussed the future yet. I think both of us were too euphoric simply basking in each other's adoration. When John held me and kissed me, all future concerns and past regrets feathered away. I'd never before lived in the moment, and each one was so precious I hated for time to march forward.

I didn't think it was possible, but each day I loved Mary more, too. When I did let myself imagine the future, the three of us were together, inseparable. And maybe one day John and I would have another child. Now I experienced all the hopefulness of people bathed in love. How blind I had been before, thinking I knew about all the most important things in life when I'd known nothing of love. How it affected me—his presence, the pull of physical attraction, and an unknown desire that before I never could have named. I would never be the same.

It wasn't until Dot had declared us "officially dating" that I finally built up the courage to ask John about his former wife. I had been holding on to questions that needed answering, and the anticipation was an anxious and unwanted burden. We were sitting in a car John had rented, waiting for Mary to wake up from her nap, and as soon as I mentioned Alice's name, a darkness came over his face. I asked if he'd ever learned anything about her whereabouts. It had been almost three months since he went in search of her in San Francisco.

"No," he answered and sat taller and stiffer. He clenched the steering wheel. "Before the divorce was finalized, I spoke to a private investigator. He would've looked for her, but he was an honest guy and told me he would do the same things I'd already done. Redoing them would have cost me a lot of money, with no guarantee of uncovering anything."

We had driven farther into Pennsylvania that day, and, with the assistance of locals and a map, had found two covered bridges, one red and one white. Both bridges crossed stony creeks overhung by leaves so colorful they brought to mind a corridor roofed with Japanese paper lanterns. I was amazed that no other Sunday drivers had made their way here, and so we had the bridges to ourselves, save for one clattering pickup truck that lumbered over the old boards. Inside the pickup truck, a weathered farmer lifted his hand to us. With Mary sleeping in my lap, John pulled me into him, kissed me, and held me. We were meant to be together. Nothing had ever felt so right, though I must confess that at times I was afraid of so much happiness.

"The aunt in Kansas?" I finally pulled back and asked.

"I finally made contact with her. She was upset over the news and knew nothing, had heard nothing. I ended up sorry I'd called her."

"You had to."

"I suppose," he said and sighed. "That was the last thing I did. Now I don't think about it so much anymore."

"You did all you could."

He squinted and looked off. "I'd never say that. I'd never let myself off the hook that easily."

"What do you mean?"

"Well," he said and turned my way. "It's hard not to believe that I somehow did her wrong."

"You didn't."

"That's kind of you . . ." he said, his voice trailing off into nothing, and he gazed off again.

"How could you possibly have done something wrong? You were off fighting in a war." I waited for a moment and then asked, "What would you do if she came back?"

"At this point?" he said. "I'd help her. She's the mother of my child, so I'd do what I could to help her, if she needed help. But I'd never take her back, if that's what you mean. I have you now."

"I think she was suffering from a mental depression. I think she was sick."

He didn't respond to that.

I waited for a moment, not sure if I should pry further, but then I said, "Are you saying that no matter what, forgiveness is out of the question for you?"

"I didn't say that. I've worried endless nights about what has become of her. I want her to be safe and happy. I'm not bitter; I fought that, and

I'm not bitter. I won't let myself go down that path. I've forgiven her already, but she made it clear how she felt about me when she walked away without a word. Obviously I meant nothing to her. And I would never be able to trust her with Mary again, don't you see?"

I allowed myself a long look at him, but kept silent.

"She left her with you, and that turned out to be the best thing she could've done under the circumstances. You are the gift from God in this sad story. But what if you hadn't been there? Where else might Alice have left her?" He shook his head. "It terrifies me to think what might have happened to her. I imagine cold orphanages, starvation, abandonment."

"I don't think—"

"I saw children like that, Gwen. Over there. I saw children who had been left with no one."

I didn't know what to say. I wanted to defend Alice, as I didn't believe she would've left Mary on the street, but John's feelings were understandable, too. And he was saying the words I longed to hear. I was safe. We were safe, together.

Mary awakened. I pulled her stuffed bunny out of my bag. She grabbed it and put her head down into its softness. Still sleepy, my precious girl.

I could feel John's eyes on me as I settled Mary down again. "I want to learn more from you, Gwen. I like your way with her so much more than my sister's way."

"Thank you."

"I don't think I could do what you did," John said, and I could still feel his eyes lingering heavily on me even after Mary fell back asleep. "I don't think I could feel this way about a child who was not my own flesh and blood."

I shook my head.

"You're rare," he said to me. "My rare special lady."

I let myself be whirled away; it was impossible to battle such a mael-strom. "John, we can live wherever you want." Only then did I realize that I'd been coming to this decision for some time now. It had slowly dawned on me that places don't make you happy; people do. And if I chose to, I could work anywhere. John meant more to me than any city.

He broke into an exquisite smile. *Oh, to make a man this happy!* He said, "We'll find a place that we both like."

He ran his fingers along my cheek, my jaw, my neck and then the neckline of my blouse, as if he'd been waiting to touch me his entire life, and I almost liquefied with love. The smell of his lemon hair oil mixed with a sweet and salty male scent I couldn't name. My head thrummed and my body trembled at his touch. His eyes glittered onto me. No one had ever looked at me like this before, with such unmitigated want. He saw me as an equal; we understood each other. When he kissed me, I tumbled into a place that I never knew existed. That night we could've pulled down all the stars from the sky and bathed ourselves in their silvery light.

During those days together, John told me all about his childhood, which had been happier than mine, and I told him about real poverty and the price one pays for it.

I said, "We nearly lost everything during the Depression. We had to get rid of most of our animals and equipment. All the paint peeled off the house, and we couldn't afford to buy more. My father forgave the land, but I did not. I'll never love it like I once did."

"You never know, Gwen. When I was in the POW camp, I dreamed about wide-open spaces. Walking a patch of land that grew things and belonged to me. When it felt so out of reach, I wanted it again. On my worst days, I felt I'd never get out of there, that I'd never feel the love of anyone again, that I'd die in that dark and solemn place."

I murmured, "I understand."

"Even on the way back across the sea, I was haunted by images. The sea opening up and swallowing us whole. It seemed impossible that I would reach home soil."

I listened to all he wanted to tell me, and he listened to me with equal enthrallment. We also shared lighter memories, such as childhood antics, tales about our eccentric family members, and our most embarrassing moments.

"I took a frog to school and hid it in my pocket, so I could scare the girls during recess. Before I ever got to do that, the damn thing peed all over my pants. Everyone found it hilarious, except my teacher, who made me stay after school and practice penmanship."

"I let Betty cut my hair into a bob once, and it ended up crooked, one side longer than the other. I couldn't face the other girls at school with it like that, so I cut it even shorter. It looked even worse. They called me a boy."

He laughed.

We talked about faith, our hopes for humanity and the future, the anguishes that would haunt us, and the dreams that had kept us muddling through. John was shelter and tenderness, strength and generosity.

I made arrangements for Mary to spend a Saturday night with Lisen, and John got us a room at the Algonquin Hotel. Neither of us lived alone; it was the only way to have privacy, and neither of us wanted to wait a moment longer. He took me first to dinner at Le Pavillon on 55th Street, as he'd heard it offered the most authentic French cuisine in the city, and he wanted me to sample a taste of Paris. The mousse of sole, pilaf of mussels, pheasant with truffle sauce, and meringue with custard and caramel were heavier than my taste buds were accustomed to, but the atmosphere was romantic and the vintage champagne soothed my nerves.

Alone . . . really alone for the first time. I had to admit that I didn't know what to do, but I placed a small towel on the bedsheet as I feared there would be blood. And I left the blinds open to the city and all its twinkling lights.

While we stood at the edge of the bed, John asked me, "Are you sure, Gwen?" When he gazed at me, I felt awash in a soft shimmering light, the way actresses glow on the screen.

A wall I'd always kept around me had crumbled, and I was ready to sweep away every last bit of its remaining brick and mortar. I answered, "You've been careful with me, and I thank you for it. But I never have been more sure about anything in my life. I want this."

He moved closer to me and very gently began to unbutton my blouse. His fingers were warm and sure, and I had to catch my breath when his fingertips brushed my skin. Slowly he undressed me, then laid me down on the bed, and twined his body around mine. I was lost, so lost, but here, so here. And then lifted to a place where we soared through the sky as if on Pegasus's mighty white wings.

For that night the world shrank down to the two of us, time stopped for us, and life waited for us. None of the little liaisons of my past—good-night kisses on doorsteps, stolen embraces in the backs of cabs, even my first kiss long ago given by one of my brother's friends behind the barn—had prepared me. Along with so many sensations I'd never felt before, came a sure feeling of goodness and rightness. With John, I finally became a woman.

When it was over, although I was sated and satisfied, I wanted more . . . and more . . . and more. If the best days were the brightest, then this one was more brilliant than a diamond; its memory would always glow incandescent through all the years ahead. I felt intoxicated, although I was not drunk, and stunned that so many of life's most meaningful moments and sensations could be contained in a single night.

Despite her own troubles, Dot was happy for me, for us, and for Mary. But each day she came up with a reason not to go home right away after our shifts ended.

One day, she took me to the Museum of Modern Art. I'd made it to many of New York's famous museums, but not that one yet. Dot couldn't believe I hadn't seen Van Gogh's masterpiece *Starry Night*, which had been acquired back in '41. We didn't have much time, so we rushed through the assault of colorful art and lingered only with the paintings that stopped us short and made us stand still, silently looking. Then we pushed ourselves onward, so we would have more time to look at the museum's most famous painting.

I knew little of art, but I loved the painting right away. I found it bold; I could feel the sweep of Van Gogh's brushstrokes on the canvas and the vastness of the brilliant night sky. I got lost in swirls and shades of blues and lavenders and light.

Dot said, "They say he was inspired by a poem. Or by God. He was looking for religion."

"He painted heaven, didn't he?" I said.

She sighed. "He was a tortured soul, you know. He sold only one painting in his lifetime and never knew his work would become so famous."

I was deep inside the moon by then. A yellow crescent moon haloed by white light. And then each of the stars dancing a dervish. The painting made me feel as I did on those sleepless nights that are gentle, when the thoughts and ideas in your head lay out long and languid on the bed beside you, and it's so peaceful there's no need for sleep and dreams, when the night itself is the dream.

Dot said in a whisper, "He painted this while he was in an asylum. One year before he died."

"It's hard to understand," I wondered. "Isn't it? That he could've been so unhappy, and yet he painted such a promising night."

She cocked her head to one side. "But the cypress adds sadness, don't you think?"

My thoughts shifted to Dennis, and Dot had to have been thinking of her husband at that moment, too. But *Starry Night* gave me hope for Dennis, for wasn't there at least the possibility of an unconquerable spirit inside those thick brushstrokes and vivid swirls of light? I could feel a reverence for quiet beauty in the sleepy, sparkling town below the billowing sky, and wouldn't a vision of such enormity, both dark and bright, be representative of hope?

And yet, Van Gogh had committed suicide.

When we had to leave, Dot had a hard time turning away, as did I.

"Why do you love it?" I asked her.

"Don't you?"

I hadn't expected to be so bowled over, and yet I was. "It's beautiful."

She said, "When I see something like this, it makes me believe in anything. I can believe that all things will fall into place."

I didn't know if Dot knew about Van Gogh's suicide, and I decided not to mention it.

CHAPTER TWENTY

As we walked toward our building, still chatting about the painting, I spotted a young woman lingering outside. Her hair had been dyed to an almost white shade, and it was cut short, Garbo style, but I recognized her right away, and it was as if I'd been cracked by a whip. Alice. The concrete under my feet melted. I found myself plunged into a nightmare. What the hell was Alice doing here? I was so astounded that when I tried to find my voice, nothing came out. In a single moment, everything had changed.

She came toward me cautiously, and then her face opened up. She grasped me in a hug. "Gwen, Gwen," she said. "I'm so happy to see you." Her voice drifted over me exactly as I'd remembered it, like soft tinkling bells.

I had to shake myself to believe it. I had always known Alice could come back, but now? My body felt sharp and cold, but I let her hold on to me. I wanted to scream at her, *Why did you come back?* But her affection took me by surprise.

She stood back and took stock of me. "You look wonderful. This year has been kind to you. Oh my Lord, it's so wonderful to be back in New York!" She was wearing a white crepe dress with pearl-like buttons, and her lightened hair moved like silk about her face. Her cheeks were rouged and her lips a lovely shade of coral red.

Dot was staring at us with a look of stunned bewilderment on her face.

"Dot," I managed to say. "This is Alice, Mary's mother." I spoke on some kind of automatic reflex, as if words were forming themselves *for* me, because I wasn't capable. How was it that I'd experienced such a strong sense of foreboding before John's arrival, and yet I'd had no premonition whatsoever before Alice's? Out of the clear blue sky, as they say, she'd come back to wreak havoc on our lives. I was already sure of that. How had my intuition failed me this time? Maybe my intense happiness had made me blind.

Dot had never been one to conceal her emotions very well. "Mary's mother? Knock it off."

Thank God Dot was there. My legs fluttered, and I was so shaky I was surprised my feet were still holding me up. "No, really," I said to her. I had to look at Alice again, to convince myself this was really transpiring. Opening night, scene one, of a surprise attack.

Alice extended her hand, and Dot eventually took it and steered the three of us upstairs. If she hadn't been there, I might have stood indefinitely, letting my imagination and all the implications of Alice's return paralyze me. I should've been happy that at least she was alive and appeared well.

Inside the apartment, Alice finally asked the question I dreaded: "Where is my daughter?"

A rising fear, hissing and hot. But I said with forced calm, "With the babysitter."

"Shall we go get her then?"

It still hadn't registered that Alice had suddenly appeared, but when I thought of her with Mary, it tore me open from throat to toes. Could this be true? I was shocked by Alice's pure gall as well. After more than a year away, she had just turned up and nonchalantly asked to pick up her daughter, as though she'd gone out for an afternoon matinee. Legally, however, Alice was Mary's mother, much as I hated to think of it that way, and she had come back. There was no way to deny her seeing Mary.

I turned to go, but Dot said, "Hold on for a moment, Gwen. I think the three of us girls should sit down for a little chat."

Thank God Dennis wasn't there and capable Dot was.

Dot made coffee and Alice used the bathroom. I sat in a stupor, numbed by this insane turn of events. I kept blinking and blinking like some deranged person trying to make myself believe it was real. Dot came back with the coffee and sat across from Alice and right next to me. Her hand found mine as she said, "So you left your child with our good-hearted Gwen here. What have you been doing with yourself?"

Alice's face was just as delicately perfect as before, and I could see right away that whatever illness had plagued her had now lifted. Now she glowed. She smiled in a way that involved her entire face and eyes. She sat very properly on the edge of the chair, her legs crossed at the ankles, her body leaned forward like a bird on a perch.

"I went to California, Hollywood to be specific. I sang in a few places, and I landed a couple of photo shoots for advertisements in magazines. Maybe you've seen me?" she asked.

I almost laughed. Dot shook her head. "No, we must have missed it."

Alice chirped out a laugh. "Oh well. It's not like I became famous or anything. Well, maybe a little famous, but only in LA."

"Is that why you're back? Things didn't work out as well as you'd hoped?" Dot asked.

Alice suddenly sobered. "N-No. I wasn't well, and I left my daughter here. I'm not proud of that, but I need to see her. I need to see my baby." She turned her gaze to me. "How is she?"

I said, "She's wonderful. She's no longer a baby. She's a toddler. She's completely changed since you last saw her."

"Healthy and sound, no thanks to you," Dot interjected, and the room became very still. A great gaping silence opened between us.

Alice looked down at her lap, but then lifted her head as if in an act of defiance. "I'm very grateful."

"So where have you been staying? How have you been taking care of yourself?" Dot asked.

"I stayed with some friends in LA. I did some waitressing, too, but only in nice places."

Dot said, "And none of these friends had a telephone or stationery you could use from time to time?"

"I had to get myself together," Alice said. Then she blinked hard. "Who are you, anyway?" she said to Dot.

Dot stiffened even more, if that was possible, and her voice lowered and intensified. "I'm the new roommate. I'm another person who has seen your daughter a lot more than you have."

Another silence descended, and the gaping space in the room widened even more.

Then Alice shrugged, as if to say no words could hurt her. But her eyes betrayed how much Dot's words had stung. How long had it taken her to build up the nerve to show up? "Well, that's why I'm here. Now. To remedy that situation."

Dot sat like a rod of steel beside me. "So you come and go as you please. That's not like any other mother I've ever known."

Alice's face finally fell, but it was almost impossible to summon any sympathy for her. The mood in the room grew even more strained.

I said to Alice, "Mary's upstairs with Lisen. You remember the lady who used to look after her for you? She's been my saving grace all this time, babysitting while I work."

"Oh, I'm so happy to hear that. I always liked Lisen," Alice said, clasping her hands in anticipation. I was amazed at how easily she was able to move past Dot's incriminations, or at least fake it. I was astounded to remember that I'd once thought her too fragile for this world. I saw little of that fragility now. Maybe she'd found what she needed in Hollywood. But if so, why had she come back now? And why hadn't I agreed to marry John when he'd asked me on that day that now seemed so long ago? We could be husband and wife right now.

"Yes, Lisen has been wonderful," I said, and then before I rose, a thought blinked in my brain. John. Alice had no idea he was here. Was I destined to always be giving important news to one of Mary's parents? Was this my new role in life, that of an unhinged messenger? Tempted as I was to keep it a secret, no good could come of hiding this news from her. "By the way, John's in town. He's been back for three months."

She paled. "John?" she said and collapsed back into the chair. Her next words came out as a gasp. "John is alive?"

"Yes."

She shook her head and gazed around as if she suddenly saw herself in a place she had never expected to be. I could see the realization filling her cells. Then she looked back at me, and there were genuine tears in her eyes. "He's alive? He's OK? Not wounded?"

"No, he's perfectly fine," I said.

And I love him, which I didn't say. *He loves me. We're together now.*

Alice touched her face in the feminine gesture I always remembered. "I-I had no idea. I was convinced he was dead. He hadn't written to me during the last part of the war."

"I remember that, too, Alice, but he couldn't write. He was in a POW camp. But he came here as soon as he could. On V-J Day. That's the first time I saw him."

"Where is he now?"

"He's sharing an apartment nearby."

Her face brightened like a flower opening.

"Can you take me there?" Alice said, suddenly shifting to the very edge of the chair and grabbing her handbag from the floor. "I have to see him. My husband. He's alive."

It wasn't my place to tell her that he'd divorced her. Divorced her quickly on special grounds because of the horrific thing she'd done, abandoning both her husband *and* her child. And I hoped Dot wouldn't say it, either. This was something John needed to disclose himself.

Instead Dot said, "What about your daughter? I thought you came to see *her*."

When I came down the stairs with the baby, Mary exhibited the same fear of her mother as she did with anyone else she didn't know. Alice simply watched her play for a little bit, but I could tell her mind had floated away on an entirely different air current. Mary's distance didn't seem to devastate Alice, perhaps because she was already envisioning her romantic reunion with John. Before I prepared Mary's dinner, I wrote John's address on a piece of paper for Alice. I found it harder and harder to ignore the bleak sense of darkness that had entered my life at Alice's return, as though a curtain had been drawn against the sun.

Alice came to Mary after I'd settled her in her high chair, and she gave her daughter a quick kiss on the top of the head. Mary cringed, and Alice laughed. "Oh my goodness," she said.

And then she left. She ran out, as if on a mission.

Dot stood with her arms crossed over her chest and studied me as I went about doing all the things I did every night, carefully, quietly. If I didn't keep myself occupied, I'd fall to pieces, and I didn't want to do that in front of Mary.

"I'll be a monkey's goddamn uncle," Dot said through a long sigh. "What now?"

Though I was filled with foreboding, I said, "I've talked about this with John. I mentioned this possibility before, and he said it wouldn't make any difference. He said he would never take Alice back." I spoke with confidence, but I was experiencing the strangest feeling, like a long slide down a slick slope.

Dot shook her head as if saying to herself, *Unbelievable.* "That woman has a whole hell of a lot of nerve."

CHAPTER TWENTY-ONE

When Dennis came home, he appeared to be sober, and, surprisingly, he wanted to take Dot to a movie. He even dressed in clean clothes and combed back his hair, which had grown too long. Dot put up her hair and wore a dress and heels.

After they left, my imagination began to flood with wild thoughts. What would Alice say to John? What would he say to her? How would he react to her? And what of John and me?

I found myself leaving the water running in the sink and the refrigerator door open. I could barely concentrate on Mary's needs. Mary cocked her head and looked at me as if to ask what was going on. "It's all right, little one," I said, reassuring myself. But my hands were trembling. I wasn't fit company for anyone.

I had hoped Dennis and Dot would stay out late, have a good time, enjoy each other, but they returned after the movie and Dennis made himself a drink. Dot watched him as he downed one cocktail and then another. I monitored my breathing as hope for them slipped away yet again.

Upon finishing his second cocktail, Dennis bumped a fresh cigarette out of his pack of Pall Malls. Without looking at her, he said to
Dot, "You remind me of a bird of prey, eyeing its next meal."

I couldn't listen to another argument, and Mary's eyes were solid
blue pools, open wide. If I had stayed in the room, I might have yelled
at Dennis to shut up and leave Dot alone. So I took Mary and we went
to bed.

I rolled over in bed and found that it was finally morning. The first
cold front of the season had moved in and drenched the city with sleet
and rain, which had left the sidewalks littered with leaves and broken
branches.

All night long I'd been imagining John's reaction to Alice and what
they would say to each other. I reminded myself over and over of the
reassurances he'd given to me, and yet nothing calmed me. I'd fought
with the sheets throughout the loud, stormy night. I kept telling myself
that nothing would change, but there was a difference in the way my
heart beat and the way I held my breath that morning, as if my body
was preparing itself for the unthinkable.

Dennis and Dot were awake before I was—I could hear their voices
in the kitchen. The sun was up, but the sense of darkness was still there,
and the day felt like a volcano ready to erupt. I hadn't heard anything
yet from John, and the sounds of pots and pans in the kitchen further
frayed my nerves. Dot was probably cooking Dennis breakfast, trying
to get some food down him instead of just liquor.

Mary stirred, and so I got up, changed her, and took her into the
kitchen to feed her. Dot was in there by herself now washing and drying
the dishes. I looked at her, and she looked back. No words were needed.
Then we heard sounds from the bedroom. Dot tossed down the kitchen

towel she'd been drying with and said to me, "Come along, please. He's scaring me this morning."

I did as she asked. Mary was safe in her high chair, and I figured Dot must be scared for a reason. So I followed her when she marched into their bedroom, where Dennis was throwing clothes into a suitcase.

"What are you doing?" she gasped at him.

He laughed and leaned back on his heels, throwing a disgusted look her way. "What does it look like I'm doing?"

She held still and kept her voice calm. "It looks like you're packing to leave."

I reached for Dot's hand.

He tossed in pairs of socks and underwear on top of slacks and shirts. "This house has ghosts."

"What?"

"There's something wrong in this place. That woman leaving her baby here and disappearing and now coming back." Apparently Dot had told him about Alice. "I bet this place has a history of things like that. I bet it wasn't the first time."

"That's just superstition. Houses don't make things happen to people. People make things happen to people."

Dennis stopped and turned to look at his wife, ignoring me completely. "People make things happen?"

She nodded.

He said, "You have no idea how little say we have in any of it."

"I don't believe we have *no* say."

He stopped for a moment. "Yeah, you're right. Some things we can change, and that's what I'm doing now."

"What *are* you doing?"

"I'm going home."

"Home?"

He tossed another pair of socks into his bag and looked at her as if she were an idiot. "That's what I said."

"Where do you mean?"

He smiled sarcastically. "I have only one home that I know of."

Dot looked stupefied. "You mean South Carolina?"

When he didn't respond, Dot said, "That's where you want to go? Back to your parents' farm?"

No answer.

Dot dropped my hand, changed her tone, moved a step closer to him, and said, "But we can go anywhere, honey. If you don't like it here, we can leave. I can work anywhere; I'm a nurse. We don't have to go back to our pasts. We can start fresh."

He threw the last items into the case and then crunched it closed. After he snapped the latches, he turned to her again and said, "You can go anywhere you want to, Dot. But I'm going home."

She seemed to rock on her heels. She eked out, "Are you leaving me?"

"I'm leaving this *place*. It's up to you if you want to come."

"To the farm?"

"Yes!"

Dot said, "Then I'm going with you."

CHAPTER TWENTY-TWO

All day I waited to hear from John. Dot and Dennis argued off and on for hours, and finally after dinner, I couldn't stand my own anxiety or their anguish a moment longer. I put Mary in her coat, wrapped mine around me, and then, with Mary in my arms, we headed for the door.

"Where are *you* going?" Dennis said to my back.

"For a walk," I answered.

Out in the hallway, I slowed my breathing. As Mary rubbed her eyes and curled up on my chest, I realized it was too late and probably too cold to take her out. So I climbed the stairs to Lisen's and asked her to watch Mary for a while.

And then I was outside in air cold as steel. My breath was a starry fog. I walked in long strides, skirting street signs and mailboxes and people, breathing deeply. On and on, strangled by thoughts that seemed to have nothing to do with what was happening to Dot or me. The first cold air of the season had never been so brutal. The sound of my heels on the pavement was hard and clacking. Everywhere happy couples strolled with their arms looped through each other's, hands in their pockets, bodies angled in close to each other. Even the buildings appeared to slant in over the street. Pedestrians walked, laughed, and tapped their shoes across the pavement, but I heard nothing but the thunder of turmoil inside.

I found that I had walked around the same block twice, and then changed my route, even though it had already dawned on me that I had no destination. Walking, moving, doing *something*, was the point. I longed to find a place of reassurance, but it was not to be found anywhere. Why hadn't I heard from John? Where was he? And why hadn't he called me?

I knew where he lived! I started walking in that direction, not sure if I would have the nerve to go to his door and knock, but heading there all the same. Maybe I would simply stand outside and wait for a sign. Pathetic, but I couldn't help myself. Even drawing closer to his apartment building made me feel a little more at ease. Along the way, businesses emitted a warm yellow glow from their windows, and happy faces were bright at window-side tables. Someone was burning paper up above, and charred remnants began to fall, floating downward like the feathers of flaming birds. They fell on the pavement and gathered in clumps I stepped over. Maybe John would be at home, see me on the street, and come out for a talk.

As I walked past another restaurant, his face materialized in front of me.

John.

He was sitting at one of those window-side tables, and I nearly tripped as the sight of him broke my rhythm. At first I saw only him, and I started to wave to get his attention. But my hand froze in the air. He was engaged in a conversation, his body leaning forward, his focus on someone across from him. My eyes darted to the shape that sat opposite—Alice in profile—her upturned nose, rosy cheeks, and hair combed back and held in place with sparkly barrettes. Her dress was pale pink.

The moment froze like a photograph. Frost on the edges of the windowpanes, music drifting from a nearby club, John looking at Alice,

Alice looking at John, and me, looking at both of them. Everything held still, even sounds. The shutter in my mind's eye clicked, capturing the moment for posterity.

In the next moment, I became aware of myself. I was like an actress who had stumbled on the wrong stage and found herself in a play she knew nothing about. I wasn't a part of this picture. John was out with Alice. At a restaurant. As if they were celebrating something.

I turned away and walked on, surprised that my legs hadn't given out. I walked along with wealthy women wearing mink and well-aligned, seamed stockings and carrying bags from Bonwit Teller. Teenagers ran down the sidewalks, their laughter trailing behind them like music. The wind picked up, and women held on to their hats. Their men pulled them close and guided them into restaurants and bars.

I was convinced that John would never do me wrong, and yet the worry that had been circling inside my head landed like a falcon with its talons open. What were John and Alice doing, dressed up, sitting in a restaurant, talking intimately, as if they were together? I tried to shake the images out of my brain, but they would not budge. The sparkle of the rhinestones in Alice's barrettes. The pale pink of her dress. The way he had been looking at her.

I tried to shake off an engulfing panic. I told myself that John had every right to sit down and talk with his ex-wife. They had a child together, after all. He was a good man, and he'd never be unkind to her. Maybe they'd simply gone out to eat to discuss what their future held. Indeed, what was going to happen to all of us now? But the fear that had clamped down on me wouldn't let go. Nothing eased it, and so I was compelled to walk and walk, as if that would scare away the frightening and unknown thing that burned beneath my skin. Onward with no direction. I walked briskly but out of sync with everything around. I nearly stumbled a couple of times, and a few passersby looked at me as if I were drunk. Instead of booze, I was intoxicated by fear.

Sometimes you know something, even when you don't want to know it.

My fingers began to burn and sting. I had rushed out of the apartment without gloves or a hat. Now my ears were numb and my teeth were chattering. My hands looked like frozen beef, and the cold tightened my lungs into fists. And it wasn't doing me one bit of good. I was going nowhere—nowhere!—in a city that played and worked and made merry around me. How could people be happy at a moment like this? All around me they were laughing and smiling.

The streets began to empty; the air was crisp, the stars so clear. And I had never been so alone.

Eventually, I headed home, retrieved Mary from Lisen, and collapsed into bed with Mary sound asleep beside me.

But how could I sleep? The image of them together, those few moments I had witnessed, played on the front screen of my mind in living color and went round and round in a loop.

CHAPTER TWENTY-THREE

Another two days dragged by, and I heard nothing from John. I could barely make myself go through the motions of living. My heart seemed to be fluttering instead of beating, and I was stunned, stunned, stunned that John hadn't called or come by. Panic rushed through my veins, and in my mind's eye, all sorts of imaginary scenarios played out, over and over.

During the first day after seeing him with Alice, I'd imagined all kinds of wonderful scenes inside my head. John coming to me and explaining that he had sent Alice packing, that she had left wordlessly, that he, Mary, and I would sail forward into a life together. John and I would marry and have twins. But the day after that, hysterical doubts began to set in. He had left with her; they had left together without a word to me, and would show up in the middle of the night to claim Mary. It had been three days; that was a fact. I had no idea what John was really doing; I was out of the picture, and utter torment filled my every waking hour. At night I barely slept, my fear a bedmate that tossed and turned and startled me awake each time I began to drift off. *John.* What had he done?

I was in no state for celebrating, but Dot and Dennis had planned a going-away celebration out on the town for the Saturday night before they were to leave. Dot convinced me I had to go, that I needed to stop pacing the floor and fretting.

"Stop torturing yourself. It will be good for you to get some air," she said.

She was right; I wasn't doing any good by simply . . . languishing.

I left Mary with Lisen, who had already decided against going out with us into the thrall of a Saturday night. Dot, Dennis, and I bundled up against the cold wind and joined the masses of people trying to get to the city's hot spots.

We ran into John in front of our building, and for a moment I couldn't move. Despite the shock of his beauty and manner and the way it pierced my heart, I knew. The bleak future I'd been imagining flashed in front of my face. I didn't want to hear this, and yet, I had to hear it. What choice was there?

"Gwen . . . ?" he said.

"Yes, we need to talk." My voice sounded so weak it shocked me.

John and I climbed the stairs to the apartment while Dot and Dennis waited for me down on the sidewalk. It was obvious by the way John carried himself that he'd come to say something important. He was dressed soberly, and his posture said he wasn't very proud of himself at that moment.

I couldn't sit. And so we stood together just inside the door of the apartment. I was having a hard time meeting his eyes, because I didn't want to see an apology there, or a good-bye. When I finally summoned the courage to look at him, I knew for sure what he'd come to say. His usually clear eyes were shrouded with a smoky shame, pain, and guilt. Anguish, more like it.

"Gwen," he started and looked about as if gathering strength. "Nothing has changed about the way I feel about you, about us."

I whispered, "I haven't heard from you in days."

"I know. I've been—"

"Why haven't you called me?"

He didn't answer, but it was in his eyes. Sick with the pain of it, full of regret. Was it regret for hurting me, or for all of it, for all that we had become to each other?

"You've been what? Reuniting with your wife?"

"Ex-wife."

"I saw you out with her."

He looked surprised, perhaps not so much by what I'd said as by my tone. He stuffed his hands into his jacket pockets and shifted from one foot to the other. "She's the mother of my child."

The most ferocious animal entered me then. "Well, maybe in the biological way. But *I'm* her real mother. I've taken care of her for most of her life, while Alice just waltzed off."

"I know that." He looked shaken, dazed. "Gwen, she was furious when I told her I'd gotten a divorce. She wants to resume our marriage, and if not . . ."

"If not, what . . . ?"

"Well," he murmured, shifted, and then looked at me again with a pleading in his eyes. "She says she'll fight me for custody of Mary."

I had to let that sink in. I had thought I'd gone over every possible scenario in my mind, but I hadn't imagined that one. "I don't believe it. She wasn't even that interested in her daughter when she was here. As soon as she found out you were alive, that's all she wanted: to get you back. She barely addressed her own child after more than a year away."

"I know that. Don't you know I know that? Don't you see why I'm so desperate that she never take Mary away from me?"

"But you were given custody, based on abandonment. And you told me something like this would never happen. I asked you."

"Yes, but I've already spoken to a lawyer. It was a difficult time, and you yourself said she was sick and believed me dead. It was wartime.

She fell apart. She can claim a nervous breakdown. I got a quick divorce without her consent."

"Because she wasn't here!"

"Yes, of course. But the lawyer said these things can be challenged and overturned when circumstances change. She could probably get another hearing, and she might get Mary back."

"I don't believe that!"

"That's what he said. It's almost unheard of for a father to get custody. You know that. The woman practically has to be in prison or something."

"She should be in prison!" I couldn't believe the venom spewing out of my mouth, and then the tears began to flow.

He tried to hold me, but I pushed him away. "So you're with her now?"

He held me by the shoulders as if trying to keep my body centered on solid ground. If not, I would've floated away.

He said, "I'm trying to give it a shot for Mary's sake. I know this is the last thing you want to hear, and it's the last thing I want to do. But I owe you this honesty. I can't lose Mary to her. I'll do anything I have to do to keep Mary safe."

I swiped at the tears streaming down my face. How had I let this happen to me?

"So, are you going to marry her again?"

"I don't know yet. She has a lot to prove to me."

"My God, you're a generous man."

"Not really. It's all about Mary."

I pulled back enough to look at his face clearly, to gauge his reaction. "Do you mean to tell me you have no feelings left for Alice? That you'd doom yourself to a lifetime of unhappiness?"

All I saw was a sad determination to do what he'd come here to do. To break my heart. Without malice, but still it was what he'd come here to do. That tic throbbed beside his eye as he said, "For Mary, maybe yes."

"You didn't answer my question. Do you still have feelings for Alice?"

He looked torn to shreds. "Some sentimentality maybe. Old times, you know? That innocence before I experienced war the way I did. But it's all about my daughter right now."

We stood for a while in silence, and finally I gathered myself and pushed away from him. I swiped at my face again. "Well, I suppose congratulations are in order. You have your little family back together. And you had the best babysitter in the world for your daughter while you *both* were away."

His eyes filled with tears at my cruelty. "I know that. And now I repay you with this."

"How could you?" I said it and couldn't believe those clichéd words had come from my mouth. And still, I said them again. "How could you?"

"I'm so sorry."

I held my head high and said through my pain and shock, "So when will my babysitting services no longer be needed?"

"We still don't have our own place . . ."

Rage reared its ugly head. "How convenient that I have a home for Mary."

"As soon as I find a place that will allow the three of us—"

I cut him off, "Let me know when you do."

"Is Mary upstairs with Lisen? May I spend a little time—"

"You're asking for my permission? My God, John, go and do whatever you want."

With that I flew past him. I ran down the stairs and joined Dot and Dennis on the sidewalk and started walking in long strides. They walked behind me, working hard to keep up, while I clutched the lapels of my coat across my throat and didn't care who on the street saw the sad gal I was, by herself, on such a lively evening. Crushed, as if some powerful thing had stomped the life out of me. People used the word "crush" to describe childish infatuations, but this was a real crush, a blow to my soul.

Finally Dot and Dennis caught up to me, and she walked at my side while Dennis led the way. I managed to eke out what John had said to me, and she was able to express all the righteous indignation that I, in my current state, couldn't. I'd lost the first man I'd ever loved. And to Alice, "that harlot," as Dot called her. As if that wasn't enough, I would also lose the little girl I loved just as much.

I drifted along in a fog of disbelief. Although the days without hearing from John had been a message loud enough that I should've heard it. I should have known, but hope had sustained me. Now I was unmoored and set adrift in a sea of misery.

Dot had earlier said I didn't know what going out on the town really was until I had done it with Dennis, and so I went wherever they took me. I'd drown my sorrow in a party, if that's what it took. Following was about the only thing I could do in my present state— follow along like some kind of suffering, blinded fool.

Thousands of sailors and soldiers on leave swarmed the city like a flock of hungry gulls, eager for food, entertainment, and drink. We joined the fray by first ordering Viktor Yesensky's savory oyster stew at the Grand Central Oyster Bar and then made our way to Swing Street, where Art Tatum was playing virtuoso swing at the 3 Deuces, and Dennis managed to finagle us a table. Inside women wore fur coats and seamed stockings, and some sported the new hooded look in hats. Dot whispered to me that the look made its wearer appear like a nun.

For a moment, we laughed like old times, while under the table I clenched my hands, open then shut.

I wanted to hate John for what he'd done to me, to us. I wanted to condemn him in the same way I'd recently come to condemn Alice. Hate them both—that would've been easier. They had used me. Now the three of them would be happily reunited while I would be left alone. Only John would not be happy. And he hadn't left his daughter voluntarily. It hadn't been his choice to go overseas, fight in the war, and get captured.

So what had I expected of John? Bravery that even I couldn't fathom? Once Alice had threatened to take Mary, it had been all over for him. He'd lost his daughter once and wouldn't let it happen again. In his shoes, I might have made the same decision. Parents make sacrifices. I tried telling myself that, but it did nothing to lessen the hemorrhage inside.

Friends of Dennis's joined us at the table. Sam and Tucker sat on either side of me. Perhaps they'd sensed that something awful had just happened to me, and they pressed next to me like two shields. The room was all cocktail glasses and champagne flutes with lipstick prints on the rims, jackets draped over chair backs, flowers beginning to droop on the tables, faces of people talking and laughing, music loud in the background, dancers working their way to and from the dance floor, the smell of cigarette smoke and too many men wearing Old Spice cologne. We drank rum and Cokes, a favorite of sailors, Dennis giving up his whiskey for the night.

I had no idea if my torment was noticeable or not and didn't want it to be, so I made myself focus on what others were saying and look directly into their eyes. But in many ways, I was not even there. Why didn't someone come to break this horrible spell? Why hadn't John come to tell me all was well?

Finally the effects of alcohol worked their magic on me, and a warmth entered my bones, along with a sense of fluidity and ease. I tried to imagine myself lighter, freer. I could finally listen to the conversations around me, anything to distract me from the turmoil and fever inside.

"Let them cut us down now?" said Dennis, leaning forward across the table, so that the rest of us could hear him. Dot was hemmed in closely at his side, and her face was filled with adoration as she gazed up at her husband. Dressed nicely and cleaned up, he was that handsome man Dot had married. His eyes flashed brightly as he spoke. "Those politicians know nothing of war. Merge the navy and the army together? Never!"

Tucker said, "It's worse than that. Some would have the army cut down to scraps, too," he said. "They think air warfare means there's no need for any of us anymore, that the A-bomb makes an army and a navy unnecessary."

"But let's not bore the ladies with this topic," said Dennis. "There will be plenty of discourse on this subject in the days to come."

Sam lifted his glass and said, "Hear, hear."

That night I could clearly see what had attracted Dot to Dennis in the first place. Out here among the revelers and overdrinkers, he didn't indulge any more than the rest of us did. He repeatedly took Dot's hand and held it to his chest as he talked and laughed and often looked over at her admiringly. He told us stories about the sirens of the sea, those bird-women of Greek mythology who lured sailing ships onto the rocks and to their doom. Here was a person more comfortable and alive in a crowd than in his home.

I ordered a Manhattan, in honor of this borough I loved, and before I knew it, the first one was gone and I had ordered another. When I took several gulps of my second Manhattan, Dennis said to me, "Whoa. Slow down there, little lady. The night is young."

I said, "It's a baby." I took another swig.

We listened to the jazzed-up music of Duke Ellington and the Dorsey Brothers. Tucker and Sam danced with other girls after I said I didn't want to, and, thankfully, Dot and Dennis didn't leave me alone at the table. I was the odd one out, and when he came back, Tucker finally convinced me to take a turn, obviously feeling sorry for me that I had no date. As I walked with him to the dance floor, I swayed and the floor beneath my feet turned liquid.

On the dance floor, I stood still for a moment, facing him, not knowing how I was going to handle the touch of another man. I remembered back when the only times John and I had touched had been accidental brushes against each other or during the gentlemanly things a man did for a woman—guiding her in and out of doors, giving a hand up out of a taxi, that sort of thing. When I first met John, I was still innocent. I let myself go into Tucker's arms, imagining them to be John's, and I breathed in, wishing Tucker's scent was the same lemony one that John used in his hair.

Tucker's right arm went all the way around my back, and his hand landed in the soft spot between my ribs and waist. With his left hand, he took my hand in his and curled his fingers around it. We were barely moving, and it was like a hug within a dance. Perhaps, a hug of consolation. Maybe when I'd gone to the powder room Dennis or Dot had relayed to him my tale of woe.

Tucker asked me where I came from, what it was like, and I answered him as best I could. He told me he'd gone to a small high school, too. "Did you date much?" he asked me, close to my ear, while we swayed and he gave my hand a gentle squeeze.

The alcohol was making my head spin, and my lips numbed as I spoke. "Not much in high school. Late bloomer, you know. The only boy who ever interested me traveled with his father in the circus that came through town."

He moved his head. "Yeah?"

"I wanted to run away with them. They were dirt poor, like all of us, and it was a ragtag affair they were hooked up with, but they seemed so reckless and free."

He said in my ear, "You could be a circus performer now instead of a nurse."

"I fancied myself a trapeze artist. My last name is Mullen, and my sister and I decided we would be called the Flying Mullenzas."

He asked, "What did your parents say?"

"About the circus boy?" I shook my head and smiled. "They never knew."

He laughed and then held me tighter.

"To my parents circus people were no better than beggars and thieves. You know, they moved around, they flew in the air, they had fun . . ."

He held me close, and we continued to dance.

He said, "My dating life was almost nonexistent, too. My first girl-friend was my best friend's sister. She was a year older. Our parents arranged for me to take her to her end-of-year dance. No one her age had asked her. Next, I dated the town tramp."

He made me laugh, for which I was grateful. But laughter was so close to crying that I had to blink away the burn of tears that threatened to flush from my eyes. Then I was fighting off dizziness brought on by the rather enjoyable but previously untested mix of different alcoholic concoctions now swimming in my blood. But it was working its magic; I hadn't suffered any brutal visions of what John and Alice might be doing together tonight in, what . . . ? A few minutes. This drunk thing was effective.

We stayed on the dance floor, and the next song was up-tempo, suitable for a jitterbug or swing. Tucker started leading me, and I did feel as though I were *swing*ing, floating around. I let myself fly freely on the dance floor, the way John had taught me. I was weightless and carefree, and the room rotated around me while Tucker twirled me. The floor was like ice, and I found myself sliding across it as if I were a figure skater.

This was just the release I needed, and Tucker was a good dancer, getting wilder and gyrating faster with the next song. He surprised me by the way he could shimmy as if his spine and joints had been greased with butter. He threw me around his back, and when I landed on feet that seemed to have disappeared, a wave of nausea sloshed over me. I grabbed at my throat, but he paid no attention and kept wiggling and tossing me about. He rolled me in and then flung me out along his arm, and then—*snap*, my hand broke free. My feet lost purchase, and my body was falling backward, staggering away from him as his blurry face got smaller and smaller. Something hit me in the hip. Or no, I hit something, and then in slow motion—the table tipped and everything on it slid—glasses, champagne flutes, little plates, silverware, even a pair of gloves, a clutch, and a man's hat—all the way to the floor in an explosion of billowing tablecloth, fractured glass, and soggy napkins. My knee joints melted, and the next thing I knew, my butt hit the floor.

The band stopped playing. Laughter was spurting out of my mouth, but when I looked up, I saw that no one else found it funny, least of all the patrons of the club who had been sitting at the table into which I had so unceremoniously careened. Through my stupor and fog, I started to realize what I had done. Tucker was apologizing to the people, who now stood around the mess trying to salvage their belongings, and the waiters were trying to clean up the broken glass before someone got hurt.

It was not one of my finer moments.

Someone said to Tucker, "Your gal needs to learn how to hold her liquor."

I stopped laughing. Poor Tucker. While he tried to smooth things over with the manager and the patrons, Dot came to my rescue. Behind her, I saw the murky figure of Dennis, laughing.

I had hit the lowest rung on the ladder. I had finally allowed what had happened to work its awfulness all the way through me. I had to admit to myself that it was really, truly over. John had made his choice, and it wasn't me.

CHAPTER TWENTY-FOUR

John called the next day to let me know that he and Alice wanted to see Mary as often as possible. He'd made arrangements to pick her up from Lisen's when he was free during the hours I was at work. It was obvious they didn't want to face me, and that was probably better for me, too.

To make matters worse, I was also about to lose Dot.

I certainly wasn't going to miss Dennis, but I would be set even more adrift without my best friend. I suppose I was holding myself together until Dot left, for her sake. Over our egg-salad sandwiches the day before her departure, Dot sighed dramatically and said, "Soon I begin my life as a farmer's wife."

I tried to smile, although I was already missing her. "You'll always be a nurse."

"Yes," she said. "I won't give it up, and besides, we'll need one of us to bring in an income."

"Where could you work?"

"Charleston isn't that far away from the family farm. I'll apply at the hospitals. I don't relish the thought of being without my own money."

"What will Dennis do?"

She paused. "Heal, I hope. He says he'll help out, but this time of year, there isn't a great deal to do on the farm. So I suppose he and his family will teach me what it's like to live the rural life."

"Don't let them take away your nylons and lipstick."

"Oh, not to worry," she said. "I'll be the life of the barn dances."

I almost laughed.

"Or maybe I'll start drinking seriously, and then Dennis and I should get along just fine."

I must have looked aghast, because she continued, "Please wipe that horrified look off your face. Dennis has been much better since we made the decision to leave. He needs his hometown friends and family around him now. Just planning this move has lifted his spirits."

"What about you?" I asked.

"I suppose I'll adjust. In between shifts at the hospital, I'll learn how to churn butter and milk cows and conduct myself in a ladylike fashion."

I could see that Dot wanted to end this conversation on a pleasant note. She was making light of it all—the move, Dennis's drinking, financial worries—but she still hadn't regained her glow from the days before she married.

I said, "And who will be in charge of your reformation?"

"Dennis's mother, I presume. Her name is Myrtle. Did I tell you that?"

"No," I smiled. "Mother Myrtle. Charming. I wish I could be a fly on the wall and watch every step of your conversion."

She looked down. "I hate to leave you now . . . it couldn't have happened at a worse time. I still can't believe that harlot came back, just when everything was going so well for you. I could kill that woman."

I smiled in the most defeated way. Lisen had told me that John, Mary, and Alice had been together a couple of times already, and when I picked her up from Lisen's, Mary had a new dress once and a new toy the next time. Probably Alice trying to buy her daughter's love.

"What will you do?" Dot asked, her eyes full of worry.

"I need to heal as well, I guess."

"I wish I could be here for you. I wish I could do something to that floozy and her Hollywood and her advertisements, too."

"But it's your place to go with your husband."

"While you stay here and continue to care for a child whose parents don't deserve her. Or you."

I suppressed a sob rising in my throat as I met her eyes. "I can't hate him, Dot."

She looked at me with the saddest expression. "I understand. That's why I'm doing it for you."

Dot and Dennis left early in the morning, when freezing rain beat the windows and the river slapped at the city's docks. The wind came from the north, pushing in clouds as dark as soot. Winter had arrived in full force, and New Yorkers armored themselves in winter wools, gloves, and boots. The smell of wood smoke now mixed with factory fumes, cigars, and cigarettes. In the morning a dense fog permeated the air down near the pavement. All the leaves had fallen and skittered across the sidewalks like empty shells; the trees on our street stood like skeletons in the mist.

While Dennis warmed the car downstairs, I had a few minutes alone with the person I considered my closest friend. She stood before me in her coat and clever hat cocked to one side and said, "I'll see you soon. I can't stay away from my city for long."

"Will you have a phone? Can we talk from time to time?" I asked. I dreaded the long-distance phone bill, but I didn't care.

"Dennis has promised they'll put one in, but they haven't had one till now. Can you imagine?"

"Then promise to write."

"Of course."

Dot whispered, "Kiss Mary for me every day." Mary was still sleeping, and Dot had said her good-byes the night before. She pulled back. "Until the evil woman and her cowardly husband come for her."

At the mere mention of him, a warmth came over me, but it soon changed to a burn. How easily John had moved on with his life.

It was time for Dot to leave. I hoped my worry about her and Dennis would go away once they were settled. I hoped I would receive cheerful letters in Dot's handwriting, which looked like coils of charms on the page, telling of her good life in the countryside. Dot had convinced herself it would work. But a rising sense of panic crawled over my skin like a rash. Dot seemed foreign to me, already.

She had wanted to keep this parting as light as possible, but I held her at arm's length by her shoulders and looked at her dead on. "Listen to me. If you ever need help of any kind . . ."

She nodded. "I know. You don't have to say it."

I continued, "If you ever need anything . . . if things don't go well . . . this is important . . . you know where to find me."

"Right back at you," she said. "If you ever need me . . . why, you could come for the first hootenanny."

"I'll hoot and holler with the best of them."

She teared up, hugged me quickly, and then flew out of the door.

If I could give Mary one gift in her life, it would be a friend like Dot. But friends couldn't be gifted; you had to stumble upon them yourself.

That evening, as Mary slept, I ran across John's Chesterfield coat. The sight of it brought burning tears in my eyes. I had never returned it to him. I had thought about it from time to time, but I'd never taken it from the closet that had once been Alice's, then Dot's. Maybe subconsciously I had wanted to hold on to it.

Shakily, I pulled the coat out and lifted it from the hanger. It was as heavy as a life in my hands. I brought it to my face, and I breathed in its scent, searching for something of him. There was only the faintest touch of that lemony stuff he combed into his hair, but it was there all the same. I buried my face into the fabric in search of more. Then I slipped both of my arms into the coat and pulled it around me like an embrace. It was not the same as having the flesh-and-blood man take me into his arms. *Oh, John, what have you done?*

When I could stand it no longer, I shrugged out of the coat and tossed it on the bed, only to collapse on top of it and finally cry. I cried like kids do, long and hard.

I called in sick the next day. Wearing my bathrobe, I took Mary to Lisen's, and then didn't bathe, didn't dress, didn't eat. I would never love another man the way I loved John. I relived each day with him, every twist and turn in our relationship, asking myself, *What if?* And then crumbled inside when I realized that I could've changed it. I could've married him when he asked me to back in September.

All gone now.

Escape from the rest of the world was only temporary. I had to function. I had to get up and go to work the next day. And my days with Mary were numbered. I couldn't squander them. I had to make each moment count. She had been mine for over a year; how was I going to live without her? I walked around with the leaden pressure of loss in my chest, but I had to do what had to be done. Life did go on, and even though I felt hollowed out inside, I had decisions to make.

Despite the financial hit I would take, I decided against renting the second bedroom in the apartment and instead gave Mary a room of her own for the first time. I'd received a raise recently, and I needed to break her habit of sleeping with me. I pushed the double bed that Dot and Dennis had left behind against the wall and used the nightstand on the other side to act as a railing of sorts. It was rather late to buy her a baby bed; besides, I could only surmise that John and Alice would be taking her away soon. I could feel it just as one feels the cold descending when night falls.

John called and asked to come see Mary at my place, and I had to try to shelve my rage and pain, as there were still many things I hadn't taught him about her yet. I swallowed down the bile in my throat and invited him over for dinner on a weeknight and asked Alice to come as well. He told me that wasn't necessary; he would come alone this time. I didn't know if Alice couldn't face me again, or if it was because John would be the new mother.

It was the first time we met face-to-face since he'd come to tell me of his decision, and I'd expected to remain furious. But with one look at his pained face, my anger dissolved; in its place came a sober acceptance of this new reality. The trap John was in was real. So was my pain. I imagined he was in a lot of pain, too. We were both wading in thick waters that had risen around us. Being angry, flapping around in all the muck, wasn't going to help either of us. And it certainly wouldn't help Mary.

As soon as I welcomed him inside the apartment, I became acutely aware of John's eyes on me, those lovely, gentle, and peering eyes that always saw through me.

Mary was playing quietly on the floor, but she smiled when she saw John and toddled over for a hug. Then she went back to her play, and John and I sat across from each other.

He was more handsome than ever. Why did he have to comb his hair in such an adorable way? Why did his cheekbones have to be so perfect? I glanced up at him and caught his gaze. He knew what I was feeling, and everything around us whispered away. The sounds of the street below, the music playing low on the radio, Mary stacking blocks at our feet. I couldn't tear my eyes away from John's. If he had opened his arms to me, in a split second I would've been like clay pressed into a palm again, just as before.

Dozens of memories swam back to my consciousness: taking off on horses on that beautiful day, playing cards at the café, dancing, laughing at Mary, the night in the hotel, his smile, our happiness. It was too much. All that I was losing. Mary. John. This love that had crept up on me so fiercely. I feared that I might crack, fling myself on him, and beg him to change his mind. It was like the most awful dream. John sitting there and no longer mine. Like me, he seemed to be holding himself back, keeping his distance, while at the same time fighting a ferocious battle to contain what he wished he could do. Or was I just telling myself that? He'd had a choice; I hadn't.

"Alice wanted to come, but I wanted to see you alone. How are you doing?" he asked me in a soft voice, his hands clasped in front of him.

I had to look away. His face summoned so many memories I would have to hide in the crevices inside my head. In that short time we had been a couple, I'd believed there was no problem big enough that we couldn't tackle it together. I said, "Just working, taking care of Mary, crying myself to sleep . . ."

He leaned forward, and I stole a glance. Upon closer observation, he looked paler, older. "I'm so sorry, Gwen. I'm like a gaping wound. To know what I've put you through, it's almost unbearable."

I knew his pain was real; I could feel it emanating from him into the room, into the air I breathed. And still I said, "Well, now you have Alice to help you."

He moved his hands to his knees, as if he were afraid of what he might do with them, of what he wanted to do with them. But between us, Alice ran like a septic river we could not cross. "The only woman who can help me through this life is you. And I can't have you."

His words washed over me, my face, through my hair, and down my spine. There was nothing dishonest about John, and his attempts to console were real. But I shivered at his words. I shrugged in a way that spoke volumes about my helplessness in this situation. "Your choice, not mine."

"An impossible choice," he said and gazed at Mary. His darling daughter.

Perhaps it had been an impossible choice. I thought back to all the decisions, right or wrong, I'd made in order to keep Mary. How could I really blame the man for doing all he could and more to keep her now? There was nothing left to do but go back to our original goal: to make it right for Mary.

"I can't come up with anything else to do. I've tried to persuade Alice that we should both start anew. I've tried to make her understand that everything has changed. I've even questioned if she's really up for motherhood, but she's determined that we get back together as a family." He paused. "I can't lose Mary to Alice, Gwen. I can't take that chance. I know that with even more conviction since I've been around her. Alice can't do this alone. But believe me, this has been the toughest time of my life. It's harder than being in that damned camp in Germany."

"So, where do we go from here?"

John whispered, "You have every right to hate me."

I gasped. "If only I could!"

"Work on it a little longer." His words seem to chew through him like sharp teeth. "Maybe you'll get there. Anger is more bearable than pain."

"You have no idea."

"I don't?" He looked incredulous, and hurt. "I lost us, too, Gwen."

So he had not had any second thoughts about his decision. Until that moment, I'd held on to a shred of hope. I pulled in a deep breath; I was still alive. A few minutes later, all that was left was the sorrow hanging in the air, lots of lovely memories, and the silent but unmistakable closing of a door. *We* were over. I had to do something or I'd start simpering like a fool. So without another word I got up and plodded off to the kitchen, made a salad, and cooked spaghetti and meatballs with garlic bread. We still had to eat. I cut the meatballs and bread into bite-size pieces for Mary and let her eat the spaghetti any way she wanted. She spread it out on her tray, patting it first and making cooing sounds, and then she had to work hard to get the slippery stuff into her clasp and into her mouth.

John acted like a man who hadn't eaten in ages. I doubted that Alice was the kind of woman who would cook for him. He attacked the spaghetti first and wound it around his fork into big, mouthful-sized bulbs, and then he speared a chunk of meatball on the end. In between bites, he tore pieces of garlic bread off the loaf and stuffed them into his mouth. He even went at the salad with abandon, digging through the greens and stabbing tomatoes with his fork. He reminded me of the way a teenage boy would eat, and it tugged at my heart. I couldn't imagine not touching him again, not running my hands through his hair, not smiling into his face as he held me. I almost couldn't believe everything that had happened, the last part a nightmare from which I never awoke.

Focusing on Mary was the way through this. Our love for her was the only common thread left. Despite the tension, we were able to laugh at her while she made a mess eating. Mary was still able to bring out the joy. She dropped a bread piece and then hung her head over to watch it fall. Then she waited for one of us to retrieve it.

John said, "Uh-oh," as if it had been an accident.

Mary cackled and dropped another lump of bread on the floor. She said, "Uh-oh."

"Uh-oh, my foot," I said and took her food away. It was time to put an end to this. "No, Miss Mary. No, no."

John was so easeful and sweet, he would surely spoil her. "You'll have to learn to discipline her."

His smile faded. "I'm not up to that right now."

"Sometimes you have to force yourself to be up to it."

We ate the rest of the spaghetti in silence.

So far I'd told no one about what had transpired with Dot and Dennis, but now that they were gone it didn't seem like so much of a break in confidence. And I needed to get it out, to breathe past the words, to cleanse the air of it. After I cleared the table, John sat there, not moving, staring at Mary, and a new conversation seemed to be in order. I brought him and Mary a bowl of ice cream. Then I said to John, "Dennis wasn't well, you know. He was drinking a lot and was angry . . . often."

"Is that why they went back to his hometown?"

"Yes," I answered, suddenly feeling pensive. I missed Dot already. "He hopes to get better there."

"Shell shock," he said and shook his head sadly, looking down. I saw a flash of recognition cross his face. "That's what they call it in the army."

"Yes," I said.

"Did he ever get angry at Mary?"

"I made sure that never happened. I kept her out of his way."

His head shot up. "You felt you had to keep her out of his way? Why didn't you tell me how bad it was?"

"I didn't want you to worry. And I had it under control."

"Yes," he said, studying me with loving eyes that made my own ache. "You always do what's best for Mary."

I inhaled deeply and asked, "Did you ever wonder about Dennis?"

He straightened his back against the chair. "I had a sense that something wasn't right, but nothing specific."

"I felt something was amiss as soon as I met him, too." I gazed around the apartment. Then I turned back to John. "Isn't it strange that others, like us, felt it, but Dot obviously didn't?"

He took his time saying, "It's a funny little thing called love, Gwen." I could see the pain and loss in his eyes. He did care for me. He had fallen in love with me. He had.

I had to look away. "I didn't realize how hard it had been. It's so much better to have this place to myself."

"Do you miss her?"

"Dot? Very much, all the time. But she's a married woman now, and she believes her place is with her husband, no matter what."

John was lifting a spoonful of ice cream to his mouth, but he stopped, the spoon frozen in the air. What had I said? I supposed that wifely obligations were not a good subject of conversation for John and me. All the strain and pain, already known to us, didn't need to be refreshed. I hadn't done it on purpose, or had I?

We should have gone out to eat.

Mary was comfortable with her father now. She went into his arms, spoke to him, and touched his face. She loved it when he sat down on the floor and played with her. She had a doll and stuffed animals but also played with trucks and cars. John ran those around on the rug with her and made motor sounds; he was trying valiantly to make the night about Mary, to keep her entertained, and also, I guessed, to keep his mind on her instead of us.

When it was time to rock her before bedtime, Mary still wanted me. She fell asleep and went down easily that night. While I was still in her room, I pulled out John's Chesterfield from the closet. I had to return it now, this moment. Otherwise, I would keep on forgetting, and forgetting, and forgetting to give it back.

John seemed surprised that I had the coat. "Thank you. I thought this was lost."

"Alice left it."

He gave me the saddest smile. "Of course she did."

As soon as we closed the door on Mary, he started to gather his things to leave.

The realization splashed over me that he had other plans, of course, with Alice.

"I need to know what you're going to do, John. I have my own plans to make."

He shoved his arms into his jacket, draped the Chesterfield coat over his arm, and then he stopped. He knew what I was asking and said as if each word pained him, "We'll leave here just after Christmas. The apartment feels like a crowded cage with Alice living there, too. But I don't think I could take Mary away before the holidays."

So Alice had moved in with John and his roommates. I felt sick but managed to say, "Where will you go?"

"We're thinking of Ohio."

"To your sister?" I asked, incredulous.

He nodded slowly. John's face showed the stress of survival. He'd survived the war and the POW camp, only to come back into a different kind of conflict. The air between us was like a long, slow sigh.

"You said you didn't like her style of mothering."

"I don't, but I can take charge of Mary now. I just need a home to take her to, somewhere stable while I figure out my next move."

"What about Alice?"

He said, "I hope she'll learn. I'm going to guide her just as you've guided me." He put his hands on his hips, and his eyes clouded. "Gwen, I'll never forget what you did. I'll never forget you—"

He reached out to touch me, but I pulled away. Any touch from him would make me worse. I pushed my thoughts away from him and instead thought of Mary. "If you're not going to leave until after Christmas, you and Alice can join us for the holidays. We'll all be together like a big happy family." That hadn't exactly come out as kindly as I'd wanted it to, so I softened my tone. "Lisen and Geoff are cooking a turkey on Thanksgiving Day. I'm sure it will be OK. That woman cooks like she has a whole battalion to feed."

"OK," he said. He slowly pulled gloves onto his hands, as if even that was a chore.

"And then maybe after that, we can put up a tree." I pointed toward the front window, where a big tree would fit nicely.

He looked that way and nodded. He was making himself step away from me. I wanted that, but then it was the last thing I wanted. I wanted him to hold me and also to never touch me again.

Eventually he said solemnly, "That would be good for Mary to have us all together. Thank you for asking."

The wind howled down the alleyways, across thresholds, and through trees.

He nodded. And I nodded in return. There was nothing else to say.

CHAPTER TWENTY-FIVE

My solid core had shattered. While I battled demons inside, the city was returning to something resembling normal. Macy's would be holding its famous Thanksgiving Day Parade complete with balloons and floats. The double-decker buses on Fifth Avenue and the city's trolley cars that Mary loved to ride were still running. We'd heard they would be retired in a year's time. Everyone was eating turkey again by the end of 1945, and Schrafft's had resumed selling its popular pumpkin and mincemeat pies, which had tempted me to buy pies instead of baking them. Penn Station and Grand Central were packed with soldiers; this time they were going home.

On Thanksgiving Day, John and Alice were to come to my apartment first. But when I opened the door, John stood alone, carrying paper bags filled with freshly baked bread and flowers for Lisen. A preposterous hope popped into me. Maybe John had sent Alice away.

As I ushered him in, Mary saw her father and her face changed. She broke into a smile and ran his way. She clung to his trousers, leaving saliva there, as she was in the midst of cutting another tooth. John was so moved by that affection that he was rendered speechless for a moment, and tears glistened in his eyes.

He passed the bread and flowers over to me, picked up Mary, and finally said, "Well, hello, my angel. Happy Thanksgiving Day." He kissed her on the cheek and made a smacking sound. "It's turkey day, did you know that? We're going to have turkey. Gobble, gobble," he said and imitated a turkey. Obviously he was determined to make this day be about Mary, and really, what else was there to do?

She laughed and curled against him, and I could've cried.

"Where's Alice?" I asked.

"She's coming along later. She has a headache she's hoping to alleviate with some aspirin." He bounced Mary again, and my hope sailed away.

"Oh. I'm sorry she's not feeling well." That was a lie, and I gulped down the sickest feeling about myself. I should have found a way to feel happy for them, at least for John. Obviously he'd loved Alice once; maybe he could find himself there again someday. But that would require a generosity of spirit that I didn't yet possess. Instead, my mood instantly lightened to know that Alice wasn't with him.

We took the pies, bread, and flowers and headed upstairs to Lisen and Geoff's apartment. The men sat down to listen to the radio and chat, while Mary played with toys on the floor and toddled about, and I helped Lisen in the kitchen.

"Are you having some more people over?" I asked as I looked around. In the refrigerator were salads of all varieties. On the counter were casseroles and vegetables waiting to be heated, and in the oven a massive turkey was turning browner by the moment. There was a fruit tray and another tray covered with nuts, pickles, olives, and cheeses. She had also made some traditional German favorites: white sausage, macaroni salad, and *Dresden Stollen*, a moist, heavy bread filled with fruit.

"I love to cook."

"You'll have leftovers galore."

"I vant to make suckling pig, but now Geoff like his American turkey better. Turkey sandwiches," she said. "Geoff love his turkey sandwich in his pail for lunch. And you must take, too."

I shook my head. I found a place for the pies and bread and then put the flowers in a vase. She had already set the table, and after we pulled out the turkey, I stood and watched her make gravy, something I'd never mastered.

My heart went out to Lisen during this, another holiday season without any word from her family. All reports were that Germany lay in virtual ruin, and almost no news was forthcoming. The army had refused to let private relief agencies operate in Germany, and individual Germans could still not receive letters from abroad. American soldiers were smuggling out letters for some, but as far as I knew, Lisen had still received nothing from her family.

Alice finally appeared just as dinner was ready. Perfect timing: arrive for the food but after all the work and preparations have been done. The outrage I'd been working so hard to suppress was pulsing throughout my body. To have to endure her presence after all she'd done. Here she was—the clear winner—back with her man and reuniting with her daughter. She got it all, and anger grew from a single drop to a wave that coursed through my every cell. This was going to be harder than I thought. I'd overestimated my generosity of spirit, after all; I had invited them over. I'd made a huge mistake.

Alice evidenced no sign of not feeling well so I surmised that maybe she didn't want to be around the two women who'd assured her daughter's safety and survival while she was off in California shooting ads, or maybe she just didn't want to help with the cooking. It looked as though she'd been well enough to make sure her appearance was perfect—under her black overcoat with a brooch on the lapel she wore a red holiday dress with a white collar, black pumps, and nylons. Despite whatever had kept her away from her daughter for so long, she'd managed to accumulate a lot of nice dresses. She had pieced herself back into a porcelain beauty—one that I imagined fracturing.

She kept her distance from Mary, because she claimed her headache had not completely subsided. I also saw no evidence that she'd been around Mary before, although I knew she had. Mary didn't look at her. Maybe those visits hadn't gone as well as Alice had hoped. Maybe she didn't want anyone to see how little progress she'd made with her daughter.

She sat on the sofa away from everyone with her legs crossed and swinging her top leg back and forth. Good, she was nervous. There was no amount of kindness I could conjure up for Alice that day, because her presence there with John stabbed me in the gut. She had come back just in time to steal the life I should've had. At least she kept her distance; thank God for that. Maybe John had admonished her to say little and to keep herself apart. Maybe he was afraid of what might erupt between the three of us. She sat by herself and gazed off as if there were something in the room that none of us could see. The last time Alice and I were together, Alice had no idea that I'd become involved with John. Now she knew; now she was cold toward me.

They didn't act like much of a couple, but I knew she had every intention of sticking with him. It was unrealistic to hope they hadn't become man and wife again, in every sense except for the wedding ceremony to formalize their union. But I hoped for it anyway. I couldn't let my imagination wander to what they did when they were alone; jealousy was such a potent poison. She was beautiful, but I found myself staring at the darker roots growing out in the part of her hair, and I thought, *Phony*. All the compassion I'd once possessed for Alice's sadness or illness or whatever it was had picked up and walked away.

I went to the restroom, and when I came out, Alice was waiting for me in the hallway, away from the others. She stood there in the dimly lit passageway like some sort of apparition, and it startled me.

"Gwen," she said and firmly held my gaze. "Could I have a moment with you?"

I smoothed down my skirt and waited, unsure and yet fearful about what she had to say. Finally I gave a quick nod of my head.

"John thinks I haven't thanked you enough for what you did for Mary, and for me."

She seemed sincere, but there was also a gleam of brutal knowing in her eyes. A tiny bit of smugness. The feeling that this was all a terrible dream came back to me, only now it was getting worse. Seeing them together, knowing they were likely sleeping together. Alice so pretty and knowing and trying to make amends.

I said, "What do *you* think?"

She pursed her painted lips together. "I think . . . that he's probably right. I should thank you more, and so that's what I'm doing. Thank you, Gwen."

I couldn't say the things people typically say, such as "No bother" or, "Oh, it was nothing." It hadn't been nothing.

I nodded again, because only words laced with poison would come from my mouth if I spoke.

"I really do thank you, from the bottom of my heart. I'd like to repay you, somehow."

A break in my composure. "That's impossible."

She took one step back and crossed her arms. "Nothing's impossible." She said it as if she finally figured out how much I hated this. Hated her. "But if you really want to know what I think . . . I think that while I was sick and lost, you helped yourself to my husband."

The ugliest thing sprang to life inside my chest. There was nothing I could do to tame this animal inside. "Your husband? Could've fooled me." I fought against the creeping of outraged tears.

She dropped her arms and forced a smile, forced a composure that surely wasn't there. She had a purpose; perhaps John had told her to stay civil at all costs. "But it's all under the bridge now. John and I are back together."

I stood perfectly still. I would not congratulate her. I would not.

Alice shifted her weight from one foot to the other, as though she was feeling the strain and maybe regretting what she'd just said. Her next smile seemed more real. "I want us to be friends again."

I took a deep breath and did battle with the rigid feeling in my face. Had Alice and I ever been friends? She had always been so mysterious and closed off, even before Mary was born. I'd never known her without the effects of a pregnancy, a husband overseas, and then a baby she couldn't handle. I'd never known Alice without problems she seemed incapable of dealing with. Was this the real Alice? Someone who sought approval and needed it, no matter what? Was she insecure and seeking, as I'd always believed? Or had John put her up to making peace with me? Maybe she didn't care at all.

"Listen, Gwen, when I was younger one of my favorite things to do was to play matchmaker. I have a good track record. Several marriages have resulted. I'd love to help you find your match."

I nearly staggered. The pure, unmitigated gall. How dare she suggest repaying me for a year of love and care for her daughter with a setup or two? The very suggestion of matchmaking was insulting. I'd never needed a matchmaker or help in that area. How I loathed her in that moment. The hallway was too small, and I couldn't take another second of her wretched presence.

"Excuse me," I said as I swept past her, then gathered myself together before I rejoined the others.

The food was wonderful, as I knew it would be, but I had a hard time getting anything to slide down my throat. The others seemed to fare much better in the presence of our odd trio than Alice and I did. Alice, apparently now recovered from her headache, wanted to sit next to Mary in her high chair and did so, but Mary turned her head away from her mother and focused on John at her other side, instead. Alice didn't eat much, either. John and Geoff talked business at the furniture store until Lisen made them stop. Lisen told us that Germans preferred goose, or *gans*, over turkey for special occasions but did stuff them in a similar fashion. She said they also often ate *der Kapaun*, a fattened, castrated rooster.

John set down his fork. "Thank you for that information, Lisen."

"That's my girl," laughed Geoff. "Never fails to entertain."

After the main dinner, we took a break before dessert consisting of my pies and Lisen's Dresden Stollen. I wanted to help Lisen in the kitchen with the cleanup, but she shooed me away. She knew what had happened and wanted to make things easier on me. Alice made no such offer.

Lisen said to me, "Go sit down. Talk. Relax." To Geoff she said, "You go, too. Rest."

He smiled devilishly. "Am I hearing this correctly? I haven't done anything in—let me see—at least an hour."

Lisen swatted at him.

Geoff looked at John. "Let's not miss this opportunity. I'm in no hurry to go back to household slavery."

She swatted at him again.

I looked at my watch; I wanted this to be over. This had not been a good idea, to see them through the holidays. Maybe we should've taken the surgical approach: make a quick, clean incision, excise, then sew up and over. But there was Mary, and each day was so precious. How could I give up even one of the days left to me? She was mine, mine! I'd been the mother who took care of her when she was ill, held her until she fell asleep at night, cuddled her when she was scared. I had been the one to endure the sleepless nights during her infancy, her bouts with diaper rash, her grumpiness while teething. I, alone, had witnessed her first smile, her first laugh, her first steps.

Unable to face sitting in the living room with Alice, I insisted on helping Lisen. After I joined the others, John got down on the floor with Mary to play blocks with her, while Alice watched. Mary's favorite game was for him or me to build a tower of blocks and then let her knock them down. Watching the two of them together brought on a barrage of conflicting emotions—happiness that John and Mary were so connected, and then despair that they would go on without me. With Alice as the mother, and me cast aside. The thought of never seeing Mary again made me teeter on the edge of collapse. I'd been doing everything in my power to avoid thinking about this, but now it was right in front of me. I was having a hard time breathing.

Geoff said, "He has a good way with people at the store. That's the most important thing. People want to buy from him. If there were more places for people to live, we'd be selling even more furniture."

I was glad the housing situation was so difficult. They couldn't take Mary yet.

Alice looked decidedly uncomfortable as she sat in the corner of the sofa, leaning away from us, as if she'd decided to put up her invisible wall. She reminded me of one of those tiny, trembling, terrified . . . dogs. Chihuahuas or some such. Had my lack of interest in her matchmaking skills hurt her so badly? She wouldn't meet my eyes now. Obviously John had told her about us. *You helped yourself to my husband.* Before tonight, I had wondered if he'd been open about our relationship. But I should've known he would be honest.

I had to blot away her existence, or I'd never get through this evening. I focused on my dear friends instead. While Lisen was still out of the room, I asked Geoff in a whisper, "Has Lisen heard from any of her family back in Germany?"

He lowered his voice, too, and leaned forward. "Only a distant third or fourth cousin. That's all."

"Do you think—?"

"I don't know. Of course they could all be gone. But we hope they just haven't had a chance to write, or maybe the mail system isn't working yet. We know they have no phones."

I nodded and looked at John, who nodded back.

We stayed until we could force ourselves to eat dessert, then packed leftovers, and took Mary downstairs. Alice stayed upstairs after finally offering to help with the dessert cleanup. John wanted to do Mary's entire bedtime routine on his own. He knew her favorite toys and games and how to distract her, how to comfort her.

That night I decided to show him how to comb her hair. She hated having her hair styled. It was always an ordeal, because her hair was terribly fine and tangled easily, plus she was tender-headed. When I brought out the soft brush and comb set, she started to whine and protest.

"No," she said and pushed my hand away.

John distracted her with squeaky toys she could chew and handle. We worked so well together; we would've made great parents together. The connection we'd once shared still zinged with electricity. Perhaps the wires were frayed, but the sparks still flared. He made hilarious sounds that she loved, and then he started singing "Onward, Christian Soldiers."

"Come now," I said. "You have to know some baby songs."

But Mary didn't seem to mind. Whenever anyone sang to her she always stilled and quieted, like a sea going smooth and silver. He kept on.

I sat down behind her on the floor and first started with the soft brush. Alice had wandered downstairs by then and sat nearby on the couch in a state of unconcerned detachment. Something seemed very wrong about her again. How dare she turn back into that fragile woman I'd once known, when now she had everything? It was as if she had dematerialized, and it was just the three of us again: John, Mary, me.

John ran out of song, and I started in on "The Old Grey Goose is Dead," which my grandmother sang to me when I was young.

When I'd finished the first stanza, John said, "Well that's a comforting thought for a child. The old goose, probably a pet, is dead."

"I'd never thought of it that way," I laughed.

"Now that I think of it," said John. "So many of those songs they used to sing to us were brutal. Think of, oh . . . you know . . . the one about daddy going hunting and killing a rabbit."

"Yes! 'Bye, Baby Bunting.' I sing it when I rock her to sleep."

"Daddy comes home with a dead rabbit. What a great thought before going to sleep and dreaming."

"Then there's 'Rock-a-Bye Baby.' The cradle falls from the tree."

"See what I mean?"

John distracted Mary with more military songs and marching about, while Alice pulled out a file and started sawing away at her nails. For a moment I was filled with such anger I wanted her to look up and see how seamlessly I fit with Mary and John. But she was almost so insubstantial that I could imagine her lifting up and floating through the window into the cold.

John seemed more at peace than I was. What was the source of John's contentment? Was it Mary? Or could it be Alice, too? Was her weirdness just because she was around me? Had she become a wife to him again? There were probably things between them that I knew nothing about, but I'd be damned if I was going to entertain those thoughts.

I got Mary's hair mostly untangled with the soft brush, but then I had to get the comb through. I used the slightest touch and first barely raked the comb on top of her hair until layer by layer I could get it through and break up all the little knots. Despite his antics and singing, John watched intently; I could feel his gaze heavy on me as though he were captivated by my every move.

I missed seeing the tenderness with which he handled Mary, because after the hair ordeal was over, I turned her over to him and went back upstairs to give the three of them time alone. My emotions were getting the better of me, and chitchat was no longer possible. I had to escape their togetherness.

When I came back downstairs, I discovered everything had been done. John had bathed Mary, brushed her teeth, diapered her, dressed her in pajamas, rocked her, and put her down for the night.

When it was time to say good-night to John and Alice, the tension between us was beastly. Alice looked ready to flee, whereas John seemed hesitant, as if he felt the need to say something. But what could he say that would mean anything at this point?

They both thanked me for including them in the holiday, and then Alice put her hand on John's sleeve, as though urging him to get on with it. For once, I agreed with Alice. *Go. Please. Get out of here.* I couldn't stand this a moment longer.

I shut the door behind them, turned, and all but buckled against the door, then I slid down to the floor. I needed this to end. If John were truly kind, he would see this and they would leave New York sooner than later. But then again, Mary. Sweet, precious Mary.

I had contained my emotions all evening long, but now I let them flood.

CHAPTER TWENTY-SIX

JOHN

John led Alice toward a former speakeasy on East 53rd Street, where they'd agreed to meet one of their roommates, Larry, for drinks. Larry had no family here and wanted to celebrate Thanksgiving night in the world without war.

John pulled the lapels of his jacket up tighter around his neck and tugged Alice closer to him. The cold of winter here had come as a surprise to him. At sea level, it shouldn't have rivaled the colds of mountain climes, and yet there was something more insidious and dense and penetrating about it; a cold day felt like walking through freezing fog instead of air.

The night before, he had dreamed of the war, again. He was back on the front, in the German woods, under fire and shell attack. When he had awakened flat on his back next to Alice, the curtains fluttered as the heating system in the apartment kicked on, and they opened like a gasping mouth to allow in a flood of silver moonlight. He studied the play of it on the ceiling and let himself remember it all then, the pain and cold and suffering, the death and disease and waste. The faces of the men he'd killed, even those he might have killed. On the surface, he'd been humble and quiet. He might even have shown moments of bravery. But in private, he'd suffered the pointless, shuddering, shadowy quality of it, again and again. He closed his eyes, and sought the comfort he always sought. A face swam out of the chemical soup in his brain. Gwen. Of course, Gwen.

He shook off that memory and continued walking with Alice toward the bar. On that night in the woods, the world had turned silver, frozen grasses listed to the side with the angle of wind, and taller blades had forged a way out of the snow and stood pale in the moonlight, leaning over, too. The moon was split in half, misty-edged and run across by fast-traveling night clouds.

The whole miserable situation was taking its toll. Alice had wanted him back, but now that she had him, she had turned distant again. She wasn't altogether *there*, though he could see her clearly in Mary, in her hair color and the shape of her mouth. Alice hadn't been pleased by all the time he'd spent with Gwen, and at first she'd seemed ready to fight to win back his heart. But now . . . he had no idea what she was thinking or feeling. He was living with a stranger again. Where was Alice, and even more importantly, *who* was Alice? He felt as if he were breathing in slivers of shale instead of the fresh night air.

He had to make a change. Something he could only describe as a fog-like smoke blew over the bloated river from New Jersey every day and brought to mind the poison gases of the war zone, blocking out the light of day like a visible plague. The streets and bridges, the ferries and parks, all bottlenecked daily with too many bodies, gave the sense that the air had to be fought for.

The idea for the atomic bomb and how to wipe out whole cities had been conceived here; hence they called it the Manhattan Project. People said it had ended the war sooner, and certainly it had. But he'd seen photos of the boxes of ashes in Hiroshima, each one containing what remained of a human being, many of them women and children. Most people saw the good the bomb had done, and still others made light of it. The latest Hollywood starlets were often called anatomic bombshells. But he wondered: Once something that powerful had been created, couldn't it be recreated again and again? And for what purposes? One day such a bomb could come down on us, he thought, and the most disturbing thought of all was that New York City would be a likely target. With much of Europe in ruins, New York was now the most powerful city on the planet.

Gwen loved it and fit; he could see that she had not only adjusted but had thrived here. But he had no sense of belonging to any of it. He hadn't hated it, but he'd had his fill of the crowds and concrete. He understood Dennis more than anyone knew. He understood wanting to go home, even if he knew it would never be the same.

What he hadn't counted on was falling for Gwen. He was fascinated by her gentleness and steadiness. Once while Mary slept in her arms, he had studied Gwen as she slowly uncurled each of his daughter's tiny fingers and watched as they folded in again. That memory brought him closer to tears than any worries about Alice. Gwen was the living pearl to Alice's empty shell.

World War II was over, and peace was supposed to be the new normal. But instead he was embroiled in battle just as before, only facing a new and more mysterious warfront. Now the fog lifted, and he knew what his next battle would be. This was his new war, and this would be his new combat grounds. He would have to fight his feelings for Gwen and suppress them for the rest of his days. This . . . was what he was battling *against*.

And there was Alice to think about, too. He didn't know if he'd ever feel the same way about her as he once did. She was a mysterious girl-woman, childlike in her emotions. She saw things in either complete darkness or bright light, without shades and tones, without nuance and the appreciation of complexities. He could see how the man he'd been before had been attracted to her mysteriousness, but now he saw it differently. He didn't know how well the distance she put between herself and others would work out, in terms of her own happiness, but what frightened him, terrified him really, was the thought that she'd turn Mary into a person like herself. So in this new battle, what he was battling for was Mary. Anything for her, at all costs.

On that holiday night, Alice said she wanted to find some fun, meet Larry, and paint the town. So he took her to some of the bars they'd once frequented when they were dating, perhaps in an attempt to rekindle that old flame. But once inside the warm confines, they talked to others around them more than they talked to each other. The bars that were open were full of people still celebrating the end of the war and Thanksgiving. On the street, John ran into an old war buddy, Finch Henry, who had always been a popular and politically minded officer, always up for news and discussion, no matter the circumstances and surroundings.

Finch, a tall redhead whose face was covered with so many freckles they almost blended together, told John he'd decided to make a career of the army and was just back from a visit to Washington, DC. He, Alice, and John decided to walk to the Commodore Hotel and visit its 165-foot-long bar, deemed to be the world's longest.

Over beers, Finch said, "Did you hear about what the FAS is telling Congress?" He raked his hand through his hair and rocked with barely suppressed energy.

John shook his head. "No. Tell me."

"The FAS, man. Federation of American Scientists. All those brilliant minds who came up with the bomb are now saying we need to share how they did it and then ban it worldwide."

Finch was still as charismatic as ever, no worse for the wear, it seemed. Three girls were already making their way toward the men at the bar. One wore a fur stole and the other a checkered coat. Both wore thick layers of red lipstick, their hair down in waves.

John said, "Share it? With everyone?"

"That's their push. They say it's only a matter of time before scientists all over the world figure it out anyway, and we can't keep it a secret. It's coming, my man. They say one A-bomb could take out all of Manhattan clear to uptown."

The air left John's lungs. Of course he knew this already, but something about Finch's certainty made it feel suddenly more real. Each week had brought more news that shook him. He wanted more than anything to clear his mind of all of it—worries about Mary, about Gwen, Alice, the future, their future, the city, and the world.

Alice stared straight ahead into the mirror behind the bar and fussed with her hair. The bartender couldn't keep his eyes off her.

Finch said, "Here they developed this powerful thing that ended the war, and now they're scared to death of it. With good reason, I'd say. I say they have the smarts to see what's coming. They're calling for a Big Three Conference in Moscow and hoping for a worldwide ban."

"So let me get this straight. The same guys who devised it now want it outlawed?"

Finch nodded. "Because they know what it can do."

John pondered that for a moment. He also tried to figure out a way to include Alice in the conversation, but by then she was talking to a girl who'd sat beside her about beauty tips. "But how do you know who to trust? Can we really trust the Russians?"

"That's what I'm talking about, man. But if everyone uses the bomb the next time there's a war, the only safe place might be under the sea. The way I see it, an agreement is the only way."

John downed his beer. "Makes you wonder what's going to happen."

"Precisely. We let the wildcat out of the bag, and now she's running rampant. We can't control what other countries do. But we can sure try."

"Hello, girls," Finch said as he turned to the young women making their way to the bar.

John took a slow slug of his beer and fully succumbed to his fears.

After Finch had politely dismissed the girls, John told Finch about Mary, and Finch filled John in on his plans to marry his high school sweetheart back home in his native Indiana. They swapped stories about the whereabouts of some of their former comrades and finally called it a night, vowing to stay in touch.

When John and Alice finally left the bar, John was overcome by a melancholy that had no name. He thought the world would be changed for the better after so many years of fighting, but even at war's end, safety was nothing but an illusion. Now there were new things to fear. Christmas was coming, so the holiday season would be over soon, and then they would have to leave and take Mary. He had to take her to a place where there was plenty of clean water and elbow room, away from a city that held too many dangers and made a perfect target. He had to take her away from Gwen and let Alice be her mother, hard as it was going to be.

They walked to the river and John watched the dark waters silently flow by. When he pulled out his handkerchief to wipe his nose, he thought he could smell the spices that Gwen had baked into her pumpkin pie, and he held the handkerchief there, inhaling the scents, while his former wife and mother to his child stood next to him, lost in a place where he could not go.

CHAPTER TWENTY-SEVEN

Desperate to formulate a new plan for my future, I started to make inquiries about entering the armed services. To my surprise, even nurses were being discharged. So I began to look into foreign service with charitable organizations, such as the Red Cross. It seemed it would be a long process to make something happen. But after Christmas, after John and Alice took Mary, nothing would really hold me here. Maybe the best thing to do would be to escape. Maybe I would apply for any and all overseas jobs. Maybe I would move to a new apartment. Maybe I would get a dog.

When I picked up Mary at Lisen's a week after Thanksgiving, Lisen was beside herself with joy. Some good news, finally! She had received a letter from her younger brother, Gunter; the letter probably had been smuggled out of Germany by US soldiers. He was now living in Hamburg, but hadn't told her any of the details of his survival or how he'd gotten there. While Hamburg had been brutalized by the so-called "firestorm" of Allied bombings, and much of it lay in disastrous condition, Gunter wrote that he was healthy and strong.

Lisen hugged me so hard it hurt. She pulled back and said some words in German, then caught herself and said, "I go to the church, the one that help get people over. He need to put his name on list for immigration. He must have job here, but Geoff take care of that. Then he has to pass tests."

"Tests? What kind of tests?"

"Medical. And then they ask questions: vhat he has done, how he believe."

"He should say as little as possible. Nothing political, that's for sure."

"I know. But vhen all is done, he can come over on ship, and church vill pay for passage. He has to learn English vhen he gets here. You and John vill help? Help him speak gud English? Maybe you become friends to him."

"Of course," I said. "Only John will probably be gone by the time your brother gets here."

Her face fell. "You think John and that voman really leave?"

"That's the grand plan."

A strange and solemn expression on her face, she said slowly, "I thought you and John maybe . . ."

"No," I told her. "He has forgiven Alice."

She looked taken aback and visibly disappointed. "I do not see how he do this."

She registered this news for a few moments, and then she showed me a small black-and-white photograph that had come with her brother's letter. Gunter had a strong, square jaw and small, deep-set eyes, and he wore a look that said he'd seen more than anyone would want to. His firm gaze burned through the photographic paper, and I could've sworn he could see me. It was like one of those paintings in which the subject's eyes follow you around the room. He was handsome in an otherworldly way, raw and unpolished but undeniably handsome.

Lisen gazed wistfully at the photo. "I might not know him. Might not know. He change so much. He is twenty-five now. The last I see him, only eighteen. Still look like a boy."

I pulled her close to me as the news sunk in. "I'm so happy for you, and of course I'll do anything to help."

"He must become citizen right away. Citizen of United States, so that no one ever can make him go back there . . ."

I didn't ask Lisen about news of any other family members. I also didn't ask her how often John and Alice had taken Mary for the day and then returned her, effectively avoiding me.

Her face lit up again. "Maybe you vill like Gunter . . ."

"I'm sure I'll like Gunter. He's your brother."

"No, I mean really like Gunter. Maybe you and he vill fall in love."

I smiled. "How can I help you get him over here?"

"Maybe you come to church vith me. The church that helps. They have meeting every veek."

"I'd like that."

Given that the army couldn't take me, I liked the idea of helping refugees move here. I needed something I could latch onto.

CHAPTER TWENTY-EIGHT

Another dreaded encounter among the twisted trio was upon me. John and I both had a day off, the last Sunday before Christmas. He and Alice wanted to take Mary shopping, and they wanted me to come along. I had tried to beg off, but John convinced me to go by saying they wanted my help picking out things Mary needed and would like.

So John showed up with Alice in tow, and even though I knew she was coming, I was at a loss for a moment. So strange to feel such resentment toward the person who had brought the baby I loved into this world. Today she pointedly said hello and smiled. I twisted my face into a smile as best I could right back at her. I wasn't sure she noticed. It seemed she paid little attention to other people, but she had paid lots of attention to her appearance. She wore a double-breasted jacket over a skirt and held a clutch bag with both hands in front of her. Her hair, which looked newly trimmed, was tucked behind her ears.

John had dressed for the occasion and wore his black suit. My heart fell into my stomach when I saw him in my favorite suit. I'd almost forgotten how handsome he was in it. He looked even better than before with his hair a little unkempt from the wind outside and grown out a little longish.

With Alice's "cold" no longer an issue, he tried to get Mary to go to Alice, but Mary did what she always did with people she hadn't gotten to know. Mary ignored her mother. Maybe they hadn't picked up Mary as often as I'd imagined. Alice didn't force herself on Mary. She smiled and held back.

I carried Mary onto the street, and Alice walked close to John in front of me, looping her arm through his, as if to say, *He's mine again.* Flaunting it, oh so unflinchingly. I imagined firing little poisonous arrows from my eyes into her back.

The streets of Manhattan were gaily decked out with Christmas lights and decorated trees, Santa figures, reindeer, and Nativity scenes. Holiday music drifted from restaurants and bars. But the holiday season in New York, which was usually magical, could not charm me.

Mary was outgrowing everything, and so we bought new winter clothes and a new red-and-white-checked coat and several warm woolen caps. One smart retailer had set out a display of teddy bears next to the children's coats and clothes, and when Mary cried for one, a brown one with a tan nose and tan ears, John bought it, even though she already had a favorite bear.

"*I've* never bought her one," he explained to me, and even though it was a first-time experience for him, sadness seemed to emanate from every feature on his face. The joy of the season wasn't working for John, either; like me, he was putting on a facade.

Alice spoke to Mary from time to time but didn't try to take her away from either John or me. She seemed to understand that this was not the time to try to bond with her daughter, and I had to admire her patience. Or was it fear? How hard must it be that her own daughter didn't want to have anything to do with her.

I felt a flicker of sympathy for her. I was a nurse; I was supposed to be sympathetic toward those in pain. She had been sick when she left, I guessed. I'd been convinced of it before. But had it been illness or just an escape for selfish reasons? I shook my head without meaning to. What difference did it make now? Whatever it had been—illness or selfishness—she was better now, and she had gotten away with it all.

We headed down Broadway, past small shops bursting with hats, coats, lingerie, and costume jewelry, past confectioners, arcades, and all manner of street vendors: shoeblacks, newspaper hawkers, fruit stands, and flower sellers. Our destination was a street corner where John and I both remembered seeing freshly cut trees.

As we passed Washington Square Park, where several sidewalk portraitists were at work, a thought occurred to me: a portrait of Mary would be an ideal Christmas present from me to John. When I made the suggestion, he loved the idea.

Alice said, "What a nice thing to do."

So I chose a charcoal artist based on the quality of the portrait he was completing, and we waited for him to become available. He was a small, wiry man who wore a black beret tilted on his head, very artistlike, and his face was full of serious concentration as he worked.

When it was our turn, Alice said, "I'll hold her."

John, who was holding Mary then, hesitated, but I could see his mind working it out. Might as well give it a try, he seemed to be thinking. He pulled out his keys, which Mary loved, and gave them to her as a distraction while he passed her to Alice.

At first the distraction was effective. Alice sat down on the stool the artist led them to, and Mary was fixated on the keys, tasting them, feeling them, jangling them. Alice looked elated, as if she thought all her problems had just been solved. Her genuine-looking smile filled me with the most confused mix of emotions. If I was a good-hearted person, I should wish Alice well. It would be best for Mary and for John. But God help me, I still felt those invisible poisonous arrows in my eyes. Nothing noble lived inside me at that moment.

Then something flashed in Mary, and she turned her head, looked at her mother, and started screaming. Alice tried to act unaffected and simply gave her to John.

"Oh, well. I'll win her back over eventually," she said as she came and stood beside me.

A tiny bit of compassion sprung out of me, taking me completely by surprise. "You'll be her mother again soon."

Alice held still beside me, her breathing deep and regular. It surprised me when she said, "Nursing is one of the best professions for a woman." Alice glanced over at me. "I can be a mother and still have a career, don't you think? You did it, Gwen. I look up to you for that. Nowadays we women can have it all, don't you think?"

Her insecurity was so huge, I couldn't strike her down, especially after what she'd just endured from her daughter.

She looked forward then and sighed. "I've always felt there was something grand out there for me. Something more than just an ordinary life as a wife and mother. I admire women like you who work and make something of themselves."

"Thank you," I finally murmured. But the word *selfish* kept swimming around inside my skull. Did she really think so much about herself? All the time? And had I been much the same before Mary? I was surprised that the conversation had come back to Alice and her hopes and dreams. Would she mature after she had Mary back? Would she realize that she would have to make sacrifices—that it couldn't be all about her—once she was responsible for her daughter? What was I supposed to say?

Alice's eyes meandered over my face. "John tells me you're the nurse in the photo taken on V-J Day in Times Square. It's such a great photo. People love it. You're going to become more famous than I could ever hope to be."

I tried to smile, but it quickly slid away. "I doubt that."

"You should come forward."

I didn't know how to respond. I'd known her, but not this side of her. Her need for fame was something I couldn't relate to. I couldn't help but like the idea that I was the nurse in that photo, but as of yet, I hadn't done anything about it. I could not match her in terms of shiny ambition. Alice's beauty was something I could never match, either. Even amid her contradictions and neediness, her loveliness outshined me as the sun does the stars.

As the portraitist began his work on a sheet of fresh, milky-white paper clamped to his easel, Alice eventually wandered off to peruse the goods of other street artists and vendors. John tried to still Mary, who was cooperating more than I would've expected.

He said, "There, there, Miss Mary. Let's hold still for the man. Let's hold still now."

He let her play with the keys some more, and when she tired of them, I handed him a toy out of the bag I always carried for her, and she sat without wiggling for quite a while, fairly contented. Of course she didn't hold still for the artist, but he said it was no matter. John, when he wasn't tending to Mary, held his face in an expression that was calm, pleased, expectant, and patient.

It had been a long time since I'd been able to stand by and simply look at John, and how bittersweet it was. His gaze drifted about and landed on me from time to time, and there was a softening and brightening in his eyes when ours met. I could detect a tiny bit of hope on his face, but what he hoped for I no longer knew.

For a blink in time there was no Alice and no leaving to be done. I imagined finding a frame for the portrait and hanging it over John's and my fireplace mantle. Fire sputtered over glowing embers in the fireplace. Dinner was in the oven. Shiny packages lay under a blue spruce Christmas tree. Another child on the way . . .

John stood up with Mary in his arms to come around and look at the completed portrait. "It's really good," he said and turned to me. "Thank you."

I couldn't take my eyes from him.

He said, "What's funny?"

I hadn't realized I was smiling. My mouth went dry, but I managed to say, "Nothing's funny."

The artist tapped me on the arm. He had rolled the portrait and put it in a cardboard tube and was handing it to me. I took the tube in my hands. My gift to John and *Alice*, not me. For a moment I had forgotten. For a moment, a dream had come to me, but like most dreams, it had been short-lived and I woke up.

As if on cue, Alice returned from her spin around the square. She rushed up to John, bearing a poinsettia plant in her arms. "Look what I've found," she said and beamed up into his face.

The air froze in my throat, and my knees turned to mud. My heart clanged in my ears. There *was* an Alice, and they *were* leaving. I shoved the tube containing the portrait at John and Alice and then said, "Excuse me," and walked away. No more torture; I was done.

CHAPTER TWENTY-NINE

Only I wasn't done. Plans had been made. Plans that others counted on me to keep. I walked back through a vast, open plain of cold December air. I didn't know if I could take another evening of seeing John and Alice together. But I didn't want to miss out on being with Mary, and this could possibly be the last time I'd have to do such a thing. John and Alice had followed me home, John carrying Mary, none of us eking out a word.

A long sigh escaped my lips as I reasoned with myself and gathered some resolve. Mine was just another sad story in the midst of the miseries of the war and its aftermath. Mine wasn't even so awful in comparison to so many others. Humanity had been tested in all degrees, and many more terrible things were being revealed. The photos of the concentration camps—the horrors—were unfathomable, and yet we went on, hurting and bleeding and still possessed of life—that was almost unfathomable, too. I had to put on a poker face of false bravado, and I managed to form it.

John went back for the tree and then, with Alice as escort, half dragged it to the apartment building while I looked after Mary. Geoff helped John lug the tree up the stairs, leaving a trail of needles behind, and then into the apartment. Finally they stood it up, and it filled my front window.

"Very big," John said as he brushed tree needles from his slacks and shirt. The simple ways he moved his body shot so many sad and also wonderful sensations through me. I would never forget us; I would never forget that time of togetherness, and that night of love. Was I sorry? I looked away for a moment. Never. Not sorry.

I said to Mary, "There's our tree. Your very first big Christmas tree." I wouldn't let the thought linger in my head that it was the last Christmas I would have with her.

She wanted down, and so Lisen distracted her with toys while I pulled out the lights and ornaments I had purchased. While the men strung the lights, Lisen told us about German Christmas traditions, about children leaving a shoe or a boot by the fireplace on December 6, St. Nicholas's Day. St. Nicholas and his sidekick, Knecht Ruprecht, then went from house to house carrying his book of sins and handing out fruits and nuts and other edibles for children who had been good and only twigs for those who had not been good.

"Vicious," I said, forcing myself to make conversation. "Did you ever get twigs?"

"No, no, no," she said.

She stopped and seemed lost for a few moments. She gazed away wistfully, and I couldn't imagine what memories of her country she was experiencing. What of her homeland now? And yet she'd never fallen into despair. How could I continue to feel so sorry for myself when I compared my life to hers? Lisen filled us in on developments with Gunter, which were slowgoing at best. But she'd been assured by the church that contact had been made.

When our tree was ready, the men plugged it in, and the tree exploded in brilliant lights of red, yellow, blue, green, and white.

Mary looked up and held completely still. I said to her, "Do you like the lights?"

And she said, "Petty," her version of *pretty*, a word I had recently taught her.

After the lights went on, we attached wire hangers to each ornament and all took turns hanging them. Alice held back at first but finally joined in. John took Mary and showed her how to hook an ornament onto a tree branch. She stared at it, enthralled. Then, while she was entranced by the big, new, colorful thing in our apartment, he passed her over to Alice, who had a peppermint stick ready for Mary to taste. Mary stayed in her arms, and a satisfied smile spread over Alice's face. She looked at John as if making sure he noticed. Mary soon wanted down, but she had stayed in Alice's arms almost as long as she would've stayed in mine. She had.

She toddled toward me, and I said, "Tah-dah. It's done. Our tree is finished."

John said, "Do you like it, my little angel?"

Mary wanted to pat the tree and play with the breakable ornaments and lights. I was going to have to keep her in my sight every single moment. But I was so pleased with the results that I couldn't complain. Finally something gave me a moment of happiness. This was the first Christmas that Mary was old enough to appreciate the decorations. Alice, seemingly content that she had shared a few minutes with her daughter, perched herself on the edge of the sofa and crossed her legs at the ankles. She said, "Last Christmas, in LA, after I got some photo gigs, I figured out what I really wanted to do was sing. My real talent is in my voice. I sang at the Creole Palace in Little Tokyo last Christmas. It's a breakfast club, stays open all night. I opened for Helen O'Connell."

As she looked around for a response, my thoughts rumbled deep and heavy. We were all painfully aware that while Alice was out singing in clubs in LA, waitressing and doing the occasional photo shoot, her daughter was here being cared for by others, and her husband was in a POW camp.

Lisen, ever gracious, said, "My, you must to be much talented."

"Music made me well," Alice said. "Being on stage, it's a feeling you wouldn't understand unless you've done it. The lights, the applause, the energy in those places. It showed me there were still good things in the world. The LA City Council has been trying to shut them down, to make them close by midnight. They want to stop all the fun."

She looked around as if for approval, but there was a weird blindness in her stare. I saw Alice then as a lost person who would always be stretching beyond her grasp, even while wonderful things were hers for the taking. She would always seek and never find. But now that John was a part of her picture, perhaps he could teach her how to be happy with what she had.

Over dinner, Alice went on about her life in LA while the others listened patiently, quietly, but awkwardly, and all the while my hands gripped and ungripped my skirt.

She ended her stories by saying, "I'm hoping to find a place to sing in Ohio."

Ohio. Something frightening was going on inside me, and it wasn't caused just by how oblivious Alice could be. Instead, I felt something close to terror stewing beneath the surface. I did the mental math and realized that I had only a week or two left with Mary. I dug my fingernails into my palms so deeply I feared I would draw blood. Each moment was the equivalent of the ticking down of a time bomb. Each one of these moments took Alice closer to John, both of them closer to Mary, and Mary and John one step farther away from me.

My time was running out.

When Mary got fussy, Alice first moved toward her and then thought better of it. I saw her insecurity take hold again, and she hesitated, then drew back. She must have felt she had done enough for one day. Instead, John got Mary ready for bed, including combing her hair.

When she sat still for him and he worked the comb just as carefully as I always did, maybe even more so, never once hurting her, I saw that she trusted him enough to let him do it. She would go with him now, and it would be all right for her. I wanted to tell him that.

But after he'd put her down for the night, John looked at his watch. "We have to be going," he said. He slipped back into his suit coat. Alice stood ready, by the door.

I'd had no idea they would be leaving so soon, and disappointment coursed through me. Of course they wanted time alone, but I felt empty, as if I'd been scooped out by a backhoe. John gulped down the rest of his cider, which I was sure had gone cold, and took his mug to the kitchen.

I said quietly, "You don't have to do that."

Geoff and Lisen were observing me, and so I wiped whatever was showing there off my face.

He put the mug away anyway and then came back. He shook Geoff's hand and thanked him for his help.

Alice said, "Thanks for having us," to Lisen and Geoff, although it was my apartment. John thanked us for dinner and then touched my arm. "It was a great day," he said and then began to shrug into his overcoat.

"Don't forget your portrait." I located the artist's tube amid the mess we'd made and handed it to him.

He said, looking down at it, "The best Christmas present ever."

"Wait a minute; what am I thinking?" I tried to pull it back from him, but he resisted. "I want to wrap this up for you."

"You do?" He had a mischievous look in his eyes.

I reached out to take back the tube, but he held it out beyond my reach. His eyes were smiling, dancing with the multicolored lights in the room, and for a moment, it was just like before. That magical connection between John and me shined on brightly, even with Alice in the room, even despite losing what we'd had.

"I'm serious," I said and tried not to smile. "I want to wrap it with Mary's help and put it under the tree for you."

"You can't have it back."

I reached around behind him, but again he switched hands and held it out of my reach. I lunged for the tube again, laughing, but he held it up high in the air now, too high for me. Alice stood without moving, grasping her clutch bag.

I tried jumping, and John laughed.

Finally, I put my hands on my hips. "I thought you were older than ten."

He laughed and gave the tube back to me.

I glanced over my shoulder at the clutter left behind after the tree trimming, and John suddenly looked uneasy about leaving us with all the cleanup.

"Don't worry. We'll handle it."

Lisen and Geoff cleaned up the tree-trimming debris while I focused on the kitchen. All day I'd worked hard to hold back waves of anger and pain and all the things I'd wished to say. I was preoccupied. I ran the dishwater too hot and scalded the fingers of my right hand. Quickly I held them under cold water as my eyes ranged over the mess around me. Tears nearly blinded me, and I groped for the countertop, looking for something substantial to hold on to. In my anger and desperation, I sent everything falling to the floor. Shattering cake plates and cider mugs made no sound for a long moment, and then I heard the crash and looked down at what I had done. Lisen and Geoff stood stock still.

Lisen finally said, "I vill clean."

CHAPTER THIRTY

As the ticking-bomb sensation that dominated my life continued, I kept myself busy while Christmas approached. I spent as much time with Mary as I could, and when I was with her, I managed to live in the present moment for stretches of time. I dressed her in Christmas clothes and had photos taken. I started thinking about a menu for Christmas Day. I let Mary "help" me bake gingerbread cookies and put up even more holiday decor around the apartment.

One day I received a long letter from Dot.

> *Dear Gwen,*
> *Greetings from the middle of nowhere! I wish I could tell you that I'm adjusting beautifully, but this house! It always seems dark and filled with dust motes. The air smells of cooking grease and some kind of meat—pork, I think. The floorboards creak. Dennis's grandfather built this place with thick walls and small, high windows in an effort to conserve heat in the winter. At least it has indoor plumbing and electricity, better than some farmhouses in the area.*

When we arrived, Dennis and I moved into the spare room, where Dennis and his brother, Joey, slept and shared everything while they were growing up. When I first looked at it, I tried not to feel despair. The room was filled with boys' things like a shrine to childhood. There were baseballs, playing cards, and model airplanes, puzzles, a few books, and twin beds. Covering the beds were spreads in a dull plaid pattern of greens and browns. Believe it or not, it still retained a teenage boy smell of sweaty socks, wet towels, and leather balls. Nothing about the room suited me, so at first I resisted unpacking and settling in. But I told myself that Dennis had been away since March of 1942, and it was only natural he'd want to come back to regain his strength—both physical and mental—in his childhood home. At least he agreed to let me put away all the "boy" things.

Dennis sleeps across from me in one of the twin beds. Only a wall separates our room from his parents'. Plenty of couples have made do with less privacy than this, but it seems that our beds will be almost exclusively used for sleeping. Dennis has lost interest in me again. He goes into the bathroom to change into pajamas at night. I have to believe he'll get better.

But he still comes to bed every night with the smell of whiskey, bittersweet, on his breath. And he's losing weight. He's getting rail thin, the skin loose on his big bones, and he almost has the look of an invalid. Most people treat him that way, too.

My new mother-in-law, Myrtle, has reddened hands and skin tracked with lines, and not much use for me. She runs the Meade household like a horsewoman cracking a whip. In between cooking, baking, and skimming butterfat, she looks after a garden, the chickens, and the milk cow, too. We still have an icebox instead of a refrigerator. We keep chickens so we don't have to buy eggs. Myrtle milks the cow, but I won't. To be fair, I do the dishes alone after dinner in what I'm beginning to think of as "the scullery."

I try to help, but I seem to be more of a hindrance than anything else. Never once does Myrtle raise her voice in protest of even the most menial chore required of her, because as she told me once, her life is "better than most." Her other son, Joey, has yet to return from the war zone, and of course she has one son back under her roof. They both survived, both of her sons, and that alone sustains her. Myrtle is just a simple woman. I should have more sympathy for her.

My father-in-law, Magnus, is a large, blond man, an older version of Dennis. But he's good-hearted with the temperament of a teddy bear and in better health than his son. The only annoying thing about him is his disorganization. He has a habit of gathering together letters and papers into piles that he lets sit forever. And he misplaces things. He often has to conduct little hunts around the house to find lost ledger books and letters. He won't ask for my help, but I often join in the search anyway. When eventually we find a displaced page or book, he always smiles, gives off a short laugh to himself, and handles the paper as if he's come upon an unexpected present. That simple joy lasts him the whole day through.

I offered to help with the farm's paperwork, and he was all too relieved to relinquish some of it. His son, after all, displays no interest whatsoever. Dennis won't do any work. He can't drive our car, because most of the time he's too intoxicated, and he can't work on the farm for the same reason.

Listen to this: I was standing on the porch, looking out to nothing during another long, tiresome evening, following a flock of birds that crossed the farm, the most exciting thing that had happened all day, when Myrtle came and stood next to me. She commenced to look out to nothing, too, her hands loosely hinged on her hips. Finally, she gave a short nod and exhaled. "Give him some time," she said.

I said, "That's exactly what I have been doing. I have been giving him time. I have been waiting. It's already been months."

"Well," Myrtle said, not moving. "That's not so long, you know."

"I'm twenty-seven years old. Months last forever."

Myrtle cleared her throat and said in a low tone, "I don't think any of us women can possibly understand what war is like."

I turned back to my mother-in-law, this dense woman. Gwen, you and I understand war better than most who'd never seen it firsthand, because we've seen the aftereffects in the hospital, the ruination it can cause, but I also know of men who lost both legs in battle and are adjusting to it, doing better than Dennis is.

I tried not to sound shrill when I asked, "What are you saying? That Dennis is entitled to do anything he damn well pleases?"

Myrtle said, "I'd prefer it if you didn't curse in this house."

I have kept my mouth shut since then.

I try to enjoy the simplicity of my days: sky, wind, and clouds. But when Dennis finally gets up and moves around the house, I can't help following him with my eyes. Sometimes he walks outside, out past the barn, out into the fallow fields, out into the mists that live along the edges of forest and swamps surrounding us. He lumbers into that gray and vanishes into his own miserable world.

The other day I drove into Charleston and applied for nursing posts. I haven't heard back yet. Pray for me. I have to find a way to spend some time away from here.

Please pardon this long list of complaints.

How are things with you, dear friend?

I look forward to hearing from you, and please let your news be better than mine.

Much love,

Dot

Nothing about that letter made me feel better. It became clear to me then: It didn't matter where Dennis lived. He was sinking and taking everyone around him to the bottom of the sea.

CHAPTER THIRTY-ONE

The magic of Christmas was lost on me. While most everyone around me walked and worked with a little more energy, a little more joy, and extra springs in their steps, I was gunned down. I dreaded Christmas Day, because once that was over, nothing held John, Alice, and Mary here any longer.

Lisen kept Mary while I went out for some errands on Christmas Eve. Even out on the street, I felt flighty, unsure of myself. Christmas Eve was festive in the city. Christmas Eves at home had been quiet, but here restaurants and bars were full, mainly with soldiers and singles, and the carolers were still out, moving about in Victorian-era outfits. Lights twinkled in windows. I tucked my chin into my coat collar against the evening wind and walked briskly toward home, wanting only to pick up Mary and spend the evening with her, alone. I'd never thought it took two to tango through this life, but now I felt so much smaller without love, without John in my life. How would I feel without Mary, too? Would I become invisible?

When Lisen answered the door, she said, "John come for her."

My face must have fallen to the floor. "He did?"

"He leave a note for you."

For a moment, it felt as though my lungs had collapsed. Maybe he had taken Mary for good. But I opened his note and read:

> *Dear Gwen,*
> *I've taken Mary out for the evening. We want to take her*
> *to see Santa Claus. I hope you understand.*
> *I'll have her back after dinner.*
> *John*

"You have plans?" Lisen asked me.

I shook my head.

"You stay, eat with us," said Lisen.

I shook my head again. "I don't want to intrude."

"It Christmas Eve. No one should be alone, Christmas Eve. I make sausages and *Thomasplitzchen*. Tastes very good. You smell it?"

"Yes," I smiled at her. "I'll go downstairs and change. Should I go out and bring something back? Bread? Wine?"

She declined all my offers, and so I went down to get ready. But when I entered my apartment, a wave of panic washed over me, a sense of so many things to do but nothing to do. I had no idea how to behave in my apartment without Mary. My heart was racing, and my pulse throbbed in my neck. I ran tap water into a glass and sat down on the edge of the sofa with it in both hands. I leaned forward and placed the cool glass against my forehead, willing my breaths to slow. I felt like the deer that had once leapt across the highway in front of my father's truck. He slammed on the brakes but struck the poor thing, a doe, anyway. Animals were supposed to have strong instincts, but something had failed that sturdy, brown-eyed lady.

Music drifted up from the streets along with the voices of people celebrating.

I cleaned up, changed, and returned for dinner. Lisen had framed the photo of her brother and had placed it on her coffee table in the living room. I picked it up and studied the face within. Deep eyes, dense hair, broad forehead, solemn expression. There were lines across his forehead that I imagined had been etched there by the ragged blade of a life lived in death and darkness. And yet the eyes showed no fear. I found I wanted to know all of it—how he'd survived, how he'd escaped, how he'd endured, and how he'd gone on without his family. I was fascinated by the idea of endurance.

Lisen had been in the kitchen, but she caught me staring at Gunter's photo. She stood in the doorway with a dishrag in her hands. "You think he is handsome?"

I glanced up at her and then looked back at the photo. I said, "Yes. I do."

"You and he have lot in common. You have to say good-bye to your farm and now Mary. He has to say good-bye to homeland."

"Yes." I set the framed photo back in its place.

"But he is not sad. He vill not be sad. He vill be ready to go have some gud fun."

I smiled at her.

She continued, "And you vill not be so sad forever."

Later, Lisen told us that on Christmas Eve in Germany, the rivers turn to wine, animals speak to each other, tree blossoms bear fruit, mountains open up to reveal gems, and church bells ring from the bottom of the sea.

Geoff said, "But only the pure of heart can witness such wonders. The rest of us must be content with lots of eating and celebrating."

Throughout the evening, I had a hard time concentrating on anything but the conversation going on inside my head. John and Alice had Mary with them, and there was nothing that said they had to bring her back. I had no claim on her. But John was not a cruel man. He wouldn't take her without a good-bye. Still, I didn't eat much when we sat down at the table.

Lisen said I must. In Germany Christmas Eve is called *Dickbauch*, meaning "fat stomach," and she warned me that those who did not eat well on Christmas Eve would be haunted by demons during the night.

Demons, indeed.

John brought Mary back while I was still upstairs at Lisen's. Alice was waiting in the taxi. Mary was asleep on his shoulder, on his nice black suit, his lovely hands holding her close to him, and I asked him to carry her downstairs to my apartment since she was already sleeping.

But she woke up, cranky and overtired. For the first time, John saw one of her temper tantrums. She started screaming when I tried to put her down. She yelled, "No," one of her new favorite words, and she kicked the mattress. She rubbed her red eyes as they streamed tears. John seemed torn up by it all and stood by helplessly as I gave her a warm bottle, rocked her, and sang to her to calm her down. He watched me the entire time. Unlike Alice, here was a parent who couldn't leave until his child had stopped crying.

I awakened Christmas morning when the slow bloom of dawn was beginning to replace the darkness. My body trembled and smarted. Mary's absence the night before had brought down reality on me like a hammer. I didn't think I could move, much less get up and pretend to be happy on this holiday. But I had to do just that. Mary was old enough now to enjoy Christmas, and I wouldn't do anything that might make this precious Christmas together any less wonderful.

In the shadow of our Christmas tree, I fed Mary her breakfast but was unable to eat mine. I'd had to distract her since she had awakened, because she wanted to tear into the wrapped presents from her father and me that were under the tree. She also had gifts from Lisen and Geoff and one from Dot. I was delaying the opening of Mary's presents until John and Alice could arrive and enjoy the experience with us, but I had already opened my presents. My mother sent me jars of her jam and preserves and an old pair of Navajo turquoise earrings she'd found in a shop in Alamosa. That was my mother, always reminding me of where I'd come from.

Around midmorning, Mary was down for her morning nap when someone knocked on the door. I opened the door to find John, by himself, wearing an enormous smile on his face, his eyes sparkling. Something had happened, and although his smile practically shouted that it was a good thing, a fishhook lodged inside my chest as I waited for him to speak.

"Alice has left again."

I almost laughed. But the joy on his face made me stop. This was not what I had expected, and it did not give me the same elation that John was obviously feeling. Instead, I had a strange feeling of something that was lost drifting even farther away.

He came toward me and tried to take me in his arms, but I held him off. "Why this time?"

His elation bled away. How had he expected me to react? Apparently not like this. "I don't think motherhood suits her."

I did laugh a little bit then, God help me. "You can say that again. No doubt it's not as glamorous as Hollywood."

He just stood there looking at me.

"What happened?"

"She can't handle being a parent. Once I thought that all women were maternal at heart, but she isn't. She never thought she was all that suited to motherhood, but she tried it as a way to keep me. But I guess

I wasn't enough. She loved the idea of being with me more than actually being with me. I suppose having to be a parent in order to keep me was too much. At least she realized it for herself."

"Are you going after her?"

He looked surprised by my question. "No. We're divorced, remember?"

"You could've fooled me."

He sighed heavily. "I understand how you feel, Gwen."

"I'm not sure you do."

He looked stricken. "I understand you thought I was a fool to even give it a try, but I did it because of Mary. I even tried to fall back in love with Alice, but I couldn't."

That feeling of having lost everything became even more acute. It had been thrown away for nothing. Perhaps if Alice, John, and Mary had been able to become a little family, there could have been a good outcome for Mary at least.

"You made the best decision you could at the time, I suppose. But you did make your decision."

"I had little choice."

"You did have a choice. You made it when it was difficult. Now it's easy to come back to me. I'm not anyone's second choice. I'm not that easy."

He took hold of my shoulders and, in a pleading tone, said, "You were never my second choice." His eyes landed on me like soft rain. "Falling in love with you was easy, but that's the only thing about you that's easy."

I stood at a loss. Then I realized something profound. I *could* forgive John for making an impossible decision. Indeed, he had been trapped.

But I took a step back. "You say that Alice was unable to be a mother, but was she able to be your wife?"

A flash of fear in his eyes. "What are you asking?"

"You know exactly what I'm asking."

He looked away. "Gwen . . . I was trying to make it work . . ."

Images of them together came into focus in the front of my mind, almost blocking my vision. His lips on hers, their bodies intertwined, the same bodies that had made Mary. And then my love-soaked night with him. Had it meant anything to him? Tears were streaming down my face, and I swiped at them.

I eked out, "So it seems."

He came toward me, but I stepped away.

"Do you have any idea how that feels to me? I thought you were mine. For a short time, yes, but I still felt you were mine . . . and it was going to be forever."

"I'm so sorry."

I pulled in a long, ragged breath and willed myself to stop. I raked my hands through my hair and then pressed my fingers against my cheeks. John and Alice had already been man and wife before. And any recent encounters were now in the past. Images that might haunt me now would gradually fade. I could eventually get over it. So, truth be told, I could also forgive what they'd done together.

But one enormous problem remained, one that seized me with claws. I would be putting myself at risk of being cast away again. It could happen over and over. Each time Alice got lonely, she could come back and try another time. John would be in the same trap as before. Alice had too much of an advantage over him. There was no guarantee that John wouldn't compromise his own happiness, and therefore mine, to be with her again, so as not to lose Mary. As before, she held the upper hand with custody. The mother always did. Yes, Alice had left Mary twice, but if she wanted her daughter back in the future, she could claim wartime stress, the agony over John's relationship with me, depression, or all sorts of other reasons. A judge could believe her and favor her.

Once I'd believed in happily ever after with John, but I couldn't believe in it for a second time. Not with this obstacle forever looming.

"She could come back, John. How could a person live happily knowing that was possible? I couldn't go through this torment again."

He stuffed his hands into his pockets. "I'm stunned. I thought you'd be so happy. I was so happy . . ."

I stood still. "What will you do now?"

"I still want to leave the city, but I want you to come with me."

Those words about leaving were like a cold clasp around my heart. I ignored the part about him casually stating that he wanted me to go with him. "Why do you have to leave the city? You can take care of her here. You can make a life here."

"Did you hear me? I said I want you. I love you. Gwen, please forgive me. Give me another chance."

"It's too late," I said and fought to swallow. A choking sensation, not breathing well. My voice was determined but shaky. "You have no idea what these few weeks have done to me."

"Tell me then. Heap it all on me. I can take it."

"You don't know how I feel . . . I can get past everything else, but I can't live wondering when she's going to show up again."

"She's gone. It's over."

"You said that before."

"Alice could see for herself that it wasn't going to work. She doesn't want to be a mother, and she doesn't really want me, because I *do* want to be a father. She's off to Hollywood again, I guess. We didn't remarry. I'm free."

I had to push the hair away from my face. My forehead was sprouting beads of perspiration. "I'm supposed to be happy she left you again? Her singing career will falter, and then she'll come back. I can't live like that. I'd always be dreading her reappearance."

I imagined being with John after this, and every time a strange car pulled up or the phone rang at an odd time, I'd be trembling, thinking it was Alice. Or one day a letter would come from an attorney informing us that Alice was suing for custody. And could I say with absolute certainty what John would do? No, I couldn't. He'd given me up once; maybe he'd do it again. It would be a life filled with fear.

John said, "I hear what you're saying. But I won't let it happen again."

I sucked in a deep breath and wished—oh, how I wished—that I could believe him completely. How wonderful it would be if we could go forward into the future together. But John was tied to Alice for life because of Mary. It killed me to think of how vulnerable he was to her future whims. Alice would always be like a storm gathering just beyond the horizon, and we'd be sitting ducks waiting for it to roll in and land.

John's gaze was still colored with expectation and hope, and blasting him down was crushing me as much as it was going to crush him. This agony had to end. I had to give up on the idea of reconciliation—the situation was too perilous—and John needed to give up on us, too. I met his gaze firmly. "I can't do it again. I just can't. I'm sorry."

He looked as though I'd hit him.

Mary had crawled out of bed. She toddled into the living room and demanded attention. She reached out to John. She said something I didn't catch, and then she said it again, more clearly, "Dada."

John's face melted as he took her into his arms and held her with closed eyes.

She pulled back and patted his face. She said again, for the second time, "Dada."

Now I had to rein in tears again.

This was what we had been working toward, what we had hoped for and waited for. Mary was completely at ease with her father now, entrenched with him, and entranced, too. John and I had done what we had originally planned. He had given his daughter the time to get to know and trust him. And clearly she did trust him. This was it. We had succeeded with one thing.

I started to gather Mary's Christmas packages together so she could begin to open them, while John held Mary and watched me. Finally he breathed out, "I'm sorry."

We had ruined Christmas Day. Alice had ruined Christmas Day. Just as she could ruin any day she chose to in the future.

"I'm sorry," he said again, softer this time. "I see that it's over. I shouldn't have even asked you to forgive me. You have every right not to trust me . . . and to go on protecting yourself. You do that so well."

"What?" I asked.

He sighed. "Protect yourself. At all costs."

Obviously shaken, John walked out, leaving before Mary opened her presents.

I went through the motions of Christmas Day activities, even though I was unhinged by what had happened. I gave Lisen and Geoff the short version, and seeing how distressed I was, they helped me through the day with the presents, the food, and the cleanup. We made the day as special as possible for Mary, and she fell into a deep sleep as soon as Geoff and Lisen left.

Alone, I stood looking out my window in my quiet apartment—I had even turned off the Christmas music that was playing on all the radio stations—when snow began to fall. It seemed that the end of 1945 would not only usher in a new year without war, but also bless us with a white Christmas. Then there was a break in the snow that left room for the wind to kick up and wail. Tiny chips of snow and ice flew everywhere like fragments of something freshly broken. Some of the flakes clung to the glass windows, despite the wind howling out there, and they mesmerized me with their ability to hold on. Endurance, again.

I had done what was necessary. It was the right thing to let John go.

But without Mary, what would I do with all this love I had inside? I had even started thinking about adoption. The newspapers were filled with stories about untold numbers of orphans languishing overseas, and President Truman had issued his "Statement and Directive on Displaced Persons," which said that everything possible should be done to facilitate entrance into the United States for orphans and other refugees in Europe. Could it help Gunter? The United States Committee for the Care of European Children had been set up to expedite adoptions, and, under these dire circumstances, would a single woman be allowed to adopt? I had no idea if it would help ease the pain of losing Mary, but regardless, I wanted to be a mother, and I knew I could love a child who wasn't my own flesh and blood.

Then, an unexpected pang of longing for home. For *my* mother. How had she felt when I'd been determined to leave the farm? And how had my sister been able to endure life there when I hadn't? How had Betty managed after I'd left? To whom had she turned? I'd kept thoughts of my family at bay for so long. How could I have explained Mary? But now, all the emotions surrounding my family came flooding back.

Just the day before I'd received a Christmas card and letter from them, and as I picked up the card and looked at the signatures—my mother, father, brothers, and sister had all taken the time to individually sign their names—homesickness struck me like a blow to the gut. I missed them all. Now I knew what it was to say good-bye to one's child. I even missed the farm. It had been dreary but solid.

I reread the letter, all the while my heart quaked. Mom wrote that Betty would be marrying the nearby town's young minister in August. A summer wedding. My baby sister was really getting married. As I pictured her a bride, a sob convulsed me, brought on by the tug of that earthly place and those people who'd known me for so long.

It had been too long since my last visit, so I thought of traveling back for Betty's wedding. By summer Mary would be long gone. I'd once imagined going on a vacation to the shore; instead, maybe I'd simply go home.

I pulled out paper and pen and wrote, "Dear Mom," on the top of the page. And then I wrote all of it—how I felt about Mary, John, his proposal, my foolishness, Alice's return, and John's plans to go. All of it, including the parts that were mine to own.

CHAPTER THIRTY-TWO

The time between Christmas and New Year's passed quickly, and my life tripped and fell into a dungeon of dread. John had called me the morning after Christmas to inform me that he would be taking Mary on New Year's Eve. They would travel by train to Ohio. After that, each day felt shorter than the one before it. I worked long shifts, came straight home, and then spent my evenings holding and playing with Mary, wanting to elongate the time I had with her. But time, of course, did not wait for me.

On New Year's Eve morning, I awoke to the horrible knowledge that this was it: my last day with her. How could a mother go through a year of loving a child and then just hand her over? How could I bear not to see her face first thing in the morning and witness all her daily advances? And yet, that was exactly what I had to do. I forced myself to pack Mary's things for the second time, all the while asking the air how John could do it. How could he take her away? First he broke my heart, and now he was taking my girl.

I filled Mary's suitcase with all her newest and most necessary things, having promised to send the rest in boxes to John at his sister's address in Ohio. In the bottom of her drawers I found a few of the tiniest things she'd worn as a newborn, things I'd planned to hold on to to remind me of how small she had been. I placed those in the suitcase, too, for John. He'd never seen her when she was tiny. Slowly as I worked, the exhaustion and fear that had enveloped me lifted. I had another one of those premonitions, a sense that something unexpected would happen today. My hands trembled as I packed. I kept a few playthings and shirts to remind me of Mary, but how long would it be before these things could no longer hold her scent?

I opened the door to John, and his face was more vivid, more intense than any scenery I'd ever seen. I would carry it with me forever.

Soon I saw what the unexpected thing about this day would be.

Something in him had changed, and it was clear he was at peace. I could see it in his movements, so smooth and easy. It was clear he had done what he needed to do in this city and had already moved on in his mind. He reminded me of the way I must have looked when I was bound for Denver and then later again when I was bound for New York. John looked expectant, relaxed, and rested. Restored and excited, bound for something new. Gone was any look of desperation and sadness, even inside my apartment and its memories of us. He was talking and smiling and enjoying himself. He had come here to say his good-byes and then move on with his life.

Whatever there had been between us, he was over it. Something left the air then; something of heaven lifted off and flew away.

John said he had reserved a sleeper compartment on the late train and would put Mary down to bed with him in there for the night. I told him I had plans to go to Times Square with Lisen and Geoff and watch the ball come down. I had no intention of spending the evening alone.

Mary was edgy. It was as if she *knew*. As if she knew what I would not yet admit to myself. That I would probably never see her again.

John seemed to be taking everything in stride, and I guess knowing you're embarking on the beginning of a new life with your daughter might do that to you. In only half a day, it would be 1946, a completely new year of freedom and the beginning of his life as an everyday father.

He said, "I'm leaving you my travel plans and my sister's address, of course." He reached into his coat that he'd hung on the back of the chair, and he handed me a piece of folded paper. I glanced at it and set it aside.

There was nothing left to say. For a few moments even Mary held still, and I could feel her eyes on me and then sense her turning to John as though waiting for something. The silence in the room became a huge screaming thing that demanded to be answered.

John finally cleared his throat. "Do you want some time alone with her?"

The moment I'd been dreading ever since I first saw John had arrived, and there was a sense of the surreal, as if I was drifting in some kind of horrible hallucination. The sensation of *the end* washed across my brain, and I felt on the verge of fainting. But I inhaled deeply and nodded. "Only a moment. I don't want her to know what's happening."

"As you wish."

Before I stood up and took her, I said, "Do you think she'll remember me?"

He looked at me sadly.

I said, "I don't remember a thing before I was about three years old, and she's only half that age. Do you remember being an infant?"

"No," he said softly. "I don't."

I looked away.

"She might not remember the specifics," John said, bringing me back. "But I'm sure she'll remember you. She'll remember the love. Experts say infants who don't get love will die. That could've happened to her had it not been for you." He paused. "You know there is no way I can ever thank you . . ."

I shook my head. I couldn't hear any more of this.

He said, "You can always come to see her. You'll be welcome any time."

I listened without listening.

"Do you think you'll visit?"

I finally answered. "I don't know. I just don't know right now."

"I understand," he said. "Take your time. I'm sure the right decision will come to you."

I rose from the table, lifted Mary from the high chair, and took her to the bathroom. I washed her face and hands and then just stood there in the quiet and held her against me. She clung to me and kept perfectly still, so quiet I could hear both of us breathing. Her body was soft and pliable, and her beautiful eyes were wide open but still. Relaxed, finally, as though she had accepted this thing.

I was determined not to drag this out. I could not say good-bye. Instead I held her against me, took a deep breath, kissed her quickly, and then took her back into the living room, where John was waiting and holding her suitcase in one hand. I put her into his other arm and let her go.

She did not resist.

She was completely at ease with John now. There was no fear or panic, even though I was sure Mary knew on some level what was happening. She was only going from one person who loved and knew her to another. This was nothing like the parting that had almost taken place four months ago with John's sister. I tried to take it that way: as success. Mary was going with her father, as it should be.

During my last moments with her, she leaned her head against John's shoulder and stared at me.

I said, "Night, night," instead of good-bye.

She said a soft, "Night, night," back.

All along it had felt unreal. I had secretly expected something to happen. I had hoped that in the end, John wouldn't have the strength to take Mary away from the only mother she had ever known. I couldn't understand his determination to leave the city. He seemed to have more strength than I'd given him credit for. How well he had done, despite what had befallen him.

A long moment of silence, and then I looked up, forced a smile, and said, "If you're ever in New York . . ." I laughed pathetically.

He gave a pained smile and said, "If you're ever in Ohio . . ." And then he dropped Mary's suitcase and drew me in, next to him, next to Mary. "Thank you, Gwen," he whispered. "You'll never know . . ." Then he released me quickly and turned away.

I opened the door and didn't look as they left. It was the only way to make it through. The door shut, and my heart broke freshly into a thousand little pieces.

CHAPTER THIRTY-THREE

I walked all afternoon. Hordes of people were out on the streets, but for happy reasons. I worked my way around all the merriment and kept forging on, because I couldn't bear the idea of being in my empty apartment. I walked past brimming restaurants and bars, parties in the streets, and couples kissing. Everyone else seemed so happy and full of anticipation about the year ahead, but I could not face my life without Mary.

After night descended, Lisen, Geoff, and I joined the throng moving toward Times Square. As we strolled along, once or twice I thought someone was calling my name. I thought I heard footsteps behind me that could only be John's. But every time I turned around to look, he and Mary were not there. So I pushed on, one step behind Lisen and Geoff.

This was my new life.

People were already celebrating, but the rallying felt oppressive to me, as if a black storm were gathering. Geoff and Lisen had dressed up for the occasion; however, I had not changed my clothes all day. Underneath my coat, this sweater and these slacks—they would always be what I was wearing the last time he held me, the last time I hugged Mary close to me, and I never wanted to remove them.

We found a spot in Times Square amid the laughter, confetti, paper horns and other noisemakers, glitter and sparkle, beer and cigarettes. The lights glared down on us while the sounds of big band music boomed over voices and horns. My mind traveled back to the moment the sailor bent me back and kissed me, very near here, on V-J Day. It had been such a glorious time of jubilation. Back then, I had still believed in happy endings. Would I ever feel that way again?

The waiting began to feel tedious and even dreary. It was as though we were a mob of people having a rousing party inside a jail cell. And John and Mary were leaving soon on the late train; they were no longer a part of this city.

The air was warmed by the masses of people and the frosty clouds of air we exhaled. But the chill was biting. I pulled my coat in tighter about my neck and buttoned the top button.

"Vhat is wrong? Not so cold tonight," Lisen said.

Geoff agreed. "Couldn't be better."

So it was only me. I was cold inside, and I needed to do something to wipe away that last look at them. Mary saying, "Night, night," and John saying, "You'll never know . . ."

I looked at my watch. It was only 10:45.

"Did you see John today?" I finally asked Lisen.

Her eyes were dewy. "Yes, he bring me flowers, again. That man, always bring me flowers."

No one spoke for a few long moments. Then Lisen said, "Ve had hoped he does not leave."

I looked away. "Me, too."

Geoff shifted his weight from one foot to the other. "He left something with me. Something for you."

"What?"

He reached into his pocket and opened his gloved hand. The sight of John's hummingbird took my breath away.

I took it and brought it to my chest. I closed my eyes, and a knife of regret entered my chest so intensely it felt like a deep twisted wound. What had I done?

My eyes flew open, and I looked at my watch. John, Mary. *Don't go.*

I couldn't explain myself to Lisen and Geoff. I said only, "I have to go," and, clutching the hummingbird, quickly turned and started pushing through the mass of people, back the same way we had come. I had to get back to the apartment to look at the piece of paper detailing John's travel plans. I made my body as lithe as possible, and all the while my heart began to trill with possibility. As soon as I broke free of the mob, I started running across town to my apartment, and a sudden upsurge of hope and faith made me almost weightless. I was a young girl again weaving through the cornfields. I was a teenager draping her fingers over moving water and dreaming of seeing the world. I was back in that place before innocence was lost, when the dreams I'd shared with Betty could still come true. I was also the nurse a sailor kissed on V-J Day, on a crazy day full of joy, innocence, and optimism. And I was the woman who galloped on a horse, danced wildly to a fast jitterbug, and loved John, no matter what.

I had to stop them. *Stop this. Please.*

I rounded the corner to head down my street, and I had to dodge a group of four or five sailors and their girls headed in the opposite direction. Through them I saw the back of a woman down at the far end of my block. The woman looked like Dot. That was curious. The way she walked, her hair color, her coat—it looked like Dot's green coat.

One of the sailors blocked my view. I said, "Excuse me," and nudged past him.

The woman turned the far corner at the end of my block and left my sight. I paused for a moment. But it was crazy to think I'd seen Dot.

She was in South Carolina with Dennis. If she'd made plans to come here, she would've written me.

I ran up the stairs to my apartment, turned the key in the lock, and clicked on the light. I rushed into the kitchen toward the drawer that held the piece of paper John had given me. But something else caught my eye.

On the kitchen counter, a folded note.

> *Dear Gwen,*
> *I came to find you. I've left Dennis. I'm pregnant. I'm*
> *desperate. I don't know what to do. I thought I would*
> *find you here.*
> *Dot*

Dot left Dennis and she was pregnant? I wasn't as stunned by Dot's leaving as I was by the pregnancy. A chill traveled up my spine and tightened my scalp. Dot never used words like *desperate* to describe herself. She had always been so strong. But she had lost much of that strength since Dennis. She had to be in terrible shape to do such a thing. *Desperate?* That word echoed in my brain.

Adrenaline rushed through my veins. This was not the Dot I knew. I couldn't imagine her leaving this note. Why did I doubt myself when I saw her down on the street? I should've followed her right then and there.

But I'd come here to find John's travel plans and stop him before he left.

My heart thumped and my head pounded. For a horrible moment, I walked a tightwire. Stop John and then look for Dot later, or race after her now?

I opened the drawer and pulled out John's travel plans, took a quick look, and stuffed the paper in my pocket. The train left in forty-five minutes, and the station was near enough. I could find Dot and still make it on time. I ran back down the stairs and outside to the corner where I'd last seen her. Even on the streets far from Times Square, lots of bundled-up people were out and about, and I had to peer past them and between them. No sign of her.

Where had she gone? Why hadn't Dot simply waited for me in the apartment? But of course this was New Year's Eve; she'd found the apartment empty, and she probably thought I'd be gone into the wee hours. I ran down the street, thinking that I could still catch up to her. But I had no idea if she had turned or where.

Nothing in any direction. Just lots of people preparing for the New Year, most of them heading toward Times Square. I was hoping her green coat would pop out of the crowd. For a moment or so, I stopped and stood still, thinking and trembling. The air was cold, but sweat gathered on my forehead. On Third Avenue was a neighborhood bar that Dot and I had ducked into from time to time. Maybe I would find her there.

I ran that way. As thoughts flashed, I became even more concerned about Dot. Could this note be her version of a suicide note? No, I couldn't think about that. I couldn't believe that. On the other hand, as a nurse I'd witnessed what despair could do to people. The deterioration of her marriage, Dennis's drinking, the move to South Carolina, and now a pregnancy—that was surely enough to bring even the toughest soul down.

I rounded the corner and swung open the door to the bar and entered the warm, stale air. The place was packed with revelers. Laughing and smiling people holding bottles of beer and flutes of champagne, their glee and carefree demeanor, together with the adrenaline surge, made me begin to feel panicky. There was a smell of fried food, beer, and overheated bodies. Or was it me? I worked my way around the bar, but she wasn't here. I had to think of something else.

I glanced at my watch. Now I had less than twenty-five minutes to reach John and Mary.

I stood at a loss, and the glances and stares of others let me know how desperate *I* must have looked. What was I to do? I had to head toward the station if I had any hope of stopping John and Mary. It was an impossible choice, like when two patients needed me at the same time. Nurses had to go to the one who was in the most dire need. I knew John and Mary were safe. Dot, however, could be lost and suicidal, and if I didn't find her now, maybe I'd never find her again.

For half a second, I saw John and Mary arriving at the train station on the back screen of my mind. *Please, let there be some kind of delay.* If I found Dot soon and assured myself that she was OK, maybe I could still get there in time.

Dot couldn't have gotten far yet, so I rushed toward the other bars and restaurants in the vicinity. Maybe Dot had gone for a late dinner and was simply passing the time before going back to the apartment. Maybe, maybe . . . but her note didn't say she was coming back to the apartment. She must have been crazy with anguish to leave me such a note and then disappear.

I entered one establishment after another. No sign of her.

This was taking too long! I glanced at my watch. I had no chance to make it to the station now, and the realization made my heart collapse and my legs turn liquid. I hadn't stopped John and Mary, and I hadn't found Dot. I could lose all of them. *No!* I couldn't lose all of them.

Oh, Dot, where are you? The word *desperate* kept ringing in my head. Another chilling thought occurred to me. Maybe Dot had come to the city to get an illegal abortion. As nurses, we knew there were underground places to do that. Not the specifics, but it wouldn't be hard to find out. Those illegal procedures were performed by God knows who. And they could end up botched and fatal.

Outside yet another establishment, I stood and tried to calm myself. People were already sitting on their horns and making noises that shook through me. It was 11:45. I'd left Times Square an hour ago and had seen Dot from the back only five or ten minutes after that. Now, she could be anywhere. How was I going to find one lone woman? I was stumped. Where would she have gone? Where would I go if I'd been away from the city and then had come back?

I ran toward the nearest station where I could catch a subway that could take me to the Village. Many of our favorite places were located there. On the steps leading down to the platform, I had to fight against a mass of people. Oh God. Another horde of them was squeezed together down below. I had to wait for one packed train to come and go, before I could get close and hope to board the next one.

The New Year arrived, and even down in this cavern, people celebrated and cheered. The sounds of horns, noisemakers, more cheering, and shouting made their way underground from the street above. I finally boarded the subway, and once in the Village I slowed my frantic pace. It was making me dizzy and breathless. It was much quieter here. Many of the coffee shops and cafés had shut down, but bars and late-night eateries were still open and lively. I checked in place after place, and another hour passed. I couldn't check them all; the area was too big.

I nearly collapsed on a bench in Washington Square Park.

In my mind, I saw John and Mary settled in their compartment. Free, starting a new life. The ground swam for a moment, but I had to get a grip. I still had to find Dot.

It was well after one in the morning now. Maybe Dot had returned to the apartment. I took another crowded subway ride and got off as close to home as possible. I walked sluggishly, spent, but with my heart still racing. Wild thoughts hit me. Was Dot really at risk of hurting herself? Could she have fallen so low? I could barely breathe. Anything was possible.

I hadn't done anything I needed to do on this night. I hadn't found Dot, and in my mind, I pictured the train John and Mary were on humming through the countryside outside the city. Mary would be tucked in for the night. John would have his hand on her back, and he would gaze out of the window into the night before he lay down next to her.

As I headed toward the apartment yet again, I had a thought. I had to try one more place. The bench in Central Park, where Dot and I had sat and discovered the photo of me in *Life* magazine. It was also the place where she'd told me about her dead sister. I picked up the pace: I dodged drunks, couples, and partygoers, stepped over trash, and ran to catch a cab. I was too tired to take another long walk. When I entered the park, I hurried toward the bench.

Sitting there, a figure hunched over and wearing a green coat.

"Dot!" I called.

She looked up. Her hair a mess, her face damp with tears, she was hardly recognizable. This was not my once strong and brave best friend. I ran to her and took her in my arms.

"You found me," she said through a sob. "How did you find me?"

I breathed out huge relief. "I just did."

She wept into my coat, then put her head on my shoulder, and I stroked her head. Tears poured from her clenched eyes. In between sobs she said, "Talk about bad luck. Dennis came out of his blues just long enough to get me pregnant." She opened her eyes, turned to look up at me, clenched my coat, and gazed at me pleadingly. Her nose was running, her face crimped. "But I can't keep this baby, Gwen, I can't. I can't bring a child into a family and a life like this one."

Never had I imagined her in such a state. I whispered, "It's going to be OK."

"I know of a home upstate, a home for unwed mothers. I could tell them I'm a single girl who got herself in trouble. But I have no idea if they'll have room for me. I have no idea how I'll live without my salary."

"It's OK," I breathed. She wasn't speaking of suicide or abortion; that was a relief. "All of this can be figured out."

"I have to get out of this marriage, and a baby will only make it more difficult. I don't think I even love Dennis anymore, and he certainly doesn't love me. It's a mess I've made."

She broke free of my embrace to blow her nose into a handkerchief. Then she leaned forward and put her head in her hands. Huge heaving sobs came out of her in waves that seemed they would never end. I rubbed her back and then simply kept my hand there, solid and still. She stopped long enough to swipe at her eyes with the back of her hands and mutter, "I don't know. I don't know . . . what to do."

"Dearest, you don't have to make a decision tonight. Just talk to me."

In between bouts of sobbing, Dot told me about the dreary house. She told me about the lack of conversation among Dennis's family members. She told me how stifled she had felt, and everything poured out of her, everything she'd had to keep contained in that family's presence.

When she wasn't crying, bless her heart, she inquired about me. "I've talked endlessly about myself. But I'm not the only one with problems. When are John and Alice leaving?"

It had been easier to listen to her. She had distracted me from my own misery. I told her that Alice had left again, and Dot wasn't surprised. I also told her that John left the city, that he had asked me to go with him, and I had refused.

"When did he leave?"

She need never know she had kept me from stopping them. "Earlier today," I lied.

"You love him. You should've gone with them. But what do I know? My life is in shambles. I'm the last person in the world to give anyone advice."

The hole in my chest tore open then. The only thing that wasn't clear to me was why. Why had forces conspired to bring John and me together for a while? Why hadn't I taken a chance and gone with him? It was splitting me apart to think of them gone. But if I'd left, I wouldn't have been here for Dot.

She cried until she was all cried out. At last, a calm came over her.

A cold wind began to sweep in, and even though we clung to each other, both of us were shivering.

Finally I said, "Let's go home."

CHAPTER THIRTY-FOUR

It was that velvet hour between the last dark of night and the first light of early morning, when the city held still catching its breath in preparation for a new day. Finally even the bars and nightclubs had shut down, and the outlines of everything were almost visible in the light of dawn. Buildings, streets and signs, trees and curbs appeared as though smudged by an artist's thumb on a chalk drawing, and moment by moment they became clearer. The streetlights changed for traffic that was not there, and steam rose silently from the manholes.

We turned onto my street, and I saw a taxi in front of my building and a man who looked like John. It stopped me in my tracks. Were my eyes playing a trick on me? Had lack of sleep caused me to be delusional? Was he a figment of my exhausted imagination, or an apparition? I had not felt his and Mary's presences here in the city any longer. I had felt them gone.

Dot squeezed my arm. "Look, it's John."

He stepped into the cab and shut the door, and I couldn't believe that once again, he was getting away. It felt like a cruel joke. I blinked hard to make myself believe it, and then I left Dot on the sidewalk and started running toward the cab—Mary was probably inside—but they started to pull away. It reminded me of the night I'd chased after the army officers. I hadn't caught them. How could this happen again?

I started to cry out, pitiful sounds unknown to me emerged from my throat, and I waved my arms as the taxi rolled away.

Then brake lights, and the cab pulled over.

I got to within a few steps of it when John stepped out of the cab. He looked just as he had when I'd first met him, only this time he wore the Chesterfield coat instead of a uniform. His face was a mess of concern, and yet he was so lovely. "Where have you been all night? And why is Dot here? I've been worried sick."

I had to lean over to catch my breath. "I thought you were on the train."

"Where have you been?"

I finally stood up straight. "I had to help Dot."

"What's wrong?"

"It's a long story. I'll tell you later."

"Are you all right? You look all shook up."

I searched his face. He looked like a man who hadn't slept. He looked like a man who had stayed up, having an intense conversation with himself all through the wee hours of the night. But what had that conversation been about? I finally stepped closer, glanced into the cab, and asked, "Where's Mary?"

He held both hands down in his coat pockets and breathed out frosty air. "Upstairs with Lisen. I was going for some coffee. When I found out you weren't at home and Lisen and Geoff hadn't seen you for hours, there was no way I was going to leave. We've been frantic."

The cab driver asked John if he was going or not, and John waved him off.

I shielded my face from the sun that had just crested over the buildings and sent rods of light down the city street. "Why didn't you leave last night?"

His soft, probing gaze fell on my skin and peered into my eyes. "That's a long story, too." His voice fell to little more than a whisper, and his eyebrows lowered with that intense look of his that always paralyzed me. "I couldn't get on that train. I just couldn't." He paused. "I don't know the end of this story. Our story."

I pulled in a deep breath and let it out.

He remained there, silent, epic, and strong.

"I couldn't go without seeing you one more time, asking you one more time. Give us a chance. If Alice ever comes back again, we'll fight her. We'll fight her together."

A new moment was born to step over the old one. And for the first time in my still-short life, the biggest blessing of all rained down. The earth tilted beneath my feet, not to the side but to the solid center, where I belonged.

"Gwen, what do you say?"

My focus came back on his face. He was waiting again, for me. Composed, standing tall. He was the most beautiful man in the world.

"Marry me. Stay here, and marry me," I said.

He waited for a moment and then said just above a whisper, "You have to forgive me all the way."

Tears welled in my eyes, and then with one blink, they fell down my face. If I had never moved to this apartment building, if I had never met Alice, if I had never loved Mary, my life would've been another life, and I would be another person. Some people believe that one decision changes a life forever. But I believe rather that it's a series of many decisions—some made by others, such as Alice, and others made on our own; some filled with risk and others seeming safe—and these taken together forge our paths.

He waited while I cried and didn't come to my aid. Finally, he said again in a soft voice, "You have to forgive me all the way. Tell me you can."

I took a step in his direction and then another. He moved his hands out of his pockets and opened his arms. I ran into that warm circle, and on that day, took what Alice had given away.

"Or show me," he breathed into my hair and neck. "That works, too."

EPILOGUE

We planned a small wedding ceremony at the courthouse. I wore a knee-length beige suit, and John wore his best black suit. Lisen stood for me and brought us flowers. Into the courthouse from high, polished windows poured sunlight so pure one wished to drink it. We dressed Mary in white, and John held her throughout the ceremony, so it was as if I married them both.

Since that day, I have learned that some things cannot be repaired, as in Dot and Dennis's marriage. After spending a few days in the city, she went to the home for unwed mothers. Months later, she moved back to New York City and sublet another apartment in our old building and shared it with another roommate. She filed for divorce. Lisen and Geoff were still there, and Gunter finally made it to the United States, sooner than most. He and Dot became fast friends. I never asked Dot exactly what happened at the home, but I could only assume that Dot signed away her rights and when the baby was born he or she was adopted.

I also learned that the same ache for Colorado that rose out of my body from time to time affected John, too. I started writing letters home every few days, and when my family finally got a phone, I called once a week. In August, we traveled to Colorado by train, where we stayed with John's parents first for a week and then went to the farm I'd once called home in time for Betty's wedding.

We went back home, together, as husband and wife.

John and I still weren't sure how we would make a life for ourselves and Mary and our future children. We didn't know whether John would go back to school for a teaching certificate, or whether he would open a business. We didn't know whether we would move to Denver with its good schools, or buy a home in the new suburbs outside New York, or whether we would return to country living somewhere in Colorado, close to our families. We didn't know whether I'd work full-time or part-time as a nurse. We didn't know where and when we would settle or for how long. We weren't sure of any of the details yet, weren't sure how we would write the rest of our story, only that together, we would find our way.

Wherever we are, John takes the hummingbird out of his pocket and sets it nearby to watch over us as we sleep. When I close my eyes, I imagine it flying, and John, Mary, and I soaring behind on some invisible and magical strings, all the days left behind, making room for more.

ACKNOWLEDGMENTS

While You Were Mine could not have been possible without the help of colleagues and friends: agent Lisa Erbach Vance, for your encouragement, which was my life raft; Christina Henry de Tessan, for her insightful editorial assistance; Rebecca Friedman, for her excellent copyediting; Kaitlin Coats, for her fine proofreading; and Jodi Warshaw and the others at Lake Union Publishing, for giving the book life. Very special thanks to Kay Elliott, Nancy English, and Lynn Callaway, for kindly and patiently seeing me through this book and the ones before it. And to Joseph Jarolim—only you know.

A few of the many outstanding resources I utilized during the writing of this novel deserve to be mentioned: *Over Here!: New York City During World War II* by Lorraine B. Diehl; *Helluva Town: The Story of New York City During World War II* by Richard Goldstein; *New York in the Forties: 162 Photographs* by Andreas Feininger and John von Hartz; *Manhattan '45* by Jan Morris; *Here is New York*, a little jewel written in 1949 by E. B. White; and numerous issues of *Life* magazine from 1945. Thanks for the information and inspiration.

ABOUT THE AUTHOR

Photo © 2015 Whitney Raines Photography

Ann Howard Creel was born in Austin, Texas, and worked as a registered nurse before becoming a full-time writer. She is the author of numerous children's and young adult books as well as fiction for adults. Her children's books have won several awards, and her novel *The Magic of Ordinary Days* was made into a *Hallmark Hall of Fame* movie for CBS.

Creel currently lives and writes in Chicago.